Space Pirate Chronicles

The Fool's Tale

Dave Fancella

Other works by Dave Fancella:

> *Fastburger!* *
>
> *The Martian Experiment* *

*Forthcoming

This is a work of fiction. Names, characters, business, events and incidents are the products of the author's imagination. Any resemblance to actual persons, living or dead, or actual events is purely coincidental.

Copyright © 2017 by Dave Fancella

All rights reserved. This book or any portion thereof may not be reproduced or used in any manner whatsoever without the express written permission of the publisher except for the use of brief quotations in a book review. Alternately, this book is also licensed under the Creative Commons Attribution-NonCommercial-ShareAlike 4.0 International Public License, the full text of which can be found at www.creativecommons.org. No other license is offered nor implied.

Printed in the United States of America

First Printing, 2017

ISBN-13: 978-1542717403

ISBN-10: 154271740X

CreateSpace Independent Publishing Platform

Austin, TX 78759

www.davefancella.com

Front cover image:

Brian Hilmers (www.brianhilmers.com)

Back cover image:

NASA

For Anthony and Julian, neither of which are actual pirates

that I know of

Chapter One

It never pays to wake up in jail. Quite the contrary, waking up in jail means you didn't get paid, and probably not laid either. It's also the start of a number of bad stories, so I'll try to be brief.

So there I was, waking up, hoping to feel my baby's body heat pressed up against mine, and instead finding a cold cell and a terrible headache. What went wrong last night? How did I end up here? Why did I drink so much? It was quite the unusual feeling for a professional drinker like me to not be able to remember the night of drinking.

I've heard it said that one jail looks much like the next. I wouldn't know, I've only been arrested one time before this, and that was years ago. This cell was very different from that one. Like the other cell, this one was equipped with a steel sink and toilet unit, a steel writing table with a steel stool attached on a steel swing arm that doesn't swing, and a steel bench with a hard as steel pad on it that I'll call my bed. Unlike the other cell, this one had nothing resembling a shower. I got out of bed, winced at the sharp pain in my temple, and stumbled over to the mirror, where I learned that I was still wearing my facepaint. This was not going to be pretty. I used a black and white pattern inspired by the yin and the yang because it matched my fool's black and silver hat. Likewise, the rest of my costume, which I was no longer wearing, consisted of a silvery vest, white tuxedo shirt, black bow tie, and black pants. Without my facepaint, I'm just another white guy with high cheekbones, long brown hair, and blue eyes that the ladies go nuts about. Like a good fool, I'm somewhat muscled, but otherwise a slender build that the ladies also go nuts over. What I'm saying is that the ladies go nuts over me, in and out of my costume.

First thing's first, leave the paint on. Whatever was going to happen next, I felt like I needed my fake face showing, because it was easier to hide behind it. Then I needed to somehow find out what was going on.

All I could remember at that initial wake-up was that I was with my sweetheart at the time I was arrested. I vaguely remembered being arraigned and informed that I had violated the rights of the people by operating a vehicle while under the influence of alcohol. I barely remembered the party. I didn't know what had happened to her after I was taken away. Did she make it home? Were we even going home? Did she feel as bad as I did in the morning?

I was coming under the impression of a feeling of danger, and the more I thought about it, the more anxious I became. I didn't think we were going home, but we were doing something dangerous. And, oddly enough, I felt like there was some sense of seediness in my girlfriend's behavior. Were we expecting a threesome at the destination? Was she planning on ditching me? Not Mary, no way. She and I were together forever, there was no way... But was there? She had clearly been deceiving me about something. Something had happened. Had she cheated on me? No, that didn't make sense. Mary was loyal to a fault, to a point where she wouldn't cheat on previous boyfriends even after knowing they'd cheated on her. It wasn't a sexual thing.

What was it, then? I started to think that my mind was playing tricks on me, because why else would I be thinking that we had angered the feds, the Illuminati, and the Belgians? That didn't make sense, but it did fit with the most common busker fantasy. There was no way I could be involved with anything like that. And yet, in the seemingly strange world of Cecil the Fool, locked up in a steel cage, it made sense. Somehow, in all of my magnificence, I had managed to get caught up in a plot that involved more secret government agencies than the cover-up of the UFO crash at Roswell! Of course, being a busker who was at the moment down on his luck and in jail, the fantasy would strongly appeal to my alcohol-adled brain.

After checking on my facepaint, I felt a bit better, and went back on my so-called bed to sleep. I must have slept for 20 hours, but since there was no clock in the cell, I couldn't tell.

When I woke up, it was meal time. I wanted to eat heartily, but the sandwich provided was sickening. I ate the orange and went back to bed, hoping the citric acid wouldn't trigger a puking fit.

After lunch, I sat there dreamily trying to remember what had happened the night before, with little flashes of vision lacking meaning parading before my eyes. I had performed at a bar that I also hang out in. I remembered doing that. And some guy was buying my drinks after the performance. Mary was there, but there was something about her, something I still couldn't put my finger on. Ah yes, there was that man! He came to our table and asked to buy her a drink, and she moved off to another table with him. I was jealous, really jealous, and I don't get jealous a lot. I realize that Mary has lots of friends, and most of them are male, and unlike a lot of men, that sort of thing doesn't bother me. Usually when they show up at the bar, she invites them to sit with us. This had the look of a man making a pass at her and she went for it. She didn't tell me what the guy wanted, later, but they did do some pad syncing. In a bar, that usually only means one thing: trading contact information to meet up later. And in context, it really looked like she was flaunting availability even though she was with me. Still, I liked to think I gave her space to be who she is, and do what she wants. I never want to be a constricting boyfriend, and she'd had enough of that with other men. As it happens, most women have had that experience. So I didn't question her. I figured she'd tell me if it was important.

Interrupting my ruminations, the guard opened my cell and informed me I had a visitor. So I roused myself a bit, got out of bed, and followed the guard down to the day room. An odd quirk of this jail, I suppose, is that they don't allow inmates out into the day room, but they have a day room anyway. Maybe I'll remember some day to ask about access to the day room, since I have heard the sentence for DUI can be pretty harsh. I might need to spend time in the day room getting help eating when both of my hands are stumps.

The guard brought me to a table in the day room and sat me down, which was a clear indication that whoever my visitor was, it was a person within the system and not my sweetheart. He walked over to his counter and buzzed in the guard outside, and sure enough, two obvious cops walked in and headed my way. When they reached me, one immediately sat across the table from me while the other stood off to the side.

"My name is Detective Johns," said the seated man. "And this is my partner, Detective Raymond. We're here to ask you a few questions about last night."

"My name is Cecil, and I'll try to answer your questions, gentlemen," I responded, "but as you are aware of my charges here, I really don't remember much of last night."

"That's fine," said the detective. "We'll try anyway. Let's start with this picture."

With that, he placed his pad in front of me. The man pictured look like your stereotypical Italian syndicate, um, "manager".

"I do not recognize this man," I said.

"Interesting," said the detective. "By all accounts, you were going to his bubble when you were pulled over." And with that, he gave me the Detective Stare.

To which I responded with the Jester Stare. Few can resist the Jester Stare, that's why jesters use it so carefully in their acts. Making the audience too nervous too often is a quick way to lose your audience. In this situation, Johns was obviously trying to make me nervous. Standard interrogation tactic, really. Just make your subject nervous, keep him nervous long enough and he'll spill his guts. Luckily for me, I had no guts to spill. I had already spilled them in the toilet.

"Ok," said the detective. "How about this gentleman?" He tapped the screen and the image was replaced with a new one. This one I recognized, he bought me my drinks last night. The scar near his right eye socket and the accompanying robot eye were a dead giveaway. Curiously, the picture was a mugshot. Obviously the man had a record. I wondered briefly if he liked the jail sandwiches.

"Yes," I said. "I recognize him. But I don't know him."

"Where do you know him from?"

"He bought me my drinks last night, after the show," I said.

"Did he give you his name?"

"Curtis," I said. "Or Jonas. I'm not very good with names. Occupational hazard."

"Well," responded the detective. "We don't know either of those aliases, but we do know his legal name is Jacob Smith, and he works as a courier for one of the big crime bosses on Jupiter. He has a string of minor offenses, and usually manages to get himself out of jail one way or the other. He must have had some reason to contact you. Perhaps you would care to enlighten me?"

Crime boss? That's who was buying my drinks? I started to wonder how much I had actually drank and why I was drinking it.

"I didn't know him at all, he just offered me a drink after the show and I accepted," I answered honestly and forthrightly.

"What happened after that?"

"Well, my girlfriend came over, and he offered her a drink," I said. "We all drank together for a couple of hours, and then my girlfriend and I left together."

"Where were you going?"

"I'm not really sure," I said. "We had been drinking, and then it was time to leave and I was driving. I didn't know where we were going, and the cop stopped us before I could find out."

"And that's it?"

"That's what happened last night," I said.

"Have you ever seen this man before that day?"

"I don't know. I see a lot of people every day," I said. "I can't track every face I see."

"Understood," said the detective. "Do you

recognize this man?"

Again, a new picture. Unlike the other pictures, this man was clearly no longer among the living. Having recognized the man, I had a fair amount of momentary shock to withhold. Being a fool does have its advantages, I just hadn't expected them to show during a police interrogation.

"I'm afraid I don't," I said. "Another crime lord?"

"No," said the detective. "This man apparently doesn't exist, but was found dead a few days ago about three blocks from your downtown spot."

"Does that mean the police are now using my downtown spot as a landmark?" I asked cheekily.

"No," said the detective with a chuckle. "But there's some sort of connection between his death and the crime boss, Julian. And with this man being killed near you, and the courier buying your drinks, that makes a lot of people wonder what your part is in all of this." Again, the Detective Stare.

I felt that the Jester Stare would be an inappropriate response at this point, so I gave him the Honest Pickings.

"I'm sorry, detective, I have absolutely no idea what you're talking about." Short, to the point, and completely honest.

"Ok, then, what about this man?" The detective dropped another picture in front of me.

I didn't recognize the individual at all.

"I don't recognize this man," I said. "Who is he?"

"He was also found dead in the same spot in which we found the other victim," said the detective.

"I've never seen this man before," I volunteered.

What followed were a few moments of silence, punctuated by the respective stares of the questioner and questionee. I had nothing: no information, no understanding, and absolutely no idea what he was trying to imply. Obviously, he had nothing either and was trying to rile me because he believed that I had something. But I had faced hostile audiences before, and this man was no effort. So, after a period, I broke the silence.

"You haven't said anything at all," I said to the man who was still standing. "Maybe you have something you'd like to suggest?"

"Watch your back," was his only response. The two detectives then exchanged a look, stood up, and beat their departure without so much as a handshake or a word of farewell.

The thing that was bothering me was that I had recognized the third man. He was in my spot, near as I can tell based on what the detectives had told me, just a few hours before he was found dead. Which means I may have been one of the last people to interact with him before he died. He had been watching me perform, and when I was finished and taking tips, he put a tip in my bag. I didn't think anything of it at first, but he had made eye contact with me. Later, I found a flasher in my bag buried among the gold coins. When I tried it in my terminal at home, it showed to be blank. So I figured he was just giving me an old flasher in lieu of currency, which is a common occurrence when you're busking. After I found the flasher, I found the man who'd given it to me, dead as a doornail.

The second dead man, I had no knowledge of. I had never seen him before, and I was completely honest about that with the two detectives.

I was curious about the "all accounts" comment. They'd obviously already interviewed other people at the bar that night, but I didn't remember intending to go anywhere but home. Mary was with me when we left. It was also unusual for us to drive at all, since we didn't actually own a vehicle of any kind, other than my bicycle which I never rode. Why was I even driving in the first place? Hell, my license was suspended already for previous bad driving habits, back when I owned a motorized vehicle. It would have made more sense for Mary to drive, except she was too drunk. She'd had a lot to drink, as had I.

Later that evening, after the detectives had gone, I was set free on personal bond. Watch your back, indeed.

Chapter Negative Seven

I was just minding my own business! I swear! I was all dressed up and ready to go. When I opened the door to my apartment, a hand reached through as soon as the there was room and pulled me against the door quickly before it had retracted too far. Then the mysterious hand moved in, followed by an arm and what I assume was an entire body, squeezing one of the hand pressure points and guiding me to turn around and face back inside my apartment. The half nelson that followed put me on my knees, and there wasn't one damned thing I could do about it.

"Give me the cash!" said a somewhat high-pitched voice behind.

"I haven't worked at all today, so I have no cash," I answered.

"Not good enough! Give me the cash!"

The epiphany I had at the moment led me to my very next move, which was to twist my body hard, throwing a leg out and sweeping my captor. He lost his grip while falling, and in 0.213 seconds I straddled his belly, confirming that this man was, in fact, male.

"You old scoundrel," I told him.

My friend laughed uproariously.

"Cecil!" he said. "Nice to see that you've kept in practice!"

"Of course I have," I responded. "Now, if I release you, are you going to attack me again?"

"Of course not," he answered. "The infamous Captain Nick Vallejo knows when he's beat."

"Great," I mumbled, getting up. "I'm off to

perform--"

"No problems," he answered. "Let's go to that Fastburger joint I saw around the corner. Have you eaten, yet?"

"No," I said. "I was planning on stopping off for something off their dollar menu."

"I thought you said you didn't have any cash?"

"I have a tab there," I answered. "Actually, because I do a little performance whenever I get there, they feed me for free."

"Ah," he said. "Then let's rock and roll, shall we?"

A few minutes later we were sitting across each other in a garishly decorated burger joint, I with my two breakfast burritos, and Nick with a gigantic jalapeño cheese burger. As we ate, I considered this old friend. Interpol had him listed as somewhat dangerous, but with only a smittering reward. They described him as about two meters tall, with long wavy black hair, usually a bit scruffy on the face, and as Mexican as the Mexican Hat Dance. He wore a lot of black, and that day was no exception. He was the stereotypical picture of a ruffian.

"So, when did you get into town?" I opened up with.

"Last night," he answered. "We set in for repairs."

"What's broken?"

"Oh, just a few things," he answered. "We're out of missiles, the aft lasers got taken out, and the aft shield generator is down."

"Sounds like you were being chased," I answered.

"Yep," he said. "Pirating just isn't what it used to be."

"Who was chasing you?"

"Dunno," he answered. "The ship wasn't in our database."

"Are you still using that outdated Russian database?"

"Nope," he said. "My netrunner managed to score an up-to-date USN database."

"Oh really?"

"Really!"

"Who'd he steal it from?"

"I cannot say," answered the pirate, "but I *can* say that if a ship isn't in that database, it's not from around here."

"Maybe it was just heavily modded?"

"Not with those weapons."

Nick looked at me pointedly, and a bit more seriously.

"Look, Cecil," he said. "I don't know what's going on, but something is going *down*. There's been a lot of covert traffic running around between here and Mars, and there's rumors out about a group of vigilantes that have started taking out pirate ships."

"Only pirate ships?"

"Only."

It was my turn to look at him.

"You definitely look more haggard than you usually do," I observed. "Chino still feeding you right?"

"Of course," he answered with a sigh. "I was just thinking that maybe piracy isn't what I ought to be doing with my crew anymore."

"These new guys really got you worked up?"

"Let me just say that if the ship that attacked us was one of them, we're fucked. We can't get three pirate crews together and defeat it."

"That much firepower, eh?"

"That much," he said. "We were lucky to get away, and that was with Shauna extending the front shields to the rear after the aft shield generator resigned and went to find a new job. We hid for three days in a comet's trail while the thing stalked around us trying to find us."

"Lucky to be so near a comet," I said.

"Well, we were following the comet when we were attacked."

"Sounds like another brilliant plan of the great 'Naptime' Nick Vallejo!"

I found it disturbing that he didn't follow that up with his usual humor. My old friend looked more tired than I had seen in him in a long time. He must have been really shaken up about the experience.

"So why were you following the comet?" I asked.

"Oh, that," said Nick. "I was breaking in a new pilot, making him match course and speed to a predictable object like a comet."

"I don't believe that to be completely true."

"Ok, it's because a random USN ship caught us on sensors during a raid, and I was hiding."

"Sloppy," I said. "Why were you pirating in the inner planets?"

"I wasn't," said Nick. "That's what makes the whole thing so weird."

Nick's comm went off right then and he moved off to answer it. A few minutes later, he returned.

"Well, looks like it's time for me to go," said Nick. "We found a buyer for our cargo, and it's time to take Shauna out shopping."

"Buy her something pretty," I told him.

"I'm going to buy her a pretty new reconditioned aft shield generator," he answered. "Until I see you again, take care, my friend."

"And also with you," I said, gripping his hand in a firm handshake. I watched him walk away and wondered what nature of combat he had been in. We had been in some rough patches together, and together, we usually found a way out of them. Ok, obviously, we had always found a way out of them or I wouldn't have been sitting in that Fastburger chatting with my friend.

Realizing that I needed to get downtown to make some money, I got up to go. On my way out the door, an old homeless guy with gray hair going everywhere bumped right into me, so hard that I temporarily lost my balance.

"Excuse me," I said politely.

He met my eyes and just stared for a moment.

"I should get going," I said, and started to move off. He grabbed my shoulder and whipped me around with surprising strength.

"Don't go downtown today," he said.

"Why the hell shouldn't I?"

"Because danger awaits you."

I didn't have any time for a crazy homeless guy

doing crazy things around me, so I told him to shove it and walked away. He didn't follow me, but I continued to be unnerved.

　　* * *

Downtown. Blah. Not a terribly exciting place. It was a large dome with tall steel buildings like you'd find in any downtown area in the outer planets. Shops, banks, the usual selection of economic activity you'd expect. I was performing for a small audience in the early evening hours, normal shopping hours for mothers with their young kids. Naturally I was in the shopping district. The people closest to me were mostly kids, with their mothers making the second row, and there were only about 5 ladies. Businesspeople were walking to and fro, headed toward the tube station or headed to work. Clothing stalls lined the corridor, and barricades were starting to go up in preparation for the considerable bar traffic that would be coming soon. What little traffic that had existed had mostly stopped, and there were only battery powered vehicles certified to use in pedestrian areas. I had just finished a double cartwheel where I borked the return and dropped into a roll. When I stood up from the roll, I found myself eye to eye with a man showing Haunted Mario. It struck me so hard, this man's most seriously harried expression, that I threw myself backwards onto my hands, did an about face, and started walking away on my hands. Losing my balance, I dropped into a roll again and kicked around to face the crowd. The kids yelled, and the man was looking behind him. I glanced to see what he was looking at and saw two men pushing people out of the way and moving this way. They were still several blocks away, but the way the corridor curves in that part of downtown, I could see them clearly. So could the man.

Not knowing what else to do, I grabbed my bag, stepped up to him, and gave my standard line about tips. He looked at me for several long moments, then dropped some money into my bag and moved away, murmuring something about trying to get away before they catch him. I moved around the mothers collecting whatever I could get, and kept an eye out for the man's pursuit. When the mothers had finished letting their kids pay me for the few minutes of entertainment they received, I strapped my bag back onto my belt, pulled out my balls, and started tossing them in a cascade pattern. I kept my eye on the men moving through the crowd and moved bombastically to interpose myself between them and their prey. It took another minute for them to reach me, at which point I ran interference, while switching to the waterfall. The two men each dropped a coin in my bag, forcing me to obey the busker convention of leaving them to continue on their journey. I figured I managed to keep them busy for about 20 seconds or so. Hopefully that was enough time for the poor guy to get away.

As the evening went on, I couldn't shake the man's expression from my mind. Why were they chasing him? It wasn't technically my problem, but something about working in the street makes you develop a certain compassion for people. Later in the evening, when I was getting ready to head home, I went off to my counting spot. I usually count my money before I leave, but after I've finished performing. For safety's sake, I always count at a different spot. That night, the spot I used was a few blocks away, opposite the tubes, farther than usual. I sat down on a bench and opened my bag. Since most people pay with paper money, it's usually a matter of pulling it out and putting it in my wallet. After sorting through the bills, I started digging through the change to get an idea what sort of coinage

I had earned. There were more gold eagles than usual, but there was a funky mass that was decidedly not coin-shaped. I pulled it out and looked at it. It was a flasher, a digital storage device. Who would put that in there? Sure, people often tip with things that aren't money. In fact, early that same evening a lady tipped me with half a sandwich. But she didn't put it in the bag. People usually show you what they're tipping you, except for the ladies who leave you their contact info. It was a surprisingly safe bet that that chased man had put it there. Careful study showed it to be well-used. It was a Samsung AJT-6100, which is a common flasher used by academics. It's practical, small, and has a lot of space on it. It's also supported by the big mainframe computers used in most research labs, and there's only like three flashers that are reliably supported. I would have to see what's on it that the man was so desperate to leave me.

I put my wallet away, closed up the bag and looked up. The security cameras in this part of town don't work so well, so it's good when you're carrying a bit of cash to keep yourself in view of the cameras that do work. When I went to stand, I noticed on the ground a bit of pinkish water. That was unusual in and of itself. Water is so common on Europa, a moon made almost completely out of water, that it's not unusual for it to flow a bit freely in some of the seedier parts of town, nor is it unusual to find bodily fluids coloring it, but pink? If that was a bodily fluid, I wasn't sure I wanted to know from where it came.

On a whim, I followed the water upstream. It wound its way around the corner, where I found a person sitting slumped over on the ground, back against the wall. I walked over and looked at the person and recognized Haunted Mario. He was bleeding from what looked like a gut wound of some sort. I guessed the good news was that he was still bleeding, so he was still alive, but he didn't look like he was conscious. I picked his head up and slapped his cheek to try to revive him, and he woke up a bit. He looked at me with glassy eyes, seeming to recognize me.

"Don't talk," he said. "If they ask, you never saw me."

"Who are you?" I asked.

He coughed a bit, and let his head drop. Then he mumbled something.

"Sorry, bud," I said, "I didn't catch that." I moved my head in closer to his mouth, where I could hear better.

"Don't let it fall into anybody's hands. You will be contacted. Leave me now."

"Who will contact me?" I whispered.

"Nobody."

Then he died.

Chapter Two

Perhaps I should introduce myself. My name is Cecil Wendbury, and I am a professional fool. I am 36 years old, and live with my girlfriend in a cabin on Europa, a republic in the Islamic Federation of Jupiter. It is a tourist area where the Jovian miners spend their weeks mining Jupiter's atmosphere for helium and their evenings on Europa enjoying the lustpots, strip clubs, and various entertainments. As a professional fool, most of my evenings are spent in the street, busking. From time to time, as had happened last night, I score a gig on a stage in a bar. Tips are usually better in bars, but much more unpredictable. Europa also attracts a great deal of tourists from Earth and Mars, being in the orbit of the closest of the outer planets and therefore the cheapest to visit. Outside of Jupiter's orbit lie mostly military bases, self-sustaining colonies that are rarely heard from, probably because there's only one person left due to a dog virus that mutated into giant monsters, or so I assumed, and a few vacation spots for the very rich that operate outside the rule of law. Jupiter is the official start of the new frontier, and serves as the crossroads for all goods imported from the outer planets and exported from the inner planets. It's also a place where the rule of law isn't quite as common as it is in the inner planets, which are in turn dominated by the United States of North America and Venus. As a result, good old high seas piracy can be a profitable adventure for crews who have the courage, chutzpah, and know better than to be cruel to their victims. So it's ideally situated for a person of my profession to do quite well, and I do. I live with my girlfriend, Mary, in a modest home in an upper-middleclass bubble.

I chose Europa as a home. When I was a kid, I lived in the asteroid belt. My dad served in the Strategic Space Force as a trainer, so we spent a lot of time living in the asteroid belt. When he got cancer and retired, we went back to Mars for awhile. When he recovered, we moved back to the asteroid belt because his position had been spun off to the civil service, and he was able to take a similar position and do his old job again. Somewhere in that mess, my older sister moved to Europa to attend the same university as her school friends, and when I finished school, I followed her. She let me stay in her place for a few months while I worked a shitty fast food job, saved up money, and moved out on my own at the naïve age of 18. The rest is history, of a sort.

In the years since then, I got married, had some kids, got divorced. I've worked as a fry cook, a fusion drive mechanic, software programmer, marketer, and during the last years of my divorce, a physics lab assistant. After the divorce, about a year before I got arrested, an old friend got in contact with me, a girl from my first job. We'd both had crushes on each other, but were too wimpy to ever do anything about it. After getting in touch with me, we started going out, and I have been considering marrying her, but she doesn't know, so do me a favor and don't tell her until I get a chance to tell her myself. In any case, during the divorce, I spent some time on a freighter of sorts with an old friend who got me into juggling as a hobby. It was fun, and relaxing, and at that time I needed something relaxing to do. Later, I found I had gotten pretty good at it, and having a generally whimsical personality, decided to try my hand at busking. I parted ways with my old friend the captain at his next Europa stop to do just that. After a few false starts, and getting involved with my girlfriend, she helped me put together a costume that, when put on, makes me feel like a completely different person, but still the same person, if that makes any sense. Trying again at busking, I did quite well, and at the time we needed money so badly we were willing to try almost anything legal. So, like my old fencing instructor used to say: when you find something that works, keep doing it until it doesn't work anymore.

And there you have it. Cecil the Fool was born.

I don't really have a downtown spot. There are actually several spots downtown that I use regularly, and when they barricade the street, I tend to go out on the road and perform out there. When I'm juggling, that is. It's actually a small part of my act. I had been studying martial arts since I was a kid in the asteroid belt with my old friend before he was a freighter captain, and now I have multiple black belts in Aikido, Judo, Tae Kwon Do, and Jiujitsu. I realize how that makes me sound like some sort of martial art prodigy, but the truth is that all of those arts are similar enough that after you get a black belt in one, getting a black belt in any of the others is easy. After the divorce, I studied Hapkido without ever getting a belt, which is a story all its own, but since it includes some acrobatics that I already knew, I worked those into my act. I'm a traditional jester, doing a bit of juggling, some acrobatics, and a fair amount of scathing satirical comedy. Most of my act is spent harassing people closest to me in the circle, and getting laughs at it all. Then I take out my bag and collect my tips, and move on to a different spot. On the street, with the kind of hours I work, you have to have something different to offer audiences when there's a chance you'll see some of the same people from one spot to the next, and over the months since I started I've picked up quite a few regulars. So, improvisation is the key to my success. I take the best of what I can remember doing in the street onto the stage about once a month, and I do alright.

Naturally, it doesn't matter which downtown spot I was in when the gentleman-that-doesn't-exist tipped me, because they're all fairly close together anyway. What does matter is that if I was one of the last people to have seen him before he was murdered, then that empty flasher could be of importance, especially if he was somehow involved with a major crime boss. Jupiter, being a crossroads planet, with Europa having the interplanetary spaceport, is a natural target for organized crime and espionage. And I, being a common street fool, should be able to do a fair amount of my own detective work.

You may ask why I didn't just tell the detectives everything I just told you. Go ahead, ask it. Thanks. The last few days had actually been quite a bit more eventful than I led the detective to believe. The police had obviously been watching me for some time, and I doubted they were going to let me know how much they knew about what I had been up to. How the flasher and the man carrying it are connected to the crime boss is unclear. Well, to be completely honest, there was no logical connection to it that I could see, yet, but whatever information was on that flasher, a man who doesn't exist was carrying it, and the cops have somehow connected him to both the crime boss and to me. Chances were, the cops think the crime boss murdered the man, and that means the crime boss is connected to the flasher somehow. Worse yet, they might even think I was associated with the crime boss because of the night I got arrested, which would make me the primary suspect in this murder. Of course, technically I didn't know for sure if it was even a murder, since he could have been killed in self-defense, but when you consider that I had observed him being chased, murder was a logical conclusion.

I wanted to revisit the original crime scene to see if there was information to be gleaned now that the cops had worked it over. Since I couldn't operate in my usual costume, I decided to use my jester-ette costume. I carry with me in my juggling bag a simple bra and a set of Almost Real breast forms. Sometimes as part of my act, I slip them on when nobody's looking and instantly become a woman. At other times, I am a woman for the entire act, but that's a completely different costume. Luckily there are gawdy clothing shops downtown, so it would be a simple matter to find a new top. I carry all my makeup together, so I was set for that. All I had to do was get suited up and then I could operate without fear of security cam footage when I visit the crime scene. So, when they let me out, I bought a new costume and went straight to the nearest restroom to get suited up. I was let out in the evening, which should bring a decent crowd.

Time to get to work.

Chapter Negative Six

I was, to put it lightly, more than a little freaked out about a man dying right next to me. It wasn't the first time that had happened, but it's not really something to which you adjust. It's frightening, especially when you don't have any idea who it is or why they just died, but they have trusted you with some prized possession that's likely the reason they were killed in the first place.

It's the same old story, told a thousand times in cheesy cloak and dagger novels.

And it just happened to me.

Interesting.

Who, exactly, is supposed to contact me? His answer wasn't exactly exact, so naturally it didn't give me the exact kind of information I'd need to determine exactly who the good guys were, assuming that the dead man was one of the good guys. Maybe I'd recognize them by the color of their hats? No good, because I think I'm one of the good guys, and my hat is exactly half black and half silver.

Anyway, there wasn't much time at that moment to think about it, because if a citizen came wondering by and saw me talking to the dead guy, I'm the suspect. There wasn't time to hide the body, and all that would do is make it possible for cops to link his death to me anyway. If the man had wanted to involve the law, he wouldn't have dropped the flasher with me and then gotten himself killed, so I decided to beat my escape as quickly as possible, but not without first going through his pockets looking for spare change. At least then I'd help make it look like a mugging that went awry. More importantly, I might find some clue as to the man's identity and whoever it was that he thought may come to contact me. While I wasn't in a hurry to help the people who did this get away, I felt some responsibility since the dead man had entrusted me with the flasher. He must have had a reason, and until I can determine what that reason is, I'd better leave the cops out of it. Luckily, I have friends that could help.

So I went through his pockets, checked under his shirt, gave his crotch a good groping, all while wearing my performance gloves. I felt a little dirty doing it, especially since I didn't have a necrophilia license, but I turned up a few interesting things.

One: He was carrying a wallet with ID guaranteed to be fake. It said his name was Jack Simpson, listed a home address, and had everything you'd expect an ID card to have. Some bills, some family photos, stuff that's obviously fake.

Two: He wasn't carrying a weapon at all. Either that or his attackers took the weapon but left the rest of his stuff alone.

Three: His pad. I'd get Larry to go through it later.

Naturally there wasn't anything to make of this just yet, so I'd have to wait until the forensics team got on it to figure out who he was and then see if I could get in and find out what they knew, somehow. Or, with any luck, his compadres would contact me, I'd instantly recognize them, give them their trinket, and my involvement would be over. Yeah, not seeing that happening, but one could hope, right?

So I moved on. I picked up my stuff and headed the long way around so that by the time anybody saw me they wouldn't be able to associate me with this gentleman, jumped on the tube and headed home. It had been a long evening, and I was looking forward to a warm shower and some cuddle time with my lady before snoring the night away. I could deal with all this cloak and dagger stuff in the morning. Luckily, being self-employed, I wouldn't have to take a vacation or deal with playing spy around a full-time job. Unluckily, the two murderous thugs didn't think my night was over yet, because they were sitting in the capsule, waiting for me.

How did I know they were waiting for me? Simple, as soon as I stepped on the capsule, they each appeared on either side of me, and one shoved a sharp object into my gut. He didn't hurt me or cut any part of my costume, but I got the point, no pun intended.

"You're with us," said the man on the right. "Get off at the next stop. We have to talk."

I didn't argue the point just yet. The doors closed, so all I could hope to do was hurt the two guys until they opened again.

The thing about the tubes is this: they're long. Really long. Each route is a single capsule that is shot through a rail gun, and then caught in, well, another rail gun. The basic idea is that for close connections, a tube isn't used at all. Instead, you would just walk or use a slidewalk. It's not that bad since with surface gravity being only 1.3 m/s^2 it takes a long walk to get tired. Also, on wider thoroughfares, you're allowed to drive electric vehicles so long as they tap into the city's wireless grid. Of course, since the city gouges you on the power rates, only people who are quite well-to-do drive the electric vehicles. The remainder? Well, let's just say that the old rickshaw is not an uncommon mode of transportation. Likewise, the bicycle has made a big comeback on Europa, and battery-powered vehicles that only go so fast have been recently approved for use in pedestrian thoroughfares. Anyway, I digress. I live pretty far north of downtown, out in the

Cedar City bubble, which isn't even directly connected to downtown except by tube. It's not even possible to go from my home to New Austin without using a tube. Reason? Apparently the people of Cedar City decided some time ago to save themselves the problems associated with being a boom town by simply not being one and instead sleeping the middle-management for the boom town. Middle-managers like the tubes, so the tubes are the connection. I like living in Cedar City because, well, I don't, really, it just happens to be where I ended up after the divorce. The tubes themselves are basic ballistic tunnels. They're kept at a high vacuum to minimize friction, use magnetic bearings to keep the capsule centered in the tube, and curve only as much as the curve on the capsule can handle. The capsule maintains its vertical orientation through the simple and effective means of having a low center of mass. The tubes aren't necessarily straight, nor are they necessarily parabolic, although some are parabolas, most curve quite a bit over their entire length even if individual curves aren't terribly sharp. At each end lies a series of coils used to accelerate the capsule on either end. At launch, obviously the capsule has positive acceleration, and at its destination it has negative acceleration. The capsule has such strong magnets in it that the system is able to recover about half of the initial energy expended to launch while the capsule is being slowed to a stop, making it a very inexpensive system to operate. Some tubes shoot through the atmosphere of Europa which is so thin that the tunnel itself doesn't have to be kept at a vacuum, but obviously lowers their efficiency quite a bit. The system is really quite beautiful, but suffers from one particularly important flaw: after launch, the riders are in free fall for most of the trip. It's only a few minutes at most, usually mere seconds, but it's still quite significant. Barf bags are not provided, so a lot of people avoid the tubes whenever they can resulting in the boom town being boomier and the middle-management-sleeper-town being more middle-management like.

What that means, of course, is that these two men were clearly off-worlders. If they were native Europans, or at least transplants, they would know that the tube only has two terminals and no stops between the two. They clearly come from a place that has more traditional public transportation, which is almost certainly Earth, since most of the off-Earth colonies and nations tend to use systems like the tube.

The thought went through my mind so fast that words became deeds in nothing flat. I watched the two men as the tube launched, and they were clearly unprepared for this. It probably wasn't their first ride in the tube, but they definitely hadn't had that many rides. Of course, I'd been riding the tubes at that point for 17 years, which ignores the fact that my first series of martial arts training happened in the asteroid belt at near free fall, so I knew exactly what to do. I just couldn't kill either of them.

So, once we were in free fall, and both men looked very uncomfortable, I moved. I grabbed the knife arm and used a little of Newton's Third Law to pull him towards me. I slipped past him and knocked him against his partner, and caught the door with my butt. The two men drifted towards the back of the empty capsule, so I launched myself right at them. This is usually a suicidal tactic when used against an opponent familiar with zero gee fighting, but these blokes obviously had absolutely no idea what they were doing, so I felt reasonably safe making the charge. I zipped past the man in front to grab the back man by the neck and pull him to the other wall, where a quick neck jerk put him out like a light. A little more pressure in the jerk and his neck would have snapped, but I used just enough to knock him out instead. Then I grabbed onto a handhold while the reverse acceleration kicked in and we slowed down at about 2.2 m/s^2. The poor guy I had knocked off the ground in free fall fell back against the back wall and failed to break his fall properly. I stepped up to him when the car stopped, grabbed his left hand in a gooseneck, and walked him out the door into the corridor.

I took him to the nearest wall, slammed him up against it, and put my other hand around his neck. Pain is a wonderful motivator, it's amazing what you can get someone to do with the right joint lock.

"All I have to do is squeeze this hand, and you will be laying here in the morning for your friends to find you. On the other hand, if I move this other hand like so..."

He let out quite a squeak at that.

"...you get the idea. So how about you tell me who you are and what you want from me, and if you answer my questions smartly, you'll be laying here fast asleep when your friends catch up with you, with all of your joints and bones intact. Deal?"

The man finally got a chance to get a word in edgewise. Lucky him. Not surprisingly, he spoke with an Earth accent. I'd guess somewhere European, probably British, but never could get the hang of distinguishing all the European accents.

"You know I can't tell you anything," he said. "You're just going to have to kill me."

So I applied some pressure, and let him squeal a

bit.

"Wrong answer, bud," I said. "What do you want from me?"

"You spoke to someone we were after, he gave you something," he said.

"Who was that?"

"Does it matter? If you give us what we came after, you will live a long and fruitful life."

"And if I don't?"

"You will die, and we will search you, and we will still have what we came for."

I suspected he wasn't sure who was in control, nor who he was dealing with. If I killed him that night, it would not be the first time I'd killed a person. I decided to make that point to him.

"This here is your jugular, and this other one here is your carotid. I would squeeze them both together, and you will suffocate. No fingerprints, barely a bruise, and you're out on a limb right now without ground support. I'll get away from both the cops and your friends, and you won't get away from me."

Now, my aikido instructor once told me that you should never play the "I will kill you card". His reasoning was that the aikidoka does not kill, so could never bluff someone into believing he could kill. But among men like this guy I had against the wall, killing is second nature, and they can smell when someone has blood on their hands. As he did so now, and I had already determined about him, even if I didn't already know he'd killed the man that belongs to Nobody.

"Maybe we can work something out," he finally said. "You give me what I came for, and I move on."

"Not so fast," I said. "Firstly, I'm not involved in whatever it is you have going on, and Lastly, I don't know who the hell you're talking about, nor do I have any idea what gift I was supposed to have received."

"Then why do you want to know who I am?"

"You've gone to this much trouble to abduct me," I said, "I'd like to know why."

"Maybe this was a simple misunderstanding, but that doesn't explain why you delayed us in the cube."

"I busk. I wanted a tip. You're cheapskates. Simple enough?"

At that point, I was in a bad way. If I kept pressing to find out who he was, he'd figure out that I was lying about the flasher. If I let him go, I'd let useful information get away from me, and right now knowing who my new enemies might be would be very helpful. Of course, after I knocked him out, I could search him, and that would turn up something, I was certain. At the very least, I could steal his pad. I decided that was the best and proceeded to knock him out. Once down, I searched him and indeed found the knife, his gun, and his pad. He had a fair amount of cash on him, but I left it there. He'd need it to get back home. While I was doing that, the tube left again, sending his buddy back into downtown. Oops.

And then I went home. Mary wasn't home yet, and I was wiped out, so I showered and went to bed.

Chapter Three

I stepped out of the restroom and left the cafe, stopping at the door to check my reflection. I love how I look when I get all dressed up. Luckily the cops had returned all of my performing equipment, except the swords, predictably. While not legally defined as weapons, they're the sorts of things cops would rather take when they can, and when you're arrested all of your belongings become property of the state. Upon release, a constable decides what you get to have back and what they keep. The Islamic Federation of Jupiter isn't the free-est place to live, that's for sure. So as soon as I was down the street, I had my balls out and flying in a simple cascade, which happens to be the easiest pattern while walking, especially when you're looking to move quickly through a crowd. It's amazing how a crowd parts when they see a juggler. Luckily for me, the crowd was thin that night.

I made my way down the street to Margo's, then snatched the balls out of the air and went inside. I went straight to the bar and waited for the bartender to attend me.

"Hello there, pretty lady," he said. "Looks like you got out of jail already."

"How did you know I was in jail?" I asked casually. "Two zeigens, while you're answering, please."

"Certainly," he replied. "There were some detectives in here earlier asking some questions, and they let it drop that they spoke to you in jail."

"What sorts of questions?"

"Photo ID, mostly," said the barkeep. "They wanted someone to say they recognized some folks, and nobody recognized them."

"Did you?"

"No," said the bar. "Can't say I have. Where were you playing the night you were arrested?"

"Homeboy's," I said. "Over in the Wells bubble. Small place, older crowd. Fun show."

"I don't get out that way much. Two eagles."

I dropped the coins in his hand and nabbed my two beers.

"With the cops sniffing around and showing the pictures they're showing, you'd do well to keep your head low," said the bar. "There's something going on, I can smell it, and it smells like trouble with a capital T."

"Good thing I don't play pool," I answered. "Thanks for the heads-up. I'll remember that when I'm famous." Then I walked away.

I went over to the table I usually sit at and placed the beers in the standard Waiting For Godot position, so that nobody would try to join me. After the second one clicked in the magnetic holder, I took a long draw from the first and took out my own pad. I dialed up Mary, got voice mail, and sent her a message. She'd answer as soon as she got it, I was certain. Then I scanned news headlines. Out in the sticks, a cow gave birth to a five-legged monster. It was killed and burned immediately, as well as the mother. Superstitious folk. Some rapes, the perpetrators being in the stocks right now. Maybe I'd head over and see if I recognized any of them. Rape is an interesting crime. It's legal in most of Jupiter, provided you have a license. Of course, to get a license, you have to prove you're not an aggressive person normally, and you can only rape people who also have licenses. It's sort of a government-funded way to let something normally considered quite kinky to happen safely. If you rape someone and don't have a license, but your victim has a license, you pay a fine. If you have a license and rape someone without a license, you lose your license and pay a fine. If neither you nor your victim have a license, you go in the stocks for three days. Few rapists survive one day of the stocks. I've always wondered how these folks figure out who has a license and who doesn't before they start raping.

I noticed one of the patrons trying to catch my eye. Figures. She probably wants me to do a little dance for her. Not happening, I'm on my beer break. So I continued scanning the headlines.

Apparently carjacking rates are at the lowest they've ever been, which is no surprise considering the price of power these days. Nobody's driving much and even carjackers don't want to steal at those prices. Some archaeological team claiming to have found proof of life on Jupiter has been thoroughly debunked and stripped of their science licenses. I wondered briefly if they got to keep their rape licenses. Now there was something interesting. Apparently a sting operation run last night turned up some drug dealers, seized a lot of windcrack, and did serious damage to a crime boss's operation. The picture of the crime boss caught my eye, because it was the same one the cops had shown to me. His name was Guido Julian. Apparently Italian crime bosses are still a thing. I read the article further, but didn't find a mention of either of the detectives I'd spoken to earlier, nor the courier that had gotten me drunk. The operation itself was in progress when I was stopped, and happened just a few blocks from Homeboy's. Curious.

About then, the lady that had tried to catch my eye

just slipped into Godot's spot. So I turned my eye up to her and gave her I'm Taken.

"Hi," she said. "Didn't I see you at Homeboy's the other night?"

"Doubtful," I said, mindful of the completely different costume I was wearing compared to the evening at Homeboy's which I was still having trouble remembering.

"I remember, you were hanging out with the Tortoise."

"Tortoise?"

"Yeah," she said. "The guy that was buying your drinks."

"Ok, what's up?" I asked. She obviously had something she was dying to tell me, and had seen through the girly costume.

"You don't remember talking to me, do you?"

Damn, how drunk was I?

"Sorry," I answered. "Normally I remember every extremely attractive woman I talk to."

"Flirt," she answered. "But let's move on. Did the Tortoise ask you at all about the possibility of performing for his boss?"

Curious question.

"No," I said. "He just bought drinks for me and my girlfriend." I obviously didn't remember any more than that happening.

"Ok," she said. "That's good. I have a very private client who would like to contract with you for your entertainment skills."

"The Tortoise's boss, I take it?" I asked.

"Let's just say it's someone who could make or break your career."

"And if I don't accept?" I asked.

"Break."

"So I'm not really being given an option, then," I responded.

"You always have a choice," she said. "Look, I have other appointments to attend. I'll leave you my contact information. The gig pays one grand, and is about 6 hours. A party. You won't go on stage, if you don't want to, but you'll wander around and entertain guests the same way you do here in the street. My client specifically wants your female ego. Send me a message when you've decided, and I'll send you details."

With that, she dropped a card and took off. Luckily, she hadn't drank any of the other beer.

I nabbed the card and switched the two beers so that now it looked like Godot had drank a bit of his beer. I looked at the card. Susan Hall, Event Coordinator. Kind of cute, but obviously quite annoying. Break my career if I refuse to play? That didn't sound like a contract I wanted to sign. I slipped her card into the card slot on my pad and let it scan. Then I thought back over the conversation.

She looked awfully familiar, and her name was definitely ringing a bell. Unfortunately, the bell brought about a headache, meaning it was likely I had met her at Homeboy's, and she had been telling the truth about that. It was obviously significant that I had been talking to this turtle person, and she knew about it. Maybe she was organizing something for a competing boss with the turtle's, and wanted to make sure I wasn't already being claimed by him? No, more likely the Tortoise was checking me out, and she was going to talk to me after getting his approval. That seemed to make more sense, but was pure speculation. She could be connected with Flasher Boy, who was in turn some sort of agent who was after Julian for something. It made more sense that she was connected with Flasher Boy somehow, but what he was about, I couldn't even begin to guess. And how she identified me as the guy who received his flasher was an open question.

Still, there was something nagging me about her. I had seen her, I was certain. It could have been at Homeboy's. I did chat up a lady when Mary was off talking to her new friend. Thought it would be worth a little jealousy to throw it back at her, and it seemed to work. Who was the lady? I checked my pad to see if scanning her card had any hits, and sure enough, I already had her contact information in my pad. I had gotten her contact information, but had no intention of contacting her. I only did it because I'd seen Mary doing the same with her new friend. I didn't really want to do a gig where I'd be punished if I refused.

Feeling a stranger to my own thoughts, I thought I'd distract myself. So I dialed up Larry to see if he'd made any headway on the flasher. He answered readily.

"Hi Cecil, how are you?"

"I'm fine, Larry," I said. "Did you make any progress on the flasher?"

"Well, that depends on how you look at it. On the one hand, I haven't managed to open up the filesystem, nor have I managed to determine if there is a filesystem, because we have to consider that the encryption may be hiding an actual application. On the other hand, I have managed to at least determine the encryption algorithm that was used. You see, every encryption algorithm has a characteristic signature, and what a lot of people will do is encrypt one time with one algorithm, and then encrypt the encrypted stream with another algorithm so that you have to, well, it's called Double Layer Encryption, and what it means is..."

I let Larry drone on in his own way. He suffers from Too Much Detail Syndrome, and I've tried to cure it for several years and failed. So I've learned to tune him out until he gets to the skinny, and took a draw from the zeigen sitting in front of me. I'm sure he has a lot to teach me if I quit tuning him out, but really at that moment I just wanted to know about the flasher. Also, in this situation at least, I was already familiar with Double Layer Encryption. It's a technique that goes back to the early digital age, but was actually used with hand ciphers for centuries before that.

As he was saying:

"...and this system was really only ever used by the CIA. It's really strange, such an old encryption system on the inside layer, especially considering that it's now something like 150 years old. And since the CIA doesn't really exist anymore, having since been replaced by the EIA, chances are there isn't anybody around who knows how to get through this."

"I would expect that such an old system would be covered thoroughly in textbooks," I suggested.

"Is the internal combustion engine in any textbooks?" Larry asked.

"Well, not that I know of, but I haven't studied that sort of engineering," I said.

"No, you were studying fusion-drive engineering, which wouldn't include any such complicated mechanical devices," said Larry. "I got my master's in physics at the Mars Science U, and we didn't cover the internal combustion engine, which is weird considering how much that engine is still used on Mars."

"If there's no information on the encryption system, how were you able to identify it in the first place?"

"..." Larry can be quite long-winded.

"So, you're saying you can identify it because you happen to have gotten some old CIA equipment in your lab as a hand-me-down?" I asked.

"That's about the size of it," he answered.

"Well," I said, "Can you get one of those old machines running and see if they know how to break this encryption?"

"I've tried for several years, off and on, to get one of these machines running. You see, it all started with the fact that it uses the outdated 20th century American AC power grid, pumping 110 volts into the thing. We've all gone positronic since then, using wireless power conductors, so there isn't really a way to..." Let the positronic engineer explain the gobbledy gook.

"So if you had a wireless power inverter, you could run it?" I asked.

"Yes," he said. "Absolutely."

"Ok, don't you have one somewhere in your lab?"

"Probably," he answered. "If not, I'll have one at the house."

"Then you should probably get on that," I said. "Have you heard from Mary at all?"

"Not for a couple of days," he said. "Last time she seemed really concerned about Ohm's Law."

"Yeah, she has trouble with algebra, and she was doing her homework while I was working, which she's not supposed to do. I've got to go now, I'll check in again in a bit."

"Do I take it then that deciphering this thing has taken a higher priority now?"

"Yes, it has," I said. "There's something amok. I don't have even a clue what it is right now. Watch your back."

"I always carry that lead pipe you're so fond of swinging."

"Keep it by you," I said. "Good luck. One more thing."

"Shoot."

"What kind of forensics did you find on the first crime scene?"

"First?"

"Yes," I said. "That one."

"Oh, right," said Larry. "Let's see, cause of death was a knife to the chest, puncturing a lung. They say he was laying there for at least half an hour before finally expiring. No fingerprints, no evidence of the scene being tampered with. Also, the man had been searched, but we already knew that. Footprint analysis only turned up that there were two people with the man when he was stabbed."

"There's no evidence of the scene being tampered with?"

"Correct," said Larry, "But there is a note from the investigating Detective suggesting that the scene was too clean."

"Too clean?"

"Yeah, not enough evidence. No DNA from the attackers, very little footprint evidence, that sort of thing."

"So the scene could have been cleaned, but without leaving evidence of the cleaning?"

"Yep," said Larry.

"Ok," I said. "Thanks. I'm going now, I'm going to look at the second crime scene. It's in the same location, and it's another John Doe."

"How do you know about this?"

"Detective in the jail that questioned me."

"Was it Detective Johns?" Larry asked.

"Yes," I said. "Why?"

"He's the investigating Detective on the first murder."

"I see," I said. "Ok, then, I'm going to get going. Keep an eye on Johns for me, will ya?"

"Will do," said Larry. Then I signed out.

I dialed Mary again and got nothing. So I sipped my beer and watched the crowd. As the crowd thickened, I moved out and went to the crime scene.

The crime scene was still taped off for police only, but I could observe from a distance. There were a few rubberneckers also observing the scene. I noted that the water leak from earlier had been repaired, so this body had left a small puddle of blood, and a blood trail. Using my binoculars, I could see the trail of blood well enough to see that it led *to* the puddle, not the other way around. I spotted a larger blood spot at the beginning of the trail, several meters from the bigger puddle. I took a close look at the white chalk outlining the body that was found. Then I moved away and found a place to sit while I considered what I saw.

The basic activity that I could figure out was that the man was probably stabbed, due to the lack of any blood spatter on the wall behind where he was injured. The first man had been stabbed, and the man from the tube had a knife that he threatened me with. So, similar MO. That links the two murders, but why would they happen on the same spot?

Chapter Negative Five

In the morning I headed over to Larry's lab armed with the two pads. I had powered them down, which wouldn't guarantee they can't be tracked, of course, but since nothing bad had happened to me in the night, I felt fairly safe they hadn't tracked me just yet. And since this was exactly the sort of thing Larry liked doing, he'd know how to prevent any tracking signals from getting out. I just had to get them to him.

I found a note from Mary saying she was sorry she missed me last night. Apparently she'd come home after I was asleep, and left before I woke up, which, while not unusual, wasn't a regular occurrence. It was a bit irksome, considering the events of last night, and I felt like I needed to talk to her. Still, I could call her later. Reasoning so, I went to Larry's lab.

Nothing untoward happened on the way to the school. I encountered no gangsters, no spies, no secret organizations, and no dogs. I thought it was weird after the way the previous night had gone, but then maybe I had just foiled a couple of muggers who in turn tried to mug me instead. You know, casual crime. In any case, I approached Larry's lab unmolested. As expected, he was sitting in his stuffed prep room, full of physics educational supplies and positronics gear, and even a fair amount of older electronics stuff. He was working his terminal, probably reading some positronic journal or other, when I came in. Larry was a fairly good shaped late '50s man, measured in Earth years, of course. His blond hairline had started its retreat over a decade ago, framing a face that was frozen in an expression of confusion.

"Larry, you really need to figure out how to lock your door."

"Oh hi, Cecil," he said. "What brings you to this part of the world?"

"I have these pads here," I said. "They might be tracked, we need to disable any tracking mechanism right away before we go any further."

"Well, nice to see you after so long," he said. "So, how's the girlfriend?"

"Larry, I just saw you last week."

"Well, it'd be nice to get a 'hi, how are you doing' every now and then," said Larry. "Nobody ever does that anymore, it's always 'Larry do this', 'Larry do that', 'Larry the air track is warped', Larry--"

"Hi, how are you doing? I have these pads here that may have a tracking mechanism that you need to disable. Girlfriend's doing fine, and I'm just knocking about the neighborhood looking for a netrunner."

"Fine," he said. "Over there is a, well, it's, uh, one of those things, what do you call it?" Larry can be quite absent-minded. I walked over to where he was pointing. "That silver plate over there, that's it. It's a tracker disabler thingee." I'm always amazed when Larry throws Layman's, because he's usually so anal about using Right Words. I set the two pads on the plate. "Now you need to flip that switch on the side, there." I flipped the switch. "So, would you mind telling me what this is all about?"

"Can't yet, sorry," I said. "Could be dangerous. Also, I don't actually know anything myself yet. Well, it's mostly that. Just a strange adventure from downtown New Austin."

"You really need to quit hanging out down there," he said. "You could get your job back here, now that what's-her-face is gone."

"I know," I said. "I'm just not ready for it yet. Sorry, but you know how it is."

"No," he said. "I don't, really. Explain."

"I'd rather not," I said. I smiled. "I'd rather find out who owns those pads. Next of kin, that sort of thing. When you get names, I'll hit up Sherry and see what she can find in her PI database."

"Alright," he said. "I won't pry. It'll only be a few more minutes worth of scanning to find out what sort of passive trackers those things have. Of course, standard pads have active trackers in them, so once we power them back up, the active trackers will start broadcasting. I have no way to shield those."

"But they can often be disabled," I pointed out helpfully.

"Not reliably," he said. "That EM suppressor should prevent the wireless towers from receiving the signal, but if there's even a small chance you were followed, well, someone with the right receiver could still pick up the tracking signals if they were in close enough proximity."

"I don't think I was followed," I said. "But it's hard to be sure, you know?"

"No, I'm naturally paranoid. I always know when I'm being followed."

"Have you ever been followed?"

"Well, there was this one time, this girl," he said sheepishly, "but you don't want to hear about it. The scan is complete, looks like there are no passive tracking devices in those pads. Let me see if I can hack into them from the terminal. This could take some time, do you want to hang around and wait, or do you have pressing matters to attend to?"

"I'll hang around a bit," I said. "But I've got to make a call."

"You go do that," he said. "I'll be at work here."

"Roger that, and thanks, Larry."

"No, thank you," he said. "You know I love this stuff."

We exchanged smiles, and I stepped outside and let him work. I rang up Mary, and she answered.

"Hey baby, whatcha doin'?" I asked.

"Talking to you, what are you doing?" she answered in that sexy contralto she uses when she talks to me.

"Hanging out with Larry in his lab, wondering what you've been up to."

"I've been working, of course," and she smiled at me.

"Where'd you end up last night while I was working?"

"I hung out after work with some friends, played some silly bar games, the usual. Didn't quite manage to make it downtown to see you this time."

"I noticed," I said. "I missed you."

"I missed you, too," she said. "Look, honey, I've got to go, I'll call you back later, ok?"

"Ok, I love you, good-bye!"

"Love you too, good-bye!"

And then she was gone. I went to see if Larry had anything for me, yet. He was hard at work, but had an obviously troubled expression on his face.

"What's up, Larry?"

"Well," he said, "it's this security system that's on here to prevent exactly what I'm doing. I know it, I've seen it. A colleague of mine developed it a number of years back, and then disappeared. I heard a rumor that he was working for the mob, which would explain his disappearance, and if true, would indicate that the gentlemen you took these pads from are, well, gangsters." He looked at me very seriously. "Cecil, I've never known you to get involved with these sort of people, what's going on?"

"Larry," I said, "I have absolutely no idea. It seems that I'm getting sucked into a plot of some sort, and I don't really know a way out just yet. So I'll have to ride the roller-coaster for a bit and see what happens."

"That zen stuff never really worked for me, you know," said Larry.

"I know," I said. "Let me know when you have more from the pads." Then I left. I didn't want to get involved in a deep conversation about the source of the pads until Larry had a chance to objectively analyze the data, and I knew how Larry was.

I went over to Sherry's office. She works in an office in a retail bubble immediately adjacent to downtown where she can conveniently visit the courthouse regularly. Sherry is an interesting character. When I first met her, I was juggling at the school during downtime between labs. She initially creeped me out a bit, and I didn't want to talk to her. But since we had to occupy the same space at certain times, I couldn't shake her, and she didn't creep me out enough for me to try. So, over time, we developed a friendship and I came to rely upon her significantly. She really helped me out with her PI resources when the psycho ex-wife had a stalker, and she's always happy to use her PI resources for her friends when they're in a bit of a bind.

It's just not the kind of resource most friends need.

I'm not most friends. She's done a fair amount of extracurricular investigation for me, and this situation definitely called for her support. And she can't avoid a good spy story, so it would be an easy sell. The receptionist was quite attractive, and obviously checking me out. For a performer such as myself, I was used to that sort of attention, but I wasn't in costume at the moment, so she was obviously attracted to me as a person rather than as a performer.

"Is Sherry in?"

"Are you one of Sherry's clients?" she asked.

"Yes," I answered. "I am Cecil. Can you let her know that I'm here to see her?"

"Certainly," she smiled broadly.

"Soooo, can I see her?" I asked.

"Sure," she said. "You can see your girlfriend."

"She's not my girlfriend," I said. "She's a good friend."

"So you're free to date?"

"No, I'm not. Sorry."

"Oh," she answered, looking somewhat disappointed. Then she saw on her little screen what she needed to see and said "Ok, Sherry is available now. Just go through that door--"

"Yeah, I know where her office is, thanks," I said. "You're new."

"Yes," the receptionist answered. "Today is my first day."

"Oh, ok. Well, have a good morning," I told her.

* * *

"You want me to do WHAT?" Sherry said.

"DNA analysis."

"On blood from a man that police are going to think you killed?"

"Yep."

"Did you kill him?"

"Nope."

"Can I really believe that? Have you ever killed anyone before? Wait, don't answer that, there are some things about you that I just don't want to know," she said. "What happens if I find out who this guy is?"

"Then we'll know," I said, matter-of-factly, "And you get to do a fairly complete workup on him. Also, how does your forensics guy compare to the police's?"

"He's generally better," she said. "He really digs his work, and does it privately because he gets more interesting cases that way."

"So, when the police start investigating the murder?"

"I won't be able to keep tabs on the police investigation, but we'll be ahead of them for information for quite a while," she said.

"That's fine," I said. "I can probably get Larry to hack into the city's system and keep tabs for us."

"You have a really odd collection of friends," Sherry said.

"Yes, I do," I said. "It's like we have all that we need to be a field espionage unit."

"Isn't that what we're doing now?"

I laughed. "Don't worry, girl, it'll be fun, you'll see."

"There's a reason I'm trying to get out of PI work," she said.

"No there isn't, you love it and you know it. It's just your current boss is an asshole, is all."

"Shut up, Cecil," she said with a chuckle. "Why don't you move along and let me get this stuff done."

"Roger that, and thanks," I said.

"It'll be my pleasure," she answered. "Now shoo."

So I left. With the transit time and the time spent talking to Sherry, Larry ought to have made some headway, so I went back to the school. Indeed, Larry had gotten into the pads.

"It wasn't really that difficult," he said. "That's mostly because the basis of the security system is something I gave to my colleague..." Then Larry went off in his most detailed manner describing the system. I waited for him to finish because that would probably give Sherry some time to get the DNA analysis.

"So, who are these people?" I asked.

"They're definitely gangsters," he said. I interrupted him before he could get any further.

"One of them is a murder victim and the other is the murderer."

"Interesting," he said. "Why are you getting involved in a gang war?"

"I don't think I am," I said. "The victim seemed to know me. He gave me something, a flasher. Said Somebody would contact me."

"Have you been contacted?"

"No," I said. "They might not even know he got murdered. Hell, I don't know if the police even know about him yet."

"Interesting."

"Did you manage to download the database from each pad?"

"Yes," said Larry. "I've got it here."

"Send a copy to Sherry so she can run down the contact list and check on anything else that looks interesting."

Larry sighed. "Roger that."

"Also, would you be able to put an agent in there that would transmit all voice calls to your own recorder?"

"I could," he said. "No guarantees it won't be found out, of course."

"Of course," I said. "But can you do it without at least getting caught?"

"Certainly," he said. "What do you have in mind?"

"I was thinking they'd track the pads sooner or later, and you downloaded everything that's on them now, right?"

"I see what you're thinking. Leave them in a cafe somewhere where they can be found by the owners, and then use them to spy on the owners. Owner, I guess, since one of the owners is dead. Gangsters aren't stupid, you know, and they probably have a protocol for when their communication devices are left in enemy hands for extended periods."

"I know," I said. "But if there's a chance we can get something out of it without risking anything, then why not try?"

"True," he said. "I could have them both ready to return to their owners in about an hour. Do you want both of them ready?"

"Yes, do that," I said. "While you're at it, how easy is it to break into the city system?"

"Easy as pie," he said. "I've, uh, *cough*, done it before," he said somewhat sheepishly.

I looked askance at him.

"It wasn't on purpose!"

"You don't break into the city system on accident!"

"Well, this was, and I don't want to talk about it," he said.

I could tell he really wanted to tell me all about it, but all that really mattered was that he could do it.

"Can you get into the police subnet?"

"Sure, why?"

"I want you to track the murder investigation."

"Easy enough," he answered. "We should be able to keep abreast of whatever they find out. Why don't you just go to the police with everything you know and let them handle it?"

"Because right now we don't even know if they're involved, and if they are, on which side," I said. "This is probably a good guys vs bad guys thing, and I want to make sure the good guys win."

"But it's not your conflict," he said.

"I've got a weird feeling about it," I said, "And when my gut tells me to get involved with something, it's usually right. That's how I wound up with Mary, doncha know."

"Fine," Larry said. "But we do know one thing about the man."

"What's that?"

"He wasn't a cop," Larry said. "If he were, I'd have found that out already."

"And they'd have identified him," I said. "And probably kicked open my door in the night. I figured that much already." I hadn't, but it's usually a good idea to let Larry think you're always a step ahead of him. That way when he's clearly ahead of me, he gets really happy and smug about it, and I really appreciate a happy and smug Larry, especially considering how often he's down and out instead.

"Yep," said Larry. "Under normal police procedures, they would have identified the victim by now, so he must be pretty far off the beaten path for them not to have ID'd him already."

"I don't think they will identify him," I said.

"So how are you going to figure out who he is?"

"I don't know," I said. "But you and Sherry need to talk."

"Sure thing," said Larry. "Always a team player, I am."

Team? Is that what's going on here? Do I really have a team? I'd have to get Mary involved if that were going on, and I'd need her sooner or later. The thing about Mary is that she actually has connections into the mob, so she might be able to get some information from them. A long time ago, she worked in several of the strip joints, and by all accounts she was very good at her job. The work got her in contact with a number of shady underworld figures, and she maintained those relationships for a number of years after that. Nowadays she's your standard mid-30s chubby hispanic woman, and as a result can't strip anymore, which is good because she doesn't ever want to return to that lifestyle. And it puts her in one of the categories of sexy that I find really sexy. Add to it that she's a really great lover, loves sex, and loves me, and we've got a good thing going. I couldn't even imagine what it would be like to lose her, certainly not after all those years I struggled in an abusive marriage. With Mary, I had a level of freedom I didn't even imagine possible. Everything is open. I can have whatever sex I want with her, I can talk to her about anything, and she does the same. She's supportive of everything I want to do, which says a lot about her temperament because I'm always finding something new to do and often discarding a previous pursuit when I haven't finished it. It takes a certain kind of woman to be able to put up with that, and a very special woman to be supportive of it. On top of all of that, she is easily one of the smartest people I've ever known. I'd need that intelligence, that certain way of simplifying problems that she has. I just don't want anything to happen to her, and keeping her at arm's length in this affair should be a good protective move until I know more about what's going on.

But what about Sherry and Larry? They can protect themselves, of course! Well, so can Mary, dammit! But I was so willing to involve Sherry and Larry so quickly, within 12 hours of the man's death even, and still didn't even want to tell Mary about it. That didn't really sit right with me, I'd have to talk to Mary and see what she thought.

I suddenly remembered that I was still talking to Larry. He was just watching me work through my thoughts.

"You're thinking about getting Mary involved here, aren't you?" he psychically observed.

"Yes," I said. "She may still have mob connections that could help."

"Don't," he said. "You have to consider the possibility that the man had advance knowledge that he was safe to give you the flasher."

"What makes you think that?"

"That's the only reason you'd be involved at this point," said Larry. "You have something from an unidentified man that was killed by gangsters, carrying a pad encrypted by gangsters, and you have to figure out how to get that thing to the proper group of people, people that you think are the Good Guys. It's obvious, really. But he can't let Mary get her hands on it, because she might pass it on to the Bad Guys."

I was dumbfounded. The way Larry talks, you hear his thought process, and he often comes up as being really smart but slow. He's not really known for his wit. When he does some quick smart thing, it's always surprising.

"Ok," I said. "How does he know I'm with Mary?"

"That's an admittedly weak part of my hypothesis, and is also a reason he wouldn't have given it to you in the first place."

"Quite weak," I said. "I don't know the man."

"Maybe Mary knows him?"

"Maybe. That's another very weak part of your hypothesis. While it would be advantageous to him if he knew her and was working with her, it seems to me that she'd be more likely to turn it over to her mob connections."

"So, what are you going to do?"

"Well, what he gave me was a flasher," I said. "That means he obviously had data he needed to prevent from falling into the wrong hands."

"Maybe he figured you would just destroy it?"

"No, he told me explicitly that I'd be contacted," I said.

"That implies that his people, whoever they are, have knowledge of his giving the device to you."

"Maybe it's got a tracker?" I suggested.

"Doubtful," said Larry. "Anything they can track can also be tracked by their enemies. No, there has to be some other sort of arrangement. I'd ask if you had any strange conversations with people recently, but that would be useless because you're always having strange conversations with people."

"Just like this one," I said and smiled. "But to answer your unasked question, no, I haven't had any conversations that lead me to think his people have already contacted me. More likely they're working on my sterling reputation for honesty and integrity and will contact me."

"Or they're expecting you to hand it over to your girlfriend," said Larry.

"Well then, if they want to find me, they shouldn't have any trouble," I responded. "I am, after all, the only fool in town."

"Maybe I should clean my gun."

"Is it registered?"

"One is. I'll use that one," said Larry. "I can give you the unregistered one for the duration of the crisis, if you want."

"I'd appreciate that, Larry," I said, "But my profession makes me subject to too many searches. I'd better keep my shit clean."

"Up to you," said Larry. "So, I take it you want me to forward ID information from the pads to Sherry?"

"Yes," I said.

My pad started singing the Sweetie-is-calling-you song, so I gestured to Larry and stepped out.

"What's up, baby?" I said.

"Not much," she answered. "I just wanted to tell you it'll be another late night. Rosa's having big problems with her husband, and I need to run and help her out. This might be the Big D for them."

"Ok," I said. "I was planning on working the shopping circuit for a few days, so I won't be downtown."

"That's good," she said. "You know how you going downtown makes me nervous. They had another murder down there last night, probably not far from you. Scary stuff. I hope you're ok."

"Scary stuff indeed, and I'm just fine," I said. "Good luck with Rosa, I've got to go now, love-you-bye."

"Love-you-bye," she said.

I closed the connection.

"Larry, how soon before you can get into the police subnet?"

"I already made it in there," he said. "That system's hopelessly simple. They found the body soon after you left it. Night patrol found it. They haven't identified the man yet, but they've started interviews. They'll probably talk to you, sooner rather than later."

"Luckily nobody downtown knows my secret identity," I said, "So I'll just avoid downtown for awhile. Shopping district tips are decent, if unreliable compared to drunk tips. If the night patrol found it, then what are the chances anybody besides you, me, and the police know about the murder?"

"Slim. Very slim. Especially with the President coming to give a speech, they'd suppress the information immediately and run damage control. You can bet nobody else knows."

"Then how did Mary know the police found the body?"

"Because she knew the victim, obviously. Maybe you should give her the flasher."

"What if Mary's mob friends are the same ones that killed this guy?"

"You're starting to over think this, I think," said Larry. "Let's stick with the known facts and go from there."

"You're right, Larry. You're right."

Chapter Negative Four

Playing the Arboretum was reasonably profitable. I made enough money, even if it wasn't a killing. A number of kids laughed at my act, and kids almost always love my act. In the time I'd been being a fool, I'd never encountered a kid with a clown phobia. Maybe I had, but I think that being a fool is enough different from a clown that I don't invoke the clown phobia. So kids love me, and their mothers do too. If I were single, I could probably get into plenty of mothers' pants. Luckily, I've never really been interested in that sort of lifestyle, and no matter what your profession, sleeping with your customers is unprofessional. So I don't, and wouldn't have even if I was single. In fact, I didn't try even when I was single, even though that was before Cecil the Fool existed and I was just a random juggler that looked like a downtown beggar.

At home that night, Mary showed up late. I was still awake when she got home, but I was tired. She muttered a little bit about her friend's divorce, took a shower, and jumped into bed. I considered fooling around with her, but I was half asleep when she got home, so I didn't get far. I think I may have left our favorite tube inside her when I fell asleep, which usually means she wakes up horny, but she wasn't there when I woke up. She had to work that day, and since I usually work evenings, I wasn't even awake until after she'd left. I found the tube, though, and it had enough of a mucus covering to tell me what she'd been up to that morning. I love Mary.

Sherry should have taken the pad databases and other identifying information from Larry and run it, so I started the day by heading out to her office. I had intended to do lunch that day at a popular hispanic restaurant, so I showed up to her office dressed for work. The new receptionist was still quite attractive, and obviously checking me out in my work uniform.

"Is Sherry in?"

"You're one of Sherry's clients?" she asked.

"Yes," I answered. "I am Cecil, the Fool. Can you let her know that I'm here to see her?"

"Certainly," she giggled. "You're a lot cuter than the friend that came in yesterday."

Being the friend that came in yesterday, I was slightly offended by that.

"Soooo, can I see her?" I asked.

"Sure," she said. "Are you, um, dating her?"

"No," I said. "She's a good friend."

"So you're free to date?"

"No, I'm not. Sorry."

"Oh," she answered, looking somewhat disappointed. Then she saw on her little screen what she needed to see and said "Ok, Sherry is available now. Just go through that door--"

"Yeah, I know where her office is, thanks," I said. "You're new."

"Yes," the receptionist answered. "I started yesterday."

"Ok," I answered. "Remember me, both in costume and out, because I have a lot of business with Sherry and really don't want to go through this little scene every time I need to see her."

With that, I left a huffy girl behind me and went straight to Sherry's office. I hate having the same conversation over and over.

"Ok girl," I said, "Whatcha got?"

"Cecil! I love it when you're in costume!"

"Settle down," I said, "This is serious. What do you have?"

"Oh, alright," she answered. "You never liked friends noticing your costume anyway."

"The costume is just a formality."

"I know," she responded. "You're a fool, and that's all there is to it."

"Shut it," I said, "And give me the scoop."

"Ok," Sherry answered. "Here's the deal:

"The guy that you assaulted in the tube is a mobster. He's on the Federale's most wanted list, which means he's a pretty serious gangster. You have to have killed a number of people to get on that list."

"Wow," I said. "And I attacked him. Truthfully, we'd already figured they were mobsters."

"You're crazy," she agreed. "But, you see, they're wanted on Earth, and while the warrants apply here and the reward can be collected here, they haven't operated here. There's no record of them having ever operated here."

"That was obvious from the way they fought in free fall."

"They?"

"Did I mention there were two of them?"

"Oh yeah? How did *they* fight in free fall?"

"They didn't," I answered. "They lost."

"Ah, that was your competitive advantage," said Sherry. "These guys are cold-blooded killers, and you took them down solely because of the situation. The real question is this: why were they assigned to this mission when they clearly don't know how to handle the gravity here?"

"Because they're the best the mob has to offer?"

"The mob has plenty of good agents on Europa," said Sherry. "These two agents were obviously imported. That usually means there's a common thread of some sort."

"Common thread?"

"Yeah," answered Sherry. "Whatever jobs they were working on Earth, or Mars, or wherever they were last at are somehow linked to this job. It's the same thing."

"Are you sure they're organized that way?"

"What do you mean?"

"Well, see, when I was on Mars," I started, "I had mob contacts. Distant family. You know. Anyway, it seemed to me that the mob never evolved into a big monolithic organization but instead fractured into families that merged in various ways. I don't know how they're distributed, but there's a fair chance the Europan family and whatever family these guys are from aren't the same families and might be competing."

"That's interesting. Then the guy they're after might be a local mobster."

"Speaking of whiches, did you get an ID on him?"

"No," answered Sherry, "I didn't. There's no record of his DNA anywhere in the system, which is usually an indication that he wasn't born in the Islamic Republic. I have some leads to pursue yet, still, so I haven't given up on ID'ing him."

"Have you scanned his contact list yet?"

"I've got the computer running through the contact list, it'll report when it's done a complete background on every entry."

"Fancy," I pointed out.

"It's an older system," said Sherry, "But it gets the job done."

"So what's the common thread here, then?" I asked.

"I don't know," answered Sherry. "There's no public record, and no police record, of what these guys have done. The only thing the police have noted is who they've killed, and most of them are people the police couldn't identify."

"That's interesting by itself," I pointed out.

"Yes, but it doesn't tell us anything," Sherry said. "Their victims could have been other gangsters from rival gangs, dealers, whatever."

"True," I said, "But if they're following a particular thread, then the guy they murdered the other night is in that thread. And mobsters usually have ID's you can find. That suggests our victim was not a mobster, even if he was using mobster encryption. Can you work up a report of their victims? Who are they, where were they killed, and what sorts of thing they had their noses in?"

"Already did," said Sherry. She's so cool. "Nothing. Their victims had birth records and death records, and nothing else. It's like they barely existed."

"What kind of jobs did they have?"

"It ranges from fusion-drive mechanic to door-to-door salesman. There's really no common thread that links them."

"No obvious common thread," I said. "Interesting."

Sherry said, "Look, Cecil, you're easily the smartest person I've ever known, and I don't doubt your instincts at all, but the evidence just isn't there to tell us about these guys. One is definitely a gangster, and the other was his target, and he may or may not have been a gangster, and that's all we've got."

"I understand," I answered, "And I appreciate your over-estimate of my abilities. Tell me more about the victim?"

"He doesn't exist."

"Doesn't exist?" I asked.

"I cross-referenced every database I've got. If he had been born on Europa, then a DNA sample would be on file. If he had served in any military, then there would be DNA to match against. He's never committed a crime for which he was arrested, and he's never really done anything. He may also be from off-world, in which case the databases I have access to wouldn't carry anything on him."

"That sucks," I pointed out.

"More than a little," said Sherry. "We'll figure it out, though. It's just going to take some more time."

"Understood," I answered. "Can I have my flasher back?"

"I'm not quite done with it," answered Sherry. "If you need it..."

"Not a big deal," I said. "If you think you might get more information from it, then keep it. I figure I'll turn it over to Larry so he can study it himself."

"You mean find out what's on it?"

"And anything that might help identify these people and why one was willing to kill for it and the other was willing to die."

"Right."

"So," I said, "When you find anything out about our victim, you're going to let me know, right?"

"Right," she answered confidently. "I'll pay a visit to the address on his ID card and work my way through the mountains of data that Larry has given me."

"Ok," I said. "So we figure out who he is, focus our efforts on that, and forget that the mob might want to kill me?"

"If they'd wanted to kill you, they would have done so already," Sherry said. "So just take a chill pill and relax, you're safe right now. Whatever they wanted from him, they now want it from you. If they kill you, they don't get it. Remember that."

"But they can torture it out of me."

"We'll burn that bridge when we come to it," said Sherry. "Really, how do you go out at night?"

"By dressing up like a fool," I answered. "Speaking of whiches, I have a performance to make."

"Go do that," Sherry said. "I'll be here, unless I'm at the courthouse."

"Ok," I said. "I'm there."

"Have fun," she said.

"I'll try," I answered.

Then I left.

The lunch at the restaurant wasn't a big take, but it was better than what I normally get for lunch: nothing. I don't work lunches normally, but under the circumstances I figured I should try to take what I can when I can to leave me free to do what I have to do when I have to do it, whatever it actually turns out to be. Near the end of my performance, Mary wandered in and took a booth by herself. When my performance ended, I gave her a kiss and took a seat with her in the booth.

"Hey baby," I said. "Guess where we are?"

"I know this place," she said. "It's where we ate on our first date." She smiled sweetly at me.

"Yeppers," I said, because while I was in costume, I said stupid things. "Look, sweetie, I have to ask you something that's a little tricky to get at."

"Ok," she said. "I slept with him."

"With who?"

"Whoever you're asking about."

"A dead guy?"

"Oh, no, I didn't sleep with a dead guy, just you." I love the way she flirts.

"You mentioned earlier on the phone that they had found the body I found last night," I began.

"Yes," she said.

"I happen to know that only me and the police know about that murder," I said. "The body was found within a couple of hours of me seeing it by the police."

"You *saw* it?" she gasped.

"Yes," I said. "Look, it's hard to describe. I didn't call the police because I didn't want to get involved.

Then, when I was headed home, these two guys followed me and tried to take me into custody in the tube."

"Ah oh," she said. "Did they use guns?"

"Yes," I said. "Tried, anyway. See, here's the weird thing. They're off-worlders, obviously from a planet with much higher gravity than our beloved Europa, so I took them down pretty easily. They killed the guy downtown, and seemed to think that he had given something to me before they got to him."

"Had he?"

"I don't know," I said. "You know how my money bag is."

"True," she said. "So, what then?"

"Well," I answered, "I took their pads and got some friends to ID them. They're mobsters."

"Cecil, dear, what have you gotten yourself into?"

"I don't know," I said. "But it seems you're somehow involved as well. How did you know about the murder?"

She stopped up short at that. Apparently she didn't see this coming.

"I read it in the news," she finished.

"Sweetheart," I said, "No you didn't. The police are keeping it quiet so that there won't be a fuss when the President plays downtown next week."

"You mean 'gives a speech'," she said.

"No," I said. "I mean 'plays'. What the President does and what I do are essentially the same thing, his tips are just counted as votes, and my costume is cooler than his. But don't distract me. I need to know how you know about the murder."

"You know I have my own friends downtown, right?"

"Mobsters?"

"No, silly," she said. Then she looked at me more closely. "I haven't been in contact with any mobsters for several years, and even then it was because they were still trying to whore me out. And you know I'll never do hooker's work."

I met her eyes with a You're Not Serious.

"I didn't find out through mobsters," she said. "Besides, the ones I did know wouldn't have anything to do with off-world mobsters. The Europan families are pretty closed to outside intrusions. So I didn't find out through mobsters."

"Then you knew the victim," I said, "And were in contact with him."

"No, sweetie, I don't know the victim," she said. "I'm sorry, you must have missed the report in the news or something. I swear I don't know anything about it other than what the general public knows."

I was having a little trouble believing her, which was odd since I trusted her so much. Was she actually lying to me? Did I really miss something like that in the news? Sherry would have mentioned it, had it been in the news. Of course, I told her all about it before she had a chance to say. I better ask her.

"Under the circumstances," I said, "You wouldn't object to me double-checking that, would you?"

She was a good poker player.

"No, of course not," she said.

I gave her Blessed Silence. She stared back at

me. This went on for several nervous moments, then she spoke again.

"So, what's going on, then?"

"I think I've brought you up to date," I said slowly.

"No, I mean, why, er, crap," she stammered. "How did you get involved in the first place?"

"Well, I was performing like I usually do, and this guy stopped to watch, and I noticed he was a bit huffy and out of breath. I noticed somehow that he was being followed, and after he left me, I used my juggling act to stall the people who were following him, hoping he'd be able to get away."

She softened noticeably at that. "You're so sweet," she said. "I love you."

"I love you, too, babe," I said automatically.

"Look, sweetie," said Mary, "I have to go. I wish I didn't, but I have class to go to."

"I understand," I said. "Give me a kiss, then."

"Ok," she said. Then she leaned across the table and gave me one of her sweet, deep kisses that always leaves me gasping for air and wanting more. It had much the same effect as usual, even with the tension in the air. I love that about her. "Ok, bye sweetie, I'll see you this evening."

And she grabbed her backpack and took off.

So, she knew about the murder and wanted to play off how she knew. I went outside and dialed Sherry. She answered immediately.

"What's up?"

"Hey, Sherry," I started. "You check the news pretty often, right?"

"Yes," she said, "But the reason I always know the news is because we get an aggregate form that has names, places, etc. It helps in our investigations."

"Oh, that's convenient," I said. "Any mention of the, uh, event we're working with?"

"Nope," she said. "Checked that after you left earlier. Nada, zip, zilch. Why?"

"Why would Mary know about it, then?"

"She's obviously involved," Sherry said. "Interesting. Does she still have her old mob contacts?"

"I know she knows *how* to contact them," I said, "But she just said she hasn't talked to them in years, and the last time it seems some one or more were trying to get her to be a hooker and she didn't go for that. On the other hand, she was clearly lying about knowing about the murder, particularly in how she found out. Does your news aggregate include everything in today's news?"

"Yes," she said. "Well, everything reported on Europa, anyway. We get some off-world news, but this sort of story would break locally first and then go off-world."

"So if there was something in today's news--"

"It would be there," she interrupted. "Mary knows something."

"Damn," I said. "Damn, damn."

"Yeah, tell me about it," said Sherry. "Hang on a sec." Then, after about a minute or so: "Looks like there's someone in here marked 'Jaclyn' that shares Mary's number."

"Jaclyn?" I asked. "Why would it say that?"

"Dunno," said Sherry. "But the PI software isn't making the connection. I'll run a background on Mary and see what we get for the dossier."

"So we can confirm that Mary knows the victim," I said. "Maybe it's time to come clean to her."

"Not yet," said Sherry. "We still don't know if she's safe. Just keep it under your hat for a little longer and let's see what we come up with, ok?"

Against my gut feeling, I agreed.

Chapter Negative Three

The lunch performance was over, and I was feeling quite unsettled by Mary's knowledge of the murder, but I pushed it out of my mind. I swung by the address on the victim's ID card. It was an abandoned compartment, set for demolition. Poking around the wreckage, I determined there was nothing of interest here, or at least nothing that I would find without a full forensics team. It wasn't unexpected. So I decided to take myself out for a few drinks. While I was walking away from the abandoned compartment, Larry called me.

"Hi Larry," I said. "What's up?"

"I wanted to let you know I've got those pads ready to drop."

"Ready?"

"You asked me to put a monitoring agent on them," he reminded me.

"Oh right," I said. "Great, I was heading out to have a few drinks out in the Wells bubble. Care to join me?"

"Sure," he said. "Just remember to power up the pads whenever you drop them, or else they won't send the tracking signal."

"No problem," I said. "Do you know where Homeboy's is?"

"No, but I can check the map service," Larry answered. "I've got one of Vali's classes just finishing up right now, so I'll be able to leave in about 20 minutes. Will that work for you?"

"Sure," I said. "You're only about 10 minutes from the bar, you'll probably still beat me there. I'm leaving from downtown."

"Ok, I'll see you there," answered Larry. I cut the connection and moved on.

I dropped in at Homeboy's right when the early evening crowd was arriving. About a kilometer from Homeboy's sits a shopping center that tends to attract a good night crowd, so I figured I'd go make some money out there, after finishing up with Larry. That would also make a good place to leave the pads for the gangsters to find the one, and for me to see who shows up for the other.

Homeboy's is an unusual place, in my limited experience with bars, sarcasm intended. On one side, it's a karaoke bar starting at 10pm every evening. On the other side, it's a sports bar with a single pool table and a few vintage game machines scattered about. Now, pool in Europa's small gravity is an interesting sport. The table itself is eight times the size of an earth table, and the walls are about a meter high. Instead of pockets, there are four gates, one in each corner, plus four more gates in the middle of each side. There are 21 balls instead of the traditional 15, and the balls themselves are made of lead. That gives them a nice high mass to prevent them from jumping too high, while still allowing them to be relatively small. To shoot, the player has to actually climb into the "table" area, get down on hands and knees, and shoot. Players are automatically disqualified if any balls touch any part of their bodies, as in traditional pool.

The karaoke side of the bar doesn't start until 10pm, so at the time I met Larry there, it was just a sitting area with a dark stage. Larry was sitting stage side, since at that time of day that table is the least noticed table. I found him with two beers already on the table.

"So, whatcha got?" I asked Larry.

He passed the pads to me, and I stuck them in my bag.

"Don't forget," he reminded me. "Don't power them up until you've dropped them off, and then get out of the area as fast as possible. You don't need to hang around and make sure they're picked up. As soon as somebody uses them, we'll know, and we'll be able to quickly determine who it is."

"Got it," I said, canceling my plan to observe whoever picked up the victim's pad. When your friends are watching your back, sometimes you do what they ask without question. "Any other interesting news?"

"Yes," said Larry. "Well, sorta. It depends on how you look at it."

"Ok, what is it?"

"The police have decided to class the, um, event, as a random mugging, so the case has been shelved for now."

"Hm," I said. "That's interesting."

"I didn't really think so," said Larry. "There's enough murders around these parts that the police don't investigate every single one."

We sat in silence for a few moments and drank our beers.

"Did they identify the victim?" I asked finally.

"Nope," said Larry. "Apparently they're having the same problems doing that that Sherry's having."

"Of course," I said. "It is curious, though. The President is going to give a speech right on my spot. How does the city figure it'll look if the President finds out later about the murder? Won't that be more embarrassing?"

"I don't understand politics," said Larry. "It's all about show, not tell, so I don't even pay attention to it anymore."

"Ah," I grunted.

"There are two possibilities," said Larry, switching back to a previous track. "Either Mary knows the victim or she knows the killer."

"Or is somehow connected to one or both," I pointed out.

"Right," said Larry. "I guess, technically, that's three possibilities."

"Four," I said. "Add to it that Sherry found Mary's number under a fake name in the victim's pad. We'll just have to wait and see."

"I could probably hack into her pad and put a monitoring agent there," he suggested.

"No go," I said. "I trust her to be doing the right thing, and if she found me spying on her, that would be a disaster. We'll just have to let her run on her own while we run on our own, and we'll see where the pieces fall when the time comes."

"Not sure I agree with that," said Larry, "But you're the boss."

I finished my beer. Larry was already finished with his.

"Want another?" I asked.

"Sure," he said.

I grabbed the glasses and went to the bar. Gomer, the owner, was working the bar.

"Heya Cecil," he said. "Are you performing for us tonight?"

"Sorry bud," I answered, "Not tonight. Got stuff going on."

"Ah," he said. "Well, you need to come in and do a show sometime. We always enjoy it when you do."

"I will," I said. "Don't worry. I love playing here, you know that."

I grabbed the two full beers and headed back to the table. Larry and I sat in silence while we finished our beers, considering what little information we had.

"I went to the address on the victim's ID. Abandoned compartment."

"That's no surprise. Look, Cecil, why don't you go to the police?" asked Larry.

"Simple," I said. "Since Mary is apparently involved somehow, I have to protect her. Police involvement would destabilize the situation even more than it already has been."

"The police may be able to stabilize the situation and keep it from getting out of control."

I laughed out loud.

"I doubt it," I said. "The cops around here can't tell a murder from a rape, even though one victim is obviously still alive."

"Bah," said Larry. "We can monitor their investigation just fine, just like we're already doing."

"To be honest, they'd probably just slap me with the murder charges and be done with it," I said. "Let's see, murder, robbery, mugging two honest citizens..."

"Only they're not honest citizens," said Larry.

"Our information that ties them to the mob is somewhat incredible," I said. "The cops won't buy it, and can't confirm it their own way."

"Sherry was able to confirm it, so the cops should be able to," Larry said.

"That's even more reason for them to back down," I said. "They avoid the mob, that's why they've risen to so much power around here."

"Oh I guess you're right," said Larry. "You're stuck in the middle of this, and so far seem to have avoided getting snagged. But you'll be on the mobster's radar again, and it won't be so pleasant the next time."

"I'll watch my back," I said. "I do it anyway."

"Yeah, I know," said Larry. "I guess it's time for me to head out, got an early morning tomorrow."

"That early class of Vali's?"

"Yep," said Larry. "Thanks for the beer."

Then he walked out and disappeared. I got another beer, sat, and thought for awhile. That last part of the conversation with Larry filled me with a sense of foreboding. When my thoughts became too ugly for me to consider, I slammed the remainder of my beer and left.

I wanted to leave the pads in the Wells bubble because that's far from my normal range. True, Mary and I liked to go to Homeboy's, but we didn't go there very often, so the likelihood of us encountering anybody associated with the pads was slim. Furthermore, the people who retrieved the pads would not be able to link them to me in any way other than knowing I had taken them and left them, if they even knew that much. In any case, they wouldn't be able to track me leaving them, and by the time they were found, I'd be long gone.

I made the decision not to perform in the Wells bubble and instead to just do the drop. There's a small shopping center with a fried chicken place near Homeboy's, so I figured I drop the pads there and get some food. What's the worst that could happen?

Chapter Negative Two

When I got home that night, I found Mary sitting on the couch. She was just finishing up a conversation on her pad when I walked around the couch and dropped into the chair. I looked at her, she glanced at me.

"We'll see you then, don't worry," she said. Then she cut the connection and looked at me. "What are you doing tomorrow night?"

"Performing somewhere, I'd imagine," I said. "Hadn't set any plans yet."

"Feel like playing Homeboy's?" she asked.

"Sure," I said. "What's going on?"

"An old friend wants to hang out," she said. "I thought you might like to meet him."

"Sure," I said. Then I dumped my bag on the coffee table and started sorting through the cash. "I always like playing at a social occasion, because then I get paid to hang out and have fun."

"Thought you'd see it that way," she said. "So, did you find out anything more about the murder you were telling me about?"

"Nope," I said. "At least, nothing other than it hasn't been in the news."

"Oh silly," she said. "Of course it was. You just didn't see it."

"Sure," I said. "I didn't see it. And I have no way of checking up on it."

"Right," said Mary.

"Right," I said.

We were at an impasse.

"You're sure he didn't give you anything before he was killed?"

"Why does it matter?" I asked.

"Well, obviously because you'd have to go to the police with the whatever it was," she said matter-of-factly.

"I disagree," I said. "He may have given me something, but I wouldn't have gone to the police. I got the impression he was a nice guy, one of the Good Guys, and if he entrusted me with anything before he died, I'd have to do whatever it took to make sure it fell into the right hands. And nine times out of ten, the police are not the right hands for information to fall into."

"So you think he might have died for information?"

"I don't know why he died," I said. "Maybe they just wanted his shoes."

"Was he still wearing his shoes when you saw him?"

"Honestly, I didn't notice. I don't usually look at the feet of a fresh corpse."

She took a sudden deep breath at that, not quite gasping, but still noticeably affected by my comment.

"You knew the victim," I said. "You found out he was dead before the police even knew."

"Well, maybe," she said. "It's complicated."

"Enlighten me," I said.

"I can't," she said. "I'm sorry, Cecil, but I can't talk about it. I just lost a dear friend, and I don't know what to do about it. He was obviously murdered, and there seems to be no reason for it. It bothers me that you were so near to him when he died, and then happened to see him before anybody else saw him, and talked to him. Did he say anything at all to you?"

Put on the spot, I could only answer one thing. "No."

"I don't understand what's happening." Then she started to cry.

Oh bother. That's just great. Now she's crying. She knows damn well that I couldn't pursue any questioning while she's crying. On the other hand, neither could she, so our impasse wouldn't resolve, but we'd at least be cuddling. Sometimes I have to admire her style, especially when it comes to keeping secrets. We ended up falling asleep together on the couch, with her cuddled up in my arms and pushing her butt up against my hips. I was very horny when I finally fell asleep, but since she was already asleep and clearly going through some problems, I left her alone.

She was gone when I woke up in the morning. She hadn't left a note or anything, just took off. My pad was ringing an incoming call, and I staggered to it and answered. It was Larry.

"Cecil!" said Larry. "Cecil! Are you ok?"

"I'm fine," I said. "What's going on?"

"Damn," said Larry. "They found another body."

"Who?"

"I don't know! I can't identify the body, and Sherry has no information on it."

"No, I meant 'who found the body'?"

"The cops!"

I've never seen Larry so alarmed at something.

"Ok, so the cops found another dead body, big deal, right?"

"They found it on the same spot our murder victim was!"

That was a little more sobering.

"Interesting," I said. "What's significant about it?"

"They've now named you as a person of interest," said Larry. "The investigation is continuing, now that there's two bodies."

"Trust our police to only investigate when there's two bodies," I said. "Is there any indication the two are linked by anything other than location?"

"Yes," said Larry. "Neither body can be identified."

"Ok," I said. "That doesn't exactly link them together."

"It doesn't matter!" said Larry. He was really worked up. "You're a suspect!"

"No," I said. "I'm a 'person of interest', which is really just the police acknowledging me for who I am, if you think about it."

"Cecil, this is no time for jokes," said Larry. "They tortured this man!"

"On the contrary," I answered. "This is the best time for jokes. Look, I need a soda. Where are you?"

"I'm at the school," answered Larry.

"Ok," I said. "I'll go get a soda, and I'll get cleaned up and head over there, and we can chat, ok?"

"Ok," answered Larry dubiously.

"I'll have Sherry meet us there, and we'll have a

little pow-wow, just the three of us. What time is it, anyway?"

"It's noon," said Larry. "Vali's got a class starting in an hour."

"Fine," I said. "We can chat while his class is working on their stupid lab."

"Just don't get picked up by the cops."

"Do they even know my secret identity?"

"Not apparent," said Larry. "But probably."

"I won't worry about it, I've got bigger fish to fry. We'll be there soon." Then I broke the connection. Sometimes hanging up on Larry is the easiest way to get him to shut up.

I went ahead and took some time getting myself cleaned up. I had apparently fallen asleep while I was still wearing my costume, so parts of it were wrinkled and my face was still painted. So I took a shower while I let my clothes hang in the dryer to work out the wrinkles. Then I got dressed in street clothes, carefully folded my costume into my gear bag, and got ready to go to the school. I dialed up Sherry and got her to agree to meeting me at the school. Then I went down the corridor to grab a soda.

As soon as I stepped outside my home, I felt the familiar prickling sensation on the back of my neck that reminds me I have an audience. Since I wasn't suited up nor performing in any way, that could only mean someone was watching me intently. I turned all the way around to the left, opened the door, stepped in, grabbed something random, then came back out. This time, I turned to the right and headed out. Spotted my watcher on the first turn. Hopefully he was convinced I had forgotten something when I turned around, and not that I was surveying. I walked down towards the tubes, staying to the right, and when I reached my turn, turned left with a glance. He was following me, sure enough. Maybe I should go to the cops. Maybe it would make my life a lot simpler.

I stopped off in a grocer's stall and poked around. I wasn't looking for anything in particular, I was giving my stalker a chance to catch up. There were three possibilities as to his identity. He's an agent of the crime boss, a cop, or an agent associated with Flasher Boy. I waited until I could see him clearly looking over the wares in a magazine shop, then shifted into the butcher's stall that stood right next to the grocer's. I continued on into the little tamale shop on the corner, slipped around the corner, and nabbed a corner seat. After a few minutes, my follower headed down the street past me, failing to see me in the hidden corner table, and on down the corridor. He'd lost me. So I slipped out and got in behind him.

Being an acrobat and a juggler and performing these things in the street 6-8 hours a day for 4 or 5 days a week for three months, I was in tip top shape. I caught up to him quickly, tapped him on the shoulder, and when he spun around with his hand in the air, grabbed his wrist and pushed him against the nearby wall.

"Why are you following me?" I demanded.

"You're my assignment," he said.

"Don't you know you're not supposed to admit following me?"

"Standard protocol," he answered.

"Who are you?"

"The guy that's assigned to follow you."

"Who are you with?"

"The organization that made the assignment."

"You're not being very helpful now," I said.

"Standard protocol," he answered.

"You know I could break your neck before you could reach that blaster of yours, right?" I answered.

"Yes, but you won't do it."

"Because I'm not a cop killer?"

"Well, I'm not a cop, so obviously that doesn't matter." Aha! Not a cop.

"Why, then? Would your family come after me?"

"My family doesn't even know I exist," he said.

Emo kid? Or one of Flasher Boy's friends? I gave him Hard Up to see how he'd react to that expression. He answered with what looked for all the world like I'm Taken. Obviously a well-trained agent.

"Which government do you work for?" I asked.

"None," he said.

Then he went to live hand, broke my hold on his wrist, jabbed me in the rib, slapped me in the face, and slipped right past me. When I turned to see in which direction he had gone, he truly was gone, disappeared into the mid-morning shopping crowd. Dumbfounded, all I could do was rub my cheek and wonder at how he had so easily gotten away from me and marveled at the speed with which he moved. If I could move that fast, I could juggle 15 balls at least.

Since he had apparently quit following me, I resumed my walk to the tubes, jumped a tube, and shortly walked into Larry's lab.

"You didn't get a soda," said Larry.

"Obviously," I said. "I was followed."

"How did that stop you from getting a soda?" asked Sherry.

So I briefly related the encounter to the two of them.

"That's interesting," said Sherry. "Hang on." And she ducked out of the prep room.

"So he knows some martial arts," suggested Larry.

"Obviously," I said. "He went to live hand perfectly, he's had some practice."

"That's not a mobster thing," said Larry. "They don't train their guys in any martial arts."

"That doesn't prevent individuals who are interested from taking up the pursuit on their own," I pointed out.

"What art was it? Could you tell?"

"Live hand is common in all the grappling arts," I said. "So it could be Aikido, Hapkido, Judo, or any number of other arts."

"Any idea how many practitioners of each there are on this moon?"

"Greco-Roman and North American wrestling..."

"Cecil."

"Old Scottish, Islamic Ground Fighting, a fairly new style..."

"Cecil!"

"Australian Aboriginal kangaroo fighting..."

"CECIL!"

"Wait, what?" I asked.

"Focus!" barked Larry.

"Ok, I'm focused! Sor-ree!"

"Fine!"

"Fine."

"Now, I'll ask again," Larry said pointedly. "Any idea how many practitioners of each there are on this moon?"

"Sure," I said. "Thousands. There may be a lead there, but you'll have to let Sherry chase it down."

Sherry came back in the room with a large caffeinated and carbonated beverage. She handed it to me. I sucked it down like a Scottish Terrier sucking down a hot dog on a cold day.

"Thank you Sherry, I love you," I said gratefully.

"So, we got nothing on the flasher," said Sherry.

"Expected, at this point," I said. "Did you bring it with you?"

"Yes," she said, and she took it out of her pocket and handed it to me. I relayed it right to Larry.

"Find out what's on this thing," I told Larry. "Since a man died for it."

"Sure," said Larry. "I'm surprised she didn't get anybody to look at it."

"My own guys can't do half of what you can do," said Sherry.

"All the more reason to send the work to me."

I detected more than a little bit of tension in the room.

"Do we know yet whether or not the pads were picked up?" I asked, changing the subject.

"No," said Larry. "Nothing, as of yet."

I coughed out of nowhere as a drip of soda went down the wrong tube. Larry and Sherry looked askance at me, and I signaled I was ok.

"Let me know as soon as you've got something," I said. "**cough** So let's talk about this 'person of interest' thing, since you were so upset about it."

"Ok," said Larry and Sherry together.

"**Cough** First, what does it mean?" I asked.

Sherry answered. "It means they've connected you with the murder. They don't know if you did it, and probably aren't making you a suspect just yet. They just know that you have some sort of connection to it."

"There were two murders," I pointed out.

"Yes," said Sherry, "And the fact that they both happened near your downtown spot means something."

"Does it? **Cough** I haven't been downtown since the first murder happened."

"The cops don't know that."

"Surely they must," I said. "There are cops all over downtown **cough** every night I'm there."

"Got a timesheet? Invoice? Anything--" **cough** "-- to indicate where you were when it happened?"

"Camera data?" I asked bleakly with a hoarse voice.

"Not good enough," said Sherry. "The camera data is ok, but is usually not a high enough resolution to identify anybody."

"My costume is pretty identifia**cough**ble."

"Can you guarantee there were no copycats on

your spot last night?"

cough cough cough

"Well, uh, I guess not," I said. "But I don't have many copycats. I'm uncopyable."

Then I hacked it up for a moment while the two watched me, my cheeks the host of matching waterfalls.

"Are you ok, Cecil?" asked Sherry.

"I'm **cough** fine." I swallowed some more soda, which soothed my aching throat a bit. "I think I'm done now. Please, continue."

"If you say so," said Sherry dubiously. "Maybe the mobsters sent someone down who looked like you just before dumping the body, precisely so you'd be fingered for it?"

"That'd be a dirty trick," I commented.

"Yes," said Sherry, "And well within the scope of mob operations."

"Ok, so, Larry, can you find out for us?"

"I already have," said Larry, "And nothing of the sort happened. I don't know why they're linking you to the second murder, there's nothing indicating a link."

"Ok," I said. "Who's the victim?"

"Another unidentifiable person," said Larry.

"Unidentifiable to whom?" asked Sherry.

"To the cops," said Larry.

"But not to me," said Sherry.

"You still haven't identified our first victim."

"I'll get it."

"You still haven't. **cough** "

"Some things take time!"

"Some things!"

"Yeah, some things! Got a problem with that?"

"We needed to know **cough** yesterday!"

"We did know yesterday!"

"Nothing useful!"

"We knew that Cecil wasn't the killer!"

"No we didn't!"

"Are you suggesting he might **cough** have killed somebody?"

The argument was getting out of hand, as was the coughing.

"STOP."

"No, I'm not suggesting that!"

"Then what are you suggesting?"

"I'M SUGGESTING YOU BOTH SHUT THE FUCK UP!" I roared.

Larry and Sherry both stopped with their mouths open, ready to retort to whatever was said. Slowly, they each turned their eyes to me and closed their mouths.

Unfortunately, at that moment I had my last bit of soda coughing to do. The two watched tearfully as I finished. At least, I like to think they watched it tearfully.

"Sherry," I croaked, "Get on identifying the second body. Ok?"

"Ok," she said.

"Larry," I said, my voice recovering a bit more,

"Figure out what's on the flasher that someone died protecting, ok?"

"Ok," he said.

"Also, Larry, please don't copycat my coughing." I gave him Rue the Day.

"No problem."

"This whole 'person of interest' thing is not interesting," I said. "I can easily conceal what I know about the first victim, but I don't know anything about the second. Got it?"

"Sure," said Sherry.

"I suppose," said Larry.

"Let's try to figure out what connection the cops think I have to the two murders. Larry, you keep monitoring the investigation and see what you come up with. Sherry, you find out whatever information about the second victim you can get, forged or not. I have no connection to the second murder, other than the location of the body when it was found, so figure out why the cops have linked us based on location. Ok?"

"Ok," said Sherry.

"Sure," said Larry, dubious again.

"In the meantime, what does 'person of interest' actually mean?" I asked.

Sherry had the answer ready.

"It means you can be taken downtown for questioning at any moment. They won't arrest you until they question you, because they're hoping to get a confession out of you when they question you."

"Which they won't," I said, "Because I didn't kill either of them."

"They'll pressure you into a confession," said Sherry. "It's how they get most of their murder convictions: by pressuring someone near the murder into confessing."

"That's not a reliable way to get to the truth," I pointed out.

"You're such an idealist," Sherry pointed out.

"Yeah, sue me," I said.

"I will," said Sherry.

"No you won't," I responded.

"I will, for getting me into this mess."

"You like it," I said.

"I love it," she answered, "But that doesn't mean I won't sue you for it."

"Good luck collecting," I said. "I'm already up to my neck in debt over the divorce. You can collect from my stool samples."

"You giving me shit?"

"Of course."

"Ass."

"Yep."

"Cecil," said Larry, "We've got bigger fish to fry."

"There are fish that are bigger than my ass? Ok," I said. "So, what else do we have?"

"Well," said Sherry, "I finished the background on Mary."

"You don't look too happy to have done that." I said.

"I want to stress that I feel like I shouldn't have done it," said Sherry. "I feel like I violated her."

"Under the circumstances," I said, "I think it had to be done. Besides, she might like that. Anyway, what did you find?"

"Apparently Mary used to cohabitate with a man named Jacob Smith," Sherry said. "About five years ago. They signed a year long lease, but he was arrested eight months into the lease. He had charges associated with mob activity, and served a two year sentence before being released."

"Were they together when he was arrested?"

"No way to tell," said Sherry. "They could have broken up a month into the lease and he could have gone to stay with friends until he got arrested. No way to tell. The paperwork says he lived there, that's all I've got."

"Any idea what his family affiliation was?"

"None, but it's likely Europan," answered Sherry.

"Got it," I said. "What are his current whereabouts?"

"Unknown," said Sherry. "He finished his probation, and then disappeared off the public record."

"Probably got a girlfriend to put him up without putting his name on the lease," I said.

"Probably," said Sherry. "That's a fairly common way to stay under the police radar."

"I believe it's called 'spanking the mattresses'. Or something like that."

"My mistake."

"Whatever, do we have any determination who our murderers are affiliated with?"

"Nothing," said Sherry, "Except that they're off-world. They may be pirates for all we can tell right now."

"I'd be able to identify them if they were active pirates."

"Really?" asked Sherry.

"Really," I said, giving her Honest Pickings.

"Hum," she responded.

"So, can we make the association between Mary and the off-worlders?"

"No," said Sherry. "We can't. Quite the contrary, it looks like Mary's not associated with the murderers because her mob connections are local. She's most likely associated with the victims."

"Interesting," I said. "When there was only one victim, she told me he was a dear friend, but refused to give any more information. Now that there's two unidentifiable victims, I wonder what she'd say."

"There's more about Mary."

"Explain."

Sherry sighed deeply. "Did she ever tell you she had a kid?"

"Yes," I said. "She's been pregnant several times. None resulted in live births, however."

"That's not technically true," said Sherry. "There was a live birth, and this Jacob Smith character was the father."

That got my attention. It also evoked The Masked Man.

"So she had a baby with a mobster, and in a year together has never told me about this kid?"

"Well, the baby died at the age of two," said Sherry. "No records other than birth and death, and the death certificate simply states 'accidental causes of death' on it."

"That's interesting," I said.

"You're not shocked?" asked Sherry.

"Oh, I am," I said. "I'm just giving you The Masked Man."

"I'll never understand your facial expressions no matter how many times you explain them to me," said Sherry.

"So what if Mary also knows the second victim?"

"Maybe you should give her the drive," said Larry.

"I'd rather know what was on the drive before I tell her I have it," I said. "I trust her, and I love her, but she's fallen in with some bad crowds in the past. I have no way to verify that she's currently involved with the Good Guys. She may think she is, but actually be with the Bad Guys."

"What will you do if she comes up on the wrong side?"

"I don't know," I said. "I don't want to dump her, but I don't really know."

"What if she dumps you?"

"What do you mean?" I asked Sherry.

"What if she determines you're on the wrong side and dumps you?"

"I don't see that happening," I said. "She doesn't even know I'm involved yet."

"Are you sure?"

"Sure," I said, "Why not?"

"The police have named you as a person of interest, why wouldn't she know you're involved?"

"She knows better? She knows where I've been?"

"Does she? How much contact have you had with her the last few days?"

"Ok, not much," I admitted. "But enough."

"Enough to what?"

"Look, Sherry," I said, "I really strongly value your point of view. You're a really helpful person, that's why you're involved with this. This paranoia shit has to stop. I love Mary, and I trust her, and whatever's going on, I'm sure she's on the side of the Good Guys. So when I figure out which side she's on, I'll throw my support to that side, unconditionally, and with my life if necessary. Got it?"

"So what if she's a mobster?"

"She's a good girl," I said. "If she's a mobster, then it's the right side to be on. Ok?"

"Ok."

"Sure?"

"Not really," said Sherry, "But I'll go along with it."

"I've heard that before."

"You've said it before."

"Figures."

"Relax," said Sherry. "I wasn't trying to get your back up."

"I know," I said, "I know. And don't worry, if she turns out to be a Bad Guy, I'll kill her."

"Cecil!"

I laughed out loud over that one. Sometimes, just taking someone by surprise really is the best way to construct a joke.

"Not really, I was just seeing if you were paying attention."

"Fine, ok, so, what now?" asked Sherry.

"Do you have a way to track a person's connections and filter by particular information?" I asked.

"What do you mean?"

"Well, like the old social networking stuff that's still around. Start with a particular person, and then search all people connected to that person for a particular skill, and then search all people connected with each of those people, etc."

"Sure," said Sherry. "Our PI databases have that feature. Larry wrote it, so it works well."

I chuckled and looked at Larry. "Ok, then, start with Mary and find someone with knowledge of a grappling art."

"Do you think that will be helpful?" asked Sherry.

"No, but it's something to do, and we're pretty much grasping at strings right now, waiting for something else to happen, such as Larry figuring out what data on that drive was so important that a man died over it, and yet so unimportant that the man that died could leave it with anybody except his pursuers. And in the meantime, we all have bills to pay."

"Indeed," said Larry.

"Sure do," said Sherry.

"So let's move out and see what happens," I said.

"Hopefully before someone else dies."

By force of habit, I walked out of Larry's prep room and into the physics lab, noting that Sherry went straight into the hall and left. She was such a college student. Vali was sitting at one of the lab tables fooling with one of the air track units.

"Cecil," he said in his best Dracula impression. "What's going on with you?"

"Same old, same old," I said.

"No, not same old, not this time," he said. "Sounds like you're in a bit of a mess."

"Yeah, I suppose," I said with a chuckle. "Nothing I can't handle."

"You're a great performer, but you still cannot lie to me," he said. "What can I help you with?"

"Um, does your physics training include any sort of espionage, or martial arts?"

"It does, in fact," he answered. "I served in a special forces unit during the revolution. I was pretty good at what I did, too."

"Really? You never told me that!" I gave him Sly Story.

"Really."

"You're pulling my leg," I said.

"No, I'm not," he said. "Cecil, you are my friend, and I care deeply about what happens to you. I stood by you through your divorce, and I was always by your side when you worked here. I will always be on your side, no matter what. Just tell me what I need to do."

I looked at him soberly for a moment before answering.

"You're right, of course," I said, watching him provide a knowing smile. Actually, it was more like he was giving me Shiteater. "At this time, the danger level is low, and there's just not much information to go on. I don't know that there's anything you can do right now, but there is a likelihood there will be some shooting, sooner or later."

"You're sure of that?"

"Not completely," I said, "It's just that people keep dying, and sooner or later we'll figure out who's who, and will have an ethical obligation to step in in a big way."

"Why not go to the police?"

"Because Mary's involved, somehow," I said, "And police involvement will probably increase her danger level dramatically."

"What is her danger level right now?"

"I don't know," I answered, giving him Awe-Inspired Ignorance. "She doesn't know I've gotten involved."

"Do you trust her?"

"Yes, I do."

"Why don't you ask her what's going on, then?"

"And risk exposing everybody at once?"

"This is something you carry from your marriage," he answered. "You trust her, but you do not trust her. You fear that she will ultimately betray you as your ex-wife did. You fear that she will hurt you by what she is doing. Do you think she will?"

"No, I don't--"

"But you can't ask her for fear of that betrayal and hurt."

"Sure."

"I'm very sorry for you for having to go through this, Cecil. Your ex-wife was a terrible person to make you feel this way, and it is impacting your relationship with Mary, the woman you need to spend the rest of your life with. When you determine what role I need to play, you will let me know. Promise?"

"Yes sir," I said. "I will do that. And thank you for all that you've done for me."

"You're sure?"

"I'm sure."

"You're not just saying that to get me out of your hair."

I gave him Honest Pickings. "Vali, when I know what you need to do, I will tell you, I promise."

"Fair enough."

We shook hands soberly, and as usual, parted ways without any sort of farewell. For my part, I had to leave, if only to hide the tear developing in my right eye.

Chapter Four

I went into the crowd in performance mode. I had three balls in the air, and I was moving to a spot. The interesting thing about juggling, in case I haven't mentioned this before, is the way Newton's Laws so aptly apply. You see, you throw one ball up in the air, and it has to go high enough into the air to give you time to catch and throw a second ball. That ball, in turn, needs to go high enough into the air to let you catch and throw a third ball. When you do that, the first ball should just barely be landing in your other hand. It's complicated. It's also tricky. There's a reason so few people can juggle. In the lower gravity of Europa, juggling is quite a bit easier in some ways. You see, the velocity required to throw a ball to a height matching your forehead is much less than on Earth. But the natural inclination is to give the ball a much higher velocity, which in turn makes it easier to juggle more balls because you have more time to deal with catching and throwing. So, juggling three balls and not throwing them any higher than your head is still impressive, even on Europa, but if you throw them higher than your head, three balls isn't that impressive. A lot of people on Europa can throw three balls above their heads, it's so simple it's taught in grade school. To be impressive, you have to throw at least six balls to match the three balls thrown on Earth. Now, you might ask, how is six balls equivalent to three when the acceleration due to gravity is less than one-sixth? The answer is simple. The height of the balls changes, but the length doesn't. Your arms don't suddenly become wider apart, and the throws require a great deal of accuracy. So you're asking someone to throw six balls with the same degree of accuracy that throwing three balls would be. It's surprisingly challenging. That's why

I, like a lot of jugglers, resorted to clubs. But clubs are their own problem! You see, when you juggle clubs, you throw each individual club with the intent that it will turn over once, rise to a certain height, and then you'll catch it in the same place you'd catch the ball. The problem is that while the height varies due to gravitation, the time it takes for the club to turn over once doesn't. It's a simple matter of mass distribution, or what physicists like to call it, moment of inertia. That is dependent on the club's mass and where it exists in the club, but not on the acceleration due to gravity.

It's not as tricky as it sounds, though. Sometimes you just have to light the club on fire and throw it, and let the audience be wowed even though you're throwing a simple cascade. Fire makes all the difference.

My torch setup was completely custom. I built the torches, and I built the extinguishing devices. So I could light a set of torches, juggle them for awhile, then extinguish them without the need for water or anything else. That gave me the advantage of being able to relight the torches at will, ignoring the need for refueling. I could usually find a discrete place to refuel. I also had electronic lighters in them so I could actually juggle them unlit and light them while throwing. Unfortunately, I hadn't figured out a way to extinguish them safely while throwing, since they were still based on kevlar wicks. I'd heard rumors about torches that used burner nozzles and a fuel tank that could be lit and extinguished at will, but I hadn't found any in real life.

Juggling wasn't my entire act, however. I also did acrobatics and told jokes and other funny stories. You see, historically, fools were never primarily jugglers. The juggling was to get attention, or to impress someone. The acrobatics were done for both flare and slapstick effects. The jesters had also invented the novelty song genre long before certain pop acts in the 20th century. The core of the act, however, is what I call the Diatribe. It's an ongoing monologue about your life, whoever I'm interacting with, that is internally consistent and completely satirical. I take age old roles and turn them around.

For example, when I went into the crowd, I found a couple holding hands. A little girl was skipping in front of them. I came up right in front of them and bumped right into the little girl, lightly.

"Why are you following me?" I demanded of her.

"I'm not following you!" the little girl answered.

"Yes, you are," I said.

"No, I'm not!"

"Well then, who are you following?"

She looked a little confused, then turned and pointed at her parents. So I hunkered down and looked her in the eye.

"Dear girl," I said, gravely, "Those two are walking behind you. You can't possibly be following them."

Now, having her attention, she was seriously thinking about what was going on.

"Look on the bright side," I said. "You've raised good, obedient parents who follow you closely and don't wander off to play without telling you."

That was the role reversal, of course, making the kid responsible for the parents. Sure, it's been done to death for all of us grown-ups, but for the kids, it's often new, and even when it's not, it's always entertaining. And, as a fool, I had to take it up a few notches compared to what anybody else would do.

"Now, did you make sure they've eaten dinner?"

"Well, that's what we were going to do next," she said.

"Oh yeah? Where are you going?"

"We're going to Fastburger," she declared proudly.

"I see," I said. "And you are aware that the average burger served there is about 1400 calories, and will raise your cholesterol levels two whole points? Are you sure you should be feeding that to your parents?"

She chewed on that for a moment.

"Well, they are bigger than me," she finally said. "They need more food than I do."

"True," I said, "But 1400 calories in one meal is a lot. That only leaves them 600 calories to have for breakfast and lunch. What did they eat for those meals?"

"Are you telling me how to raise my parents?" the little girl demanded.

"Of course not," I said, "I am merely a fool trying to engage your attention. Would you like to see a trick?"

"Ok," she said dubiously.

"Would you like to see it again?"

"What? You didn't do a trick!"

"Oh yeah, forgot," I said. Then I did a back extension, which is basically a back roll with a handstand thrown in, and at the end I kick my feet down and land on my feet.

"Would you like to see it again?"

"Can you do a back flip?"

"No," I said, even as I threw myself backwards onto

my hands. Then I kicked up the same way you'd do in a tip-up, moving forward instead, and landed on my feet. "See, I keep forgetting which direction I'm going."

The little girl was giggling at this point. I had also drawn a small crowd of kids, their parents standing behind them and smiling.

So, at this time, I whipped out my light-up balls and started throwing them up in the air. Several kids started giggling uncontrollably. Kids are impressed by juggling much more than adults. I started with a cascade, then switched it to a waterfall, then smoothly transcended back through a cascade into a waterfall moving the other direction. You know, basic stuff.

"Can you--" started one of the kids.

"ACK!" I yelled out, while throwing a ball way up into the air. "Great, kid, you broke my concentration. Now, where did the ball go?"

The kid pointed up into the air. I looked up over his finger.

"I don't see it."

The whole group of kids laughed. Several started pointing fingers up in the air, with voices murmuring things like "Look up!" and "It's over your head!"

So I turned around, took a step, and looked up. Of course, I didn't see it.

"I don't see it!"

At which point the ball came down quite fast and landed in a hand I'd slipped out behind my back. I threw them all back up in a cascade.

"Oh, there it is, right where I left it."

And so on. You get the idea.

I worked my way through the crowd in this fashion, heading over to Old Blarney's spot. Old Blarney is a crazy old guy who plays a guitar badly, and only knows half of one song. He'd been living down there for years, and barely made any money, but he always knew the gossip.

"Say, Blarney," I said.

"Blarney," he responded.

"What's up?"

"Not much," he answered. "Cecil? Is that really you?"

"In the flesh!" I declared. "Surprised to see me?"

"Well, with all the dead bodies turning up, we thought you were a goner," he answered.

"Dead bodies?"

"Yeah, apparently they've found like three in the last four days, all near your spot. Say, you didn't kill any of them, did you?"

"No sir," I said, "But tell me more."

"Rumor has it these people don't even exist!" said Blarney. "Now, just between you and me, I have a hard time believing you could have killed someone who didn't exist, and the bodies are real, so obviously you couldn't have killed them."

I love Blarney's screwed up logic.

"You're right," I said. "But what do you mean about them not existing?"

"No records, no identification, nothing," said Blarney. "A bunch of John Does."

"Interesting," I said. "Why were people who don't

exist wandering around downtown?"

"Probably looking for drugs," said Blarney. "I don't know. It was the first one that's the mystery, the others were looking for him. They actually asked me about him. Then there were some guys in suits asking, then more guys in suits, it's like the whole world wants to find out what the first guy did that night."

"Any scars or tattoos or identifying marks?"

"Well, the guy that talked to me had a funky scar on his face like he'd been burned or something," Blarney said. "He's the one that turned up dead later."

"Weird," I said, thinking it was doubly weird that the guy that turned up dead attacked me hours after he was found dead.

"Yeah, weird," he said. "Hey, don't kill me, ok?"

"I'll think about it," I said. Then I dropped a couple of eagles into his cup. "Have a good night, Blarney. Play your heart out!"

"I will," he said. "It's good to see you, Cecil, take care of yourself, alright?"

"I will," I said.

So the second victim was the guy that followed me from my home a few days ago, but apparently was murdered before he followed me. That didn't make any sense. He's also obviously linked to the first victim. In that case, why didn't he ask about the flasher when I had him? Probably he just wanted to get away since I'd obviously read him.

I spent the evening hitting people up and asking questions, but there wasn't any new information to be had. I kept performing off and on since I still had bills to pay, but eventually decided I was just going home. So I went and found a new money-counting spot and sat to sort through what I had. After finishing, I dialed up Susan Hall.

"Hey lady," she said, looking at me. "So, are you going to play?"

"Sure," I said. "Maybe. Who am I going to be playing for?"

"You've already figured it out," she said. "Don Julian."

"I see," I said. "Is there a particular reason he wants me?"

"You know something about these murders," she said. "That's all he told me."

"So this is a covert way for him to get me into his house without anybody suspecting."

"Yep," she answered. "And that's really all I know. Look, I'll send you the details on when and where later. You just be ready."

"Roger that."

So I jumped on the tube and headed home.

When I walked in the door, my lovely little home was a disaster area. Clothes, shoes, data units, all sorts of things were thrown everywhere. Clearly someone had ransacked my home while I was out. Something was definitely wrong here, I decided, getting a sick feeling in my stomach when I realized that Mary wasn't in the cabin at all. Maybe she had gone home with that guy from Homeboy's after all? Then I found her note, written on old-fashioned paper with an old-fashioned pen.

Dear Cecil,

I'm sorry to say that I can't date someone irresponsible enough to drive while drinking. I will remember the fun times we had together, but we're through.

Mary.

To say that I was angry, frustrated, and rapidly filling with hate would definitely have been an understatement.

Chapter Negative One

When I left the school, I still had to make some money for the day, so I figured I'd go down to the Triangle and see what sort of business I could scare up. My take there usually wasn't very good, but it was reasonably quiet, private, and well-secured, so I wouldn't be overly exposed there. More importantly, I would still be close to the school. I found it odd that even though I had stopped working at the school over a year ago, embroiled as I was in some crazy drama, my life still revolved around that school. I had a completely different life than any I'd ever imagined, and yet there I was, still tracking the school. It stayed high in my thoughts, and at that time, involvement there was critical to my own security and possibly my girlfriend's security. I had spent six years of my life at that school. I had been one of the late-comers to secondary education and had even managed a two year degree in engineering. Vali had first been my physics instructor. Then we worked together in a physics lab, where he became a close friend and confidant. He had opposed me going to serve on the freighter, but extracted a promise to reconnect when I returned. I returned back to my old job, where another employee at the school filed a sexual harassment claim after I refused to have sex with her. It was weird, but they took her side and I was dismissed. She was subsequently fired when she was caught extorting sex acts from students in exchange for favorable treatment. Anyway, back to Vali.

By his quick humor and permanently deadpanned expression, you'd never think he had ever been anything but a nerdy physics person. Yet, I had just found out he'd served in special forces. He told me when my divorce started that 'when the bullets rain on the house, you have to act.' It was a neat metaphor that really hit the spot, but it was several months before I found out where it came from. When his people started the revolution over their communist masters, he had been living in the capital city, and bullets had literally rained on his house. He had to act. He defected from the nation's military and fought alongside the rebels in a bloody two year revolutionary war. And just a few moments ago, he told me that he'd used his special forces training to aid the revolutionaries. Before that, he had played guitar in a successful touring rock band, which at one time had been the most famous band in his country. But he put it aside to pursue his passion, which is teaching physics to people who are afraid of math, and he's damned good at it. I loved him as an instructor, and later as a coworker. And now, I was realizing, I loved him as a friend. He had stuck by me through some of the hardest times of my life, and here he was, ready to fight with me against all comers, when none of us knew the score.

That was friendship. That was love. My heart surged when I realized that it was directed at me. I had felt that way as a direct result of stuff Mary did plenty of times, which is why I was still with her. But in the wake of a divorce, after having spent so many years feeling like nobody gave a shit about me, least of all my wife, I found that it was still taking some time to realize that I was a person worth loving and that people loved me. You see, my ex-wife had been emotionally abusive. Even today, people have a hard time accepting emotional abuse as its own form of abuse, let alone the idea that women can be every bit as abusive to men. Physical abuse and sexual abuse are instantly recognized, but emotional abuse? You're just being mental! But it's real, and it happens in many relationships. My ex-wife didn't want to love me, she wanted to dominate me. She went through a lot of histrionics to get that dominance, too. For the first few years, she failed. Let's face it, I have a strong personality and don't give in to dominance. I don't have a problem taking orders, but I do have a problem having someone else run my life. But the most common way a person dominates another is by cutting off their relationships with other people so that their emotional needs can only be satisfied by the abuser. I had experienced some of that. The reason Mary and I went so long without me initiating contact with her was because my ex-wife managed to cut that thread. My parents spent some time estranged, as well as one of my brothers. And yet, my ex-wife had failed to dominate me. It wasn't until she showed that she would and could cut me off from my kids that I started to give in. I only gave a little, at first, thinking it was an acceptable cost to be a father to my kids. But she kept demanding, and I kept giving, until finally, when it was all falling apart, she discarded me because I didn't have a life worth living. That was the ultimate insult, really. When someone spends every moment of their life making yours not worth living, to the point where you're actively contemplating suicide as a way to provide for your family, and then dumps you for not having a life, well, it's quite insulting, to say the least. To rub salt into the wounds, she left the moon and no amount of investigation has turned her up. That was three years ago, and I have not had any contact with my kids since.

What you're left with when all the cards finally hit the table is an overwhelmingly empty feeling. You feel like there's nothing in your life, nobody who cares, hobbies that aren't worth a shit, and a job that's hardly respectable. Your kids won't talk to you, and probably don't even know you still exist. Your entire life is worthless to everybody you care about, including yourself. And all of this is done without a single punch, kick, or scratch. It's emotional, and it's abuse, hence the phrase 'emotional abuse.' Anybody who thinks this doesn't exist is probably an abuser.

Vali stepped into that void and was the first to speak to me on my own behalf. I had failed to study for a test he was giving because of trouble with my wife and showed up to his class crying and asking if there was any way I could take the test later. He agreed, and had me take the test at work a few days later. He trusted me not to cheat, knowing I was in a physics lab prep room surrounded by all the tools and information that was on the test. I made damned sure he placed his trust in the right person, because at that time I needed to be someone worth caring about. I didn't cheat. I scored fairly low on the test, earning a C, but I didn't cheat. He asked me later why I didn't just use the books that were sitting there, and I told him I wouldn't cheat. When I got my grades back for the semester, I had scored an unlikely B for his class, when I knew damned well I had earned a C. I didn't cheat.

One thing I learned from my marriage: Good wives are hard to come by. But I sometimes feel like I should thank her for the divorce, because it was then that I learned that good friends are hard to come by, and proceeded to enumerate a list of good friends that I had come by. Even now, I still find myself surprised, although I shouldn't be any longer, at how much my friends really care for me. Larry and Sherry had jumped off the deep end to provide whatever assistance I needed, and now Vali was offering his own support. None of them had any idea what was going on, and what we did know indicated we might all be killed for meddling! And yet there they were, offering themselves solely because I needed the help.

Good friends, indeed. I couldn't help but wonder what the attraction was for them.

At the same time that I was so expecting of their help, I had to wonder why I couldn't open up to Mary on this matter. Was it fear of her betrayal? Did I really harbor fears of what dark things might be lurking in her past? I trusted her implicitly, so why couldn't I just tell her about it? I resolved to find out by the most simple expedient possible and tell her about it the next chance I got. I didn't know that I wasn't going to get a chance before the situation blew up in my face and I would carry the guilt for the rest of my life.

The Triangle was an interesting place. New Austin had a weird layout. You see, the downtown area and a few surrounding areas were planned out, and thus had consistent naming schemes. That was the first dome. When originally constructed, New Austin had been expected to simply provide water for Jupiter's floating domes colonies. As the import/export business grew, and mankind moved out into the outer planets, New Austin found itself the city at the crossroads between the frontier and the home worlds. As a result, it grew in lurches followed by periods of stagnation. New domes were planned for one purpose, fulfilled that purpose for a few years, then their economies crashed. Later, they were repurposed. The cross-corridors reflected this overall non-strategy of assembling a domed colony, and also created the worst traffic problem in the outer planets. More recently it had gotten even worse, with something like 12 people on average moving into town every week.

The Triangle was built at the confluence of two domes: the North Lamar dome and the Guadalupe dome. Some big development company came in, spent a shitload of money to expand the inter-dome area to accommodate a shopping center that had a series of luxury apartments on top of it with the intention of leasing those apartments to the workers in the shopping center. This new feudalism worked for awhile, but then the company went bankrupt after over-extending itself in other developments. As a result, the area sank into a depression for a time, but when it emerged, the luxury apartments had become Paragraph B, Section 302 apartments, while the shopping center area upgraded to clothing stores and restaurants that catered to the upper-middle class. So you had the weird juxtaposition of people living under poverty with government assistance tending to the stores selling their wares to families who earned ten times what the workers were earning, and to whom they would be invisible if they'd encountered each other on the street. Simple plebes serving the aristocracy, they called this plan Smart Growth.

Suffice it to say, I made more money by targeting the residents of the Triangle rather than the customers, because their customers were cheapskates.

When I was finished performing and on my way home, Larry rang me.

"What's up, Larry?" I asked.

"I found something I thought you should know," said Larry.

"Ok, what's that?"

"I've been monitoring that pad, and it's exchanged messages with a few people, and apparently gone through a screening process. It appears that my agent has made it through, and the pad is in regular usage again."

"Ok, so did you find anything new from that?"

"Yes," said Larry. "Their boss is on a ship that is currently in orbit around Europa."

"Not surprising," I said. "Is it?"

"Well, it sort of is," said Larry. "There isn't an obvious mob connection with the boss. I mean, there's the dialect, and the nature of the conversation, but other than that, they look like they're not mob operators."

"That's interesting," I said. "Can you determine which ship they're in contact with?"

"No," said Larry. "Unfortunately the agent cannot determine who the receiver is, except by the address book entry on the pad. What I've learned is from listening in to the conversations."

"Is there an address book entry on the pad?"

"Nope."

"Any way to extract a hardware address or anything like that?"

"Yes, but I'd have to have the pad here to do that," said Larry. "The agent can't do that."

"Can your agent automatically update its software?"

"Nope," said Larry. "I realize you would have written that into the agent, but I frankly didn't think of it in time."

"No problem," I said. "You've got some good information there. Pass it on to Sherry and see what she can do with it."

"Ok."

"Got anything else?"

"Nope," said Larry.

"Then I'm going home, I'll talk to you tomorrow," I said. "Good night. And good work, Larry. Thanks for being there for me."

He had an awkward look on his face, and looked relieved when he saw me reach for the controls that ended the conversation. He never was good at emotional stuff.

Chapter Zero

The following day passed relatively quietly. There was no new information from Larry or Sherry, and Mary hadn't shown up. She sent me a message asking me to meet her at Homeboy's at 9 rather than going with me, something about being tied up in her divorcing friend's fight. Under the circumstances, I decided not to perform during the day, especially since I usually do well at Homeboy's. I figured I'd show up at 6 and work the dinner crowd before the drinking crowd and Mary showed up.

So it went. With the low ceiling and low gravity, I was limited to three balls thrown, but I could juggle five if I bounced two. That relatively easy feat was visually quite impressive, especially in the low-light conditions at Homeboy's and the fact that my balls were light-up balls. It would do even better when the drug addicts came in. I entertained every table, be it family, date couple, or frat boys. Without counting I couldn't be sure of my take, but it felt like quite a bit based on the weight of the bag. At nine, I took a break, knowing that Mary would probably be slightly late on account of her friend's relationship trouble. So I sat down and ordered a beer. As I sat there, a guy came over and sat with me. I should have done Waiting for Godot since I didn't really feel like talking to anybody just yet. I really had to talk to Mary.

"Want a drink?" the man asked.

"Sure," I said. "That's why I just ordered one."

"Ah," he said. "You're Cecil the Fool, aren't you?"

"None other," said I. "Freak of magnificence, and the greatest swordsman in all the land. Would you like me to put on my cap and wizard gown?"

"That won't be necessary," he said.

"I'm afraid you haven't dropped a name, friend."

"They call me the Tortoise," he said. "Just that."

"Why?" I asked. "Is it because you're unbelievably slow?"

"It's because I won a race against a snail," he answered, somewhat gruffly.

My beer arrived at that point. This Tortoise character spoke a few words to the waitress who smiled and blushed, and then quickly departed.

"I told her to get you a drink more suited for a man," he said. "You know, something not quite so dickless as a beer."

"That's awfully sweet of you," I said, fluttering my eyelashes at him.

Before we could engage in more horn-ramming, Mary sat down on the side of the square between me and my erstwhile friend.

"Hi Tortoise," she said. "You look well."

"The years have done me good, dear lady," he said.

"Have you met my friend Cecil?" she asked him.

"We just met," I said. "You two know each other?"

"Yes," said the Tortoise. "We were supposed to meet here to do some catching up. I had no idea she was with you."

"Neither did I," I said, feeling a bit miffed that she introduced me as a 'friend'.

"Oh yes you did, dear," said Mary.

Then our drinks arrived, and there were three of them. I slammed mine while the waitress was collecting and asked for another. Then I continued nursing my beer while the two old friends continued chatting. They started with the inane and moved to the downright silly pretty quickly, so I sort of tuned them out and started people-watching. It didn't take long for me to spot the attractive leggy blonde with the cleavage that glared at me. She was sitting alone, and for all appearances was also people-watching. Great, another cougar. I continued surveying the room.

All the normal people were here. There was the alcoholic who couldn't pay his tab, the know-it-all, the country bumpkin, and the collection of rednecks that sat and glared at our table occasionally. I suppose there were still lingering racial tensions between would-be cowboys and hispanics. White people still had trouble accepting that some of their proudest traditions were taught to them by Mexico. I spotted the slutty teases that were guaranteed to go home and seduce their boyfriends after they got good and toasted. There was some usual friction between them and the group of girls that really were trying to get a group of guys to go home with them, with the rednecks caught in the middle trying to figure out which group would get them laid fastest, if at all. I made eye contact with some friends, most of which were really just people I knew at Homeboy's that Mary had introduced me to. Those times, at least, she had called me her 'boyfriend'. I wondered what was different with the Tortoise.

Looking at the two, it seemed like the Tortoise might actually be making headway with my woman. Maybe I should step up and be a jealous boyfriend? Nah, that's not my style. If she wants to be the kind of bitch that takes someone else home right under my nose, she can do that. I can take care of myself. Odd that my feelings of love had so quickly changed. Of course, while I was musing that one, yet another man came over, sat down next to Mary, and offered to buy her a drink, which she gladly accepted. Maybe she should join the girls that were taking home a group of guys. Then she and the new guy stepped away and went to their own private table.

The Tortoise was staring hard at me at that point. I gave him Honest Pickings.

"You'll have to get used to it," he said. "Sometimes she'll introduce you as her best friend in the whole wide world, and sometimes you're a nobody. She's obviously not here to be with you, tonight."

"What do you mean?"

"Oh, she won't cheat," he said. "She's not looking for sex. In fact, that's why you're here, to make sure she gets sex tonight."

"Then why is she here?"

"Only she knows," he said.

"She was obviously here to meet you for a reason," I said.

"She hasn't told me," he said.

I started to feel like I was just an appendage to Mary to be used as is convenient, and put away when not needed. Kind of like a penis would be to a woman.

Well, two can play at this game. I scanned the crowd again and spotted the cougar, made eye contact. She seemed to be giving me Come Hither, so I went.

"Hi," I said. "Is this seat taken?"

"After you sit it in, it will be," she said. So I sat.

"What name can I give to the woman who has such a great pair...of eyes?" I asked. "Should it be Mindy?"

"Susan," she said. "Susan Hall. I watched your performance tonight, you're an excellent performer."

"Thank you," I said. "You obviously have low taste in performers."

"Or high taste in men," she riposted.

"So what brings you to this part of town on this particular night?"

"I'm looking for someone like you," she said. "I have a client that needs someone like you."

"So you're also an entertainment consultant? Like an escort?"

She laughed. Then: "No. I'm an event coordinator."

"That's convenient, because I'm an event," I said. "And you'd like to attend."

"I don't think your girlfriend would appreciate that," she said.

"Tonight she's apparently just a friend," I said.

"Well, then, she should know that I find her quite attractive," she answered. "Let's exchange information."

We got our pads out and did the deed. Then she got up.

"I've got to get home," she said. "Have a good rest of the evening, Cecil."

"Thank you, Susan," I said. "Enjoy your sexless night."

"Fool," she laughed, swaying her hips as she walked away. After she left, I ordered two drinks from the waitress and stayed at that table, setting up Waiting for Godot so that none of Mary's 'old friends' would interrupt me to ram horns, and moving so that my back was against the wall.

Mary was still conversing with her newest friend, and the Tortoise was sitting all by himself. I made it through my drink and signaled for another. Then another. Then another. At no time did the waitress ask me to pay, which was quite unusual. After what felt like the 47th drink but was probably only the fourth, Mary came back to me.

"We need to leave now," she said. "Apparently the Tortoise knows someone I need to speak with."

She was obviously blasted beyond belief.

"You're driving," she said.

I stood, swayed, and moved with her to the table the Tortoise was sitting at. He was waiting for us. He put the keys in my hand and we all left together without speaking. When we got into his car, we continued the silence. Mary was projecting icicles at me, and the Tortoise was trying his hardest to look like someone who didn't see the tension in the couple sitting in front of him.

I put the little electric car in gear and drove out. I suppose we made it all of three blocks before the police stopped us. I was in a squad car in no time, on my way to jail. I hadn't told Mary what was going on, and I felt like I shouldn't.

Chapter Five

I spent the night at Larry's house. Larry himself had stayed in the lab all night, and I let myself into his compartment by myself and crashed on the couch. In the morning, I woke up hollering. I wasn't in jail, and I wasn't at home, and Mary's note came back to me in a flood of emotion. How could she do this? Why would she leave me? We were doing fine! DUI is an occupational hazard when both people in a couple work bar crowds, and she knew it! She didn't even take much of her stuff, if any, so why trash the apartment? The scene looked something more like what my first wife would have done, which is quite different than anything Mary would have done. It didn't make sense. And here I was, laying on Larry's couch, and my whole life had gone completely topsy-turvy. When did that happen? I was just finding my feet again after the divorce, and now everything's a mess again.

Maybe I should just take the flasher to the cops and forget about everything. Go drown myself in a pool of alcohol, and if I survive the alcohol poisoning, move back out to the asteroid belt. Not much call for fools there, but I can turn a wrench like there's no tomorrow. No, I couldn't leave until the DUI case was finished, and when that happened, I probably wouldn't be able to drive, which would definitely preclude me from working on flying cars. My best bet would be to keep fooling for now, and try to keep myself busy. Since the compartment was leased to Mary, I would have to move my stuff out anyway, which would explain why she didn't take anything of hers out of there.

My pad started singing at me, so I picked it up. Larry.

"What's up?" I asked.

"Got one of those old computers running," he said. "It took all night, but I finally managed to build a wireless power inverter of sorts, and it's running fine. Trying to figure out how to use it now. Those archaic systems..." Larry, first thing in the morning for me, and apparently after an all-nighter of his own. I hope nobody ever tries to interrogate him with torture, he'd never survive.

"So, should I come down there and see what you've got?" I asked.

"Sure, if you want, it's up to you. Where are you now?"

"Your place, trying to take a shower."

"Don't do that! There's no water!" Larry exclaimed. "Some time ago--"

"I know, I was just poking fun," I interrupted. "I'm on my way, I'll be there in a bit." Then I signed off, threw some regular clothes on, and headed out.

Larry's place was in a weird place. It was one of the original domes built in the sticks, and it still stood. Recently, developers had moved in with the intent of buying up all the old domes and building one gigantic dome containing shops, restaurants, and more than a few of Europa's notorious fleshpots. The developers thought it was a good place to build another gigantic megadome shopping district because there was a new tube being extended that way, a special tube, one that would have a stopping point in the middle. At that stopping point, which was just a few kilometers from Larry's place, they wanted to make some money. Couldn't really blame them, of course, but it meant they were using tried and true predatory techniques to run off the indigents. In the process of doing so, they'd cut off water to the old domes, as well as numerous other tricks. Larry had told me a few weeks before about a snake that he'd found in his dome, and there weren't that many ways the snake could have gotten there, especially since Larry didn't keep any pets.

The new tube station had been built, and it connected near downtown, but getting to the school meant a lot of walking. Larry had made it a habit of carrying a lead pipe with him while walking, but I suspected he was carrying other weapons as well. The predatory nature of the development happening around him meant that he needed to be a little extra prepared.

It took about an hour to get there, during which I'd had more than enough time to consider the ultimate answer to life, the universe, and everything, and still came up with a base-10 number.

"Hi Larry," I said. "Whatcha got?"

Larry took two glances, as he always did when I showed up *en femme.*

"Well, I've got the computer working on the decryption. Apparently the computer is about a decade newer than the data, but had the decryption algorithm in a legacy app somewhere. It's working, now."

"Can we get an early look?"

"The whole stream has to be decrypted before we can see any of it," said Larry. "I'm sorry."

"How long will that take?" I asked.

"A few hours," said Larry.

"Ok, then, I'll go get us some food."

"Good idea," said Larry. "There's a taco stand about two blocks from here that has like the best green chile tacos I've ever eaten."

"Sure thing," I answered him. "Drink?"

After taking his order, I retrieved the food and drinks and we ate in silence, listening to the old computer's fan wheezing like a dying squirrel while clicking in the exact same way that a dead squirrel doesn't. Larry was right about one thing: the green chile tacos were damned good. As far from Mars as we were, green chiles were a little hard to come by. After we were done, we drank our drinks, again in silence.

Finally, his computer sounded the "I'm finished decrypting" sound, and we both jumped.

"Looks like we've got something," said Larry.

We sat in front of his ancient computer to see what we could see. Larry opened a window to point at the directory, and we started reading file names.

"It looks like one of those big CIA reports," said Larry.

"Find the executive summary," I said.

Larry scrolled the window a bit, then said "There it is."

He tapped his controller a couple of times for no discernible reason, and then the document appeared in front of us. Both of our jaws dropped to the floor when we saw the title.

Larry was the first to talk.

"What does 'extraterrestrial civilization' mean, exactly?" Larry asked.

"Well," I said, "it means a civilization that isn't bound to Earth in any way, I'd imagine."

We were both silent for a few moments while we read the executive summary.

"Ok Larry," I said. "Obviously the CIA back in the 21st century was researching extraterrestrial civilizations, which is really quite odd. The fact that there's some sort of intrigue over this information certainly means something, so why don't you go through the report and find out whatever you can learn?"

"It'll take awhile," said Larry. "You don't really think there's a government cover-up conspiracy thing about this report, do you?"

"I don't think that the secret organization in the report are ufologists, if that's what you're asking."

"Not exactly," said Larry, "I'm more concerned with government agents showing up soon. So far we've got us, the mob, a super-secret organization of some sort, and the police. It would make sense for one or more intelligence agencies and militaries to get involved."

"No way to tell where this information even came from, Larry," I said. "Not until you read the report, which will tell us what we need to know."

"Do you suppose this civilization might actually exist?" said Larry.

"I don't know," I said. "I just don't know. But all this does is confuse the matter. Why would the mob care?"

"Because if this civilization does exist, that would be a potential expansion of their market?"

"Or through trading with a more advanced civilization, they stand to gain quite a bit of power. The mob suddenly becoming the most technologically advanced criminal organization would be a disaster for the solar system."

Larry looked dumbfounded. "It's not very often you beat me to the punch," said Larry, "But that was some fine reasoning there. Think of what sorts of vices they could tap into with superior technology."

"Sure," I said. "Stuff that's still classified research by our government might be available at every corner store to another civilization."

"So who's the secret agency that's involved here, then?"

"I don't know," I said. "Read the report."

"Ok, but I have one more question."

"Shoot," I said.

"Why did you sleep at my place last night?"

I stopped up short and looked at him. How do I tell him what happened? He was one of the people who took inspiration from me and Mary's relationship. Having been through his own nasty divorce, Larry had never really dated again and certainly never married. He was quite cynical about it. But when he saw me and Mary together, he slowly started to believe, again. Now? Sorry Larry, it's all over?

"Well," I said, "you see, I, uh, went home, found my home in some disarray, and had a note from Mary."

"What did the note say?"

"It said she was dumping me because she couldn't handle dating a jailbird," I said. "So..." I sighed. "I couldn't handle being there all by myself, especially considering the mess, so I went over to your place to stay."

"Hmmmm, interesting," said Larry. "And she dumped you for going to jail?"

"Yep."

"But wasn't she involved in the activity that sent you

to jail?"

"Yep."

"And your home was in a fair amount of disarray?"

"Yep."

"Had she taken anything of hers with her?"

I took a few moments to think about that. For one, it was really difficult. You have to understand that I was madly in love with Mary, and the thought of losing her just devastated me. In a way, all that I had done that day was a way to distract myself from facing the reality that the only woman ever suited to be with me had rejected me. I realize that didn't really justify my behavior at the bar, but she really had been pushing me away. Sometimes, to be a loving boyfriend, you just have to push back and see what happens. But there was something about the way Larry was asking, some urgent matter, something I should have noticed when I was there. Something...

Then it hit me.

"She didn't take her coat," I said. "She always takes her coat. Everywhere she goes, she takes it. She's always complaining about how cold it is all over New Austin."

"So if she didn't take her coat..."

"It usually means she's in the apartment somewhere. I've gotta go check it out."

"Wait! Wait for me!"

I didn't wait, I just took off. I didn't even notice if Larry had followed me, I just left. I ran down the hall, jumped down the stairs 12 at a time, and took off out the door past the finely manicured fake lawn. I reached the tube station in 5 minutes where it normally took 15, and stood there waiting for the next tube. While I was waiting, Larry came up to me.

"Cecil," he huffed. "We can't just go barging back in there."

"Why the hell not?" I demanded.

"Because if they've been there, they ransacked the place. They're watching it! They've been watching you!"

"They're still watching me, then," I said, "And I *have* to know." Wait, what? Ransacked? Yes, that's exactly what my home looked like! Somebody had ransacked it!

"Fine," said Larry. "Take this."

He handed me his gun. I assumed it was the unregistered gun.

"It's not the unregistered gun," said Larry, "But as soon as the sensors pick up my gunfire, you'll be free to fire. I don't want you to do anything rash, but I want you to be able to protect yourself with it."

"I thought you didn't keep the unregistered gun at work, and you haven't been home."

"I thought I should change my modus operandi for the time being," Larry answered.

I understood, but I was understandably pissed that he felt he needed to second-guess my firing decisions. The idea that someone would ransack my home...

"Larry," I said. "Did you secure the drive?"

"Yes," he said. "That's why it took me so long to catch up to you."

"If they were after the drive..." I started.

"Then they might go into the lab," finished Larry, "But they won't find anything. And don't worry, I've secured it tightly."

I didn't ask how he'd secured it. Partly it was because I didn't care, I trusted him. But mostly it was because the capsule arrived at that moment, and we boarded it. Twelve minutes later we were 40 miles away in the tube station, and hurrying, albeit a bit more slowly than when we'd rushed out of the lab. I tried to think about that prisoner comment while we ran, but couldn't really focus. If Mary was in trouble, I had to find her. All this other crap was just crap at that point, I had to find Mary. I desperately hoped that my involvement in this stuff that wasn't any of my business didn't get her abducted. I didn't think I could deal with the idea that my own actions had put her in mortal danger. I had tried to shelter her!

In any case, we finally reached the corner two blocks from my home, where Larry signaled a stop.

"Cecil," he said. "We need to approach cautiously. If your place is being watched, there's a chance we're already spotted."

"I understand," I said. "I had no intention of barging in through the front door."

"They'll have the fire exits covered," he said.

"Not if it's simple surveillance," I said.

While we were discussing how to approach my own home, a figure came up behind us.

"Hi guys!"

We both jumped about 2 meters in the air. Then I turned and saw my friend Sherry.

"Sherry? What are you doing here?" I asked.

"Stopping you from doing something stupid," she said. "I've got information that you need to know before you go charging in there."

"But--"

"No buts," she said. "Let's go into that cafe over there. Do you go there ever?"

"No," I said. "Never been a fan of coffee joints."

"Good," she said. "They'll never look there for you, then. Come on, guys."

We had no choice but to follow her. She found us a nice table in the corner, where we could watch all the entrances and had a quick exit through the back door. All three of us sat down.

"Ok," I said, "Spill it."

Sherry smiled a bit.

"You remember when I told you some time ago that in my work we had stumbled across an organization that doesn't exist?"

"Yes," I said. "I thought you were giving me some crackpottery."

"Well," she said, "I thought it sounded like that, and the evidence we had was pretty thin anyway, but it looks like the organization *does* exist, and are active on Europa."

"Evidence?" I asked.

"Your murder victim," she answered. "He's part of that organization."

"How do you know?"

"Simple," she said. "My guy finally managed to identify him. He was declared dead on Mars ten years ago in a terrible industrial accident. Scars on his body matched wounds in the injury, as well as dental records. More importantly, there was a clear attempt to wipe all mention of him from public records. All that's left is a birth record and a death record. I found him by studying the scars on the body and searching for any press mention of any accident that would have caused such injuries. From there, I found the accident report--"

"Ok," I said. "I'll stipulate that the information you have on the guy is correct and you have the right identity, but how does that prove there's a secret organization?"

"Several other people involved in the accident also disappeared and had their public records wiped. You see, whoever did the wiping couldn't just erase all traces, because there's a press account of these people being in that accident. So they wiped everything else. So apparently all these people did amounts to being born, being in that accident, and dying in the accident."

"Right, and then?"

"Two of the people resurfaced later. One was arrested in the asteroid belt, charged with espionage, and thrown in Ganymede Central Booking. The other was found on a pirate ship when it was captured, and the captain and first mate mysteriously disappeared. Authorities are still looking for the captain and first mate. But the third person is more interesting. You see, unlike the other two, he had a family."

"A family?" I asked.

"Yep, a family," she said. "And his name should interest you more than a little bit."

"Ok, what is it?"

"Jack Eastcreek."

I was stunned. That was Mary's father. She was still having trouble recovering from his loss. He had been very important to her. The problem with the timeline, however, was that Mary had told me her father died three years ago. If there's a public record of his death ten years ago...

"Did he die in the accident?"

"According to the records," she said, "Yes."

"But Mary said she was there when he died three years ago," I answered.

"Really?"

"Yep," I said. "So..."

"It seems that Mary's got her own secrets," said Larry. "I'll bet you dollars to dimes that Mary is involved with this secret organization."

My vision swirled. I felt like I had been hit with a 10 tonne brick, its mass carefully concentrated at my right temple. I was having trouble staying up. Sherry grabbed my shoulder and spoke again.

"Cecil," she started, "This is good news. It means that this secret organization are the Good Guys."

I teared up, I must admit. Sherry was right. Mary wouldn't be involved with an evil organization, no matter how secret this one was. They couldn't be evil, Mary wouldn't have anything to do with it, and her father wouldn't have been involved in this organization and raised a woman as wonderful as Mary. But that still left the open question, and I had to ask.

"Then why would she dump me?"

Larry had the answer, and it was obvious as soon

as he said it.

"Obviously she was put in a situation where she had to rank the organization over you, and had no choice. Either it was a standing order, or they couldn't admit you into the organization because of their vetting process, or something. But whatever it was, she obviously ransacked her own home looking for something, and then dumped you to cover for it."

"He's right, Cecil," said Sherry, "As much as I hate to admit it."

I took out my pad and opened up Mary's directory entry. I looked askance at Sherry, and she didn't move or even make a facial expression. She had a pretty good poker face, I must admit. So I looked at Larry. He subtly nodded. So I hit the "send" button and waited. It took a full 10 seconds before I got an answer. It looked like she was laying in bed. I felt a pang of jealousy at that.

"Cecil!" said Mary. "Why the hell are you calling me?"

"Why did you dump me?"

"Didn't you read the letter?"

Yes, I read the letter. "It doesn't add up," I said. "Your father died 10 years ago."

She looked like she'd been hit with the same 10 tonnes with which I had been hit. I smiled inwardly, but maintained an outward poker face.

"How did you know that?" she asked, finally, and slowly.

"I've got my own friends, you know," I said.

"I *so* love you, Cecil," she answered. "I'm so so so sorry. I didn't want any of this." And she broke down crying.

"Mary," I said, "Please. You know I hate it when you cry, but more importantly, the game is afoot. And I don't even know what the game is. So, talk."

"I c-c-c-c-can't t-t-talk," she stuttered. She only did that when she was really upset. "I love you, and I don't want you to ever think otherwise." And she went off crying again.

I began to suspect she had been drafted into this secret agent thing against her will. She really wasn't cut out for this cloak and dagger stuff, she's just too emotional.

"Sweetheart," I said, "I love you, and today, thinking you had dumped me, has been the worst day of my life. Now that I know you didn't dump me, I have to know what's going on."

"But that's the thing," she said. "I did d-d-d-d-dump you. I have to. I'm sorry, Cecil, I'm really sorry. I can't see you anymore." And she broke the connection.

And I cried. I couldn't help it. I was being dumped by a woman that loved me, and who I loved more than anything in the world, and we were still breaking up. I wanted to marry her! I knew damn well she wanted to marry me! And here we were, breaking up, and she wouldn't tell me why! What kind of shit was this? How do you find the person ideally suited to be your mate, and to whom you are ideally suited to be her mate, spend a year together, and then break up? What the *fuck?*

I started to notice my surroundings again largely because Sherry was holding me. Sherry was always a good friend, and her embrace was definitely helping me to feel better.

"Thank you," I said as I pulled away from her. "I think I'm ok now."

"I hope so," she said, "We need you to keep yourself together, Cecil. You're usually the rock that breaks up the current and holds strong. It's disturbing to see you lose it like that."

"Sorry," I said. "But apparently I'm still dumped. That's a little hard to take."

"It has to do with this weird plot thing that's going on," said Sherry. "Don't take it personally, she still loves you. She's trying to protect you the same way you were previously trying to protect her."

"Why can't we work together to protect ourselves together?" I asked.

"Because she knows things you don't know, and you know things she doesn't know," said Sherry. "Let's work this out on our own, and somewhere along the way, you and Mary will be together again. Trust me. You two are meant for each other, this will work out."

It would take something pretty damn special for me to believe her, and luckily, I had something pretty damn special. I had, in my possession, a flasher that contained data on an extra-terrestrial civilization that apparently the mob was interested in, enough to kill. The drive itself was associated with a secret organization that apparently was a family tradition of Mary's, and somehow whatever was going on over this drive required her to dump me. And by the way, the mob was interested in all of this stuff, and knew about it to some extent. People had died, I was in danger, and I had my own underfunded team studying the problem.

And I was about to storm my own apartment, not having any idea what I would find.

I was definitely having a bad day.

Chapter Six

Sherry was packing, unsurprisingly, and furnished me with a blade. It was a ridiculously-sized 30 centimeter blade, double-sided, with a nice little scabbard. More appropriately described, it was a big-ass stiletto. I attached it to my belt, and jammed Larry's registered pistol into my belt on the other side. I'd prefer the knife, since I wouldn't have to wait for somebody else to fire before I could use it. Sherry's pistol was registered, but she had a private investigator's license, allowing her to fire first in some situations. Of course, since the gun had no way to know if the current situation was such, PI's were allowed to carry guns that can always fire first, and are then subject to intense investigation should they ever discharge their weapons. Sherry was going out on a limb for me by carrying it.

Sherry had another neat device. It was a comm device that let us all stay in touch with each other and didn't use the wireless network to communicate. It used an older technology that was, strictly speaking, usually only used for specialist purposes, such as when a group of agents has to remain in voice contact with each other even if the power went out. So it was equipped with some sort of electrical energy storage device, a "battery", as Sherry calls it, and some sort of wireless transmitter that connects directly to the other units. Sure, we could have used our pads for the same purpose, but with Sherry there, why not use her fancy PI gear?

So, since I was in tactical command of the group, I decided to send Larry to the fire escape while Sherry and I took the front door. We waited until Larry reported he was in position, then took the lift up to the floor.

Stepping out of the lift, I took in the hallway and saw nothing. Good for us. I motioned to Sherry to move up to the corner and I quietly followed. She poked her head around the corner and turned back to me.

"Looks like all clear," she said.

"Roger," I responded. "Bracket the door."

With that, I dashed around the corner and took up a position on the right-hand side of my apartment door. Sherry came in behind me and took the left-hand side.

"You go first, try not to kill anybody you find there."

"Yessir," said Sherry.

I ran my hand over the lock device and watched the door slide open. Sherry glanced around the jamb, then signaled the all clear to me and moved in with her gun pointing in front of her. I moved in behind her, ready for anything. Sherry's initial call was right, there was nobody in the room. However, it was definitely a mess. It was even worse than it had been when I left the night before. It looked like if Mary had ransacked the place before dumping me, someone had come in behind her and finished the job. Probably they didn't find what they were looking for, since Larry still had the flasher locked up in his lab. I stepped over discarded old-style paper books and approached the bathroom. Sherry stood watch while I slid the door open and looked inside. Also clear. She stayed in the living room while I moved into the dining area and scanned the kitchen. Clear here, as well. The bedroom was all that was left. I hadn't gone into the bedroom, Mary could very well still be in there.

I signaled to Sherry to take up the front position and be ready to fire, since she had the only gun capable of firing on demand. Dammit, Larry, why did you have to give me a gun I couldn't fire until someone else shoots me? I hit the lock and let the door slide open, and Sherry darted inside. I came in right after her, while she hit the lights. There was only one occupant of the room, and my heart jumped into my throat and started choking me when I saw her.

"Oh my fucking God," Sherry said. "Good sweet Jesus in a pickle fuck, what the fuck just happened?"

Mary, tied up to the bed using the same rope I had tied her up with many a time, but this time, she was bleeding, bruised, and completely naked. I ran to her and started cutting the ropes with my big-ass blade. She was conscious, but barely.

"Mary," I said, "What the fuck? Who did this?"

"Cecil," she said, "Go. Leave me."

"The hell I will!"

"You must, they'll be back any minute. They stepped out on the balcony for something, you have to GO."

"Soon as we get you out," I said. "Sherry, stand guard!"

"Right!" Sherry moved to the door and watched the outer room.

I had slashed her wrists free and moved down to her feet.

"Can you sit up?"

"I can barely move, I'm hurting everywhere."

"I'll kiss it all later, when we get you to safety," I said.

"Cecil, they want you."

"Me? Why?" Did they really torture her to find me?

"Because they believe you have something they want," she answered.

"I do," I said. "And you know what it is." After all that time agonizing over telling Mary, that one sentence was all it took.

There, I finished cutting the rope, now she was free. I moved up and put her arms around me. I kissed her square on the lips.

"I love you, baby," I said, "And we're going to get out of here if I have to kill every fucking mobster on Europa."

"I love you so much, Cecil," my sweetie told me. "I hope you understand that I had to dump you. It was for your own good."

"But obviously not for yours. Let's do something different in the future, babe. No more secret societies or any of that crap, ok?"

"Ok."

I pulled her up off the bed and stood her up. "Can you stand?"

"It's a little late to ask that question," she answered. I was heartened to hear that.

"Then let's get moving."

"I need clothes," she said.

I went to the closet and pulled out a dress we usually only use for dress up. It was a one-piece strapless deal that accentuated her curves, all of them, and drove me nuts when she wore it and danced for me. She was so unbelievably hot when she wanted to be. I pulled it over her head and brought it down. Then

I grabbed some panties out of the drawer and pulled those up on her.

"You're going to have to go barefoot, sorry babe," I said. "We'll get you some better clothes later. Let's get moving."

I signaled to Sherry to start moving out.

"Larry's coming around from the fire escape," Sherry explained. "He's going to meet us in the foyer, we just have to get there."

"Has he been exposed yet?"

"No signs that anybody's identified him yet," said Sherry.

"Great, let's go," I said.

Sherry poked her head out of the room and then pulled it back in quickly.

"They're in the dining area," she said. "Sitting at the table."

"Is this a situation where you can shoot first?"

"If there are mobsters, I can always shoot first," was her answer.

"Take them out," I said.

"It's going to be loud," Sherry said. "If they have friends nearby, they'll hear us for sure."

"Damn," I said. "We need a distraction, then."

"What sort?"

"Something to cover the noise I'm going to make when I roll over behind the couch."

At that moment Mary started yelling out. She was making fake sex noises! Loud sex noises! I would have gotten turned on by it if it weren't for the fact that she seemed to expect it to only cover up the noise of the roll. Well, as I've learned from dating this particular lady, it's usually best to ask questions later, so I rolled over behind the couch, being careful not to slap the ground when I got there. That meant I took a little more force on my back, but also made the roll pretty quiet. Since I came up into a crouch, rather than a standing position, the silence was more important than the force. Hopefully Mary's loud sex noises covered up whatever noise I did make. I crawled to the other side of the couch and listened.

"...that slut," said one of the mobsters. "Listen to her, she's so excited by being tied up and tortured that she's finally starting to get off."

"Maybe we should go do what we did earlier, now that she's all turned on?"

"Nah, that would eliminate the terror. Boss said to question her and rape her, leave her terrified and unable..."

I stopped listening at that point. Instead, I ran out with my knife in my right hand and thrusted it into the speaker's neck. Quickly I moved around and grabbed the other man's head and twisted it sharply to the right to a satisfying crack. With both men dead, I retrieved my knife, wiped it on the speaker's jacket, and idly noticed they were the same men I had fought in the tube. I did a quick look-around and determined there were no other opponents in the area. Then I walked back to the bedroom and signaled it was time to go. I said nothing, and neither did the girls.

We made it down the hall with no trouble, with Sherry and I playing leap frog and Mary moving at a fairly constant pace. She was pretty tore up and having trouble moving. We went down the lift, and Sherry finally spoke enough to tell Larry we were on our way down. Larry waited for us at the bottom of the lift, and we moved out from there. Once we were out of the foyer, we put our weapons away. I put Sherry on point, with Larry on rear guard. I took up the middle with my sweetheart, holding her hand, and supporting her weight from time to time as she struggled to make it to the tube. Once on the tube, she collapsed into a chair and enjoyed the free fall. The other passengers mostly ignored us, but one in particular made a point of touching his wallet while he looked at Mary. Sherry floated over to him and slapped him, and he quit trying to pick her up.

Presently, we made it to the lab.

"What the fuck happened here?" Sherry asked.

There were bodies, oh shit there were bodies. Security was everywhere, and medicals were all over giving triage. It looked like a small war had started in the school, concentrated on the lab. We made our way in, being relatively inconspicuous when surrounded by dead and dying students and faculty. Once in the lab, our senses were assaulted with a horrifying amount of carnage. Apparently the class that was using the lab while we were gone, which Larry would have normally assisted had he not been dealing with my personal crisis, was more or less completely slaughtered. The Romanian instructor had taken cover behind the instructor's lab desk, and was left relatively unharmed.

"What happened?" I asked him.

"Two people did all of this," he said in his Dracula accent. "Just two. I tried to stop them, but they went into the prep room. They stole your computers. Bastards."

"Why did they shoot so much?"

"I don't know," said the instructor. "I just don't know."

His failure to make a light joke was enough to tell of the unspeakable horror he had just experienced.

"Would you like a chance to fire back at him?" Sherry asked.

"Absolutely," said the physics instructor. "I'll kill them all, for what they've done."

"Easy, boy," I said. "You're dealing with professional killers."

"You know who they are?" he asked.

"I know who they're working for," I said. "We're about to understand things a lot better, and if you'd like to jump in, now's your chance."

"What were they looking for?" asked the instructor.

At that moment, Larry came out of the prep room with a shocked expression on his face.

"They didn't take the flasher," said Larry. "They took the computer I downloaded all of the data onto."

"Does that mean we don't have a copy of the report anymore?"

"No, we still have the flasher, and the ancient CIA computer," said Larry. "It means they have the report, too."

"This is bad," said Mary. "This is really bad."

"Larry," I said, "Grab the flasher and get the storage device out of that computer. Let's get the hell out of here ourselves. Mary, do your people have the ability to read an ancient storage device?"

"Yes," she answered. "We can read the flasher

directly, in fact."

"Fine," I said. "Grab the storage device anyway to prevent it from falling into someone else's hands."

"It'll only take a few minutes to pull," said Larry. "I'll get right on it."

"Sherry," I said.

Sherry looked at me with an unrecognizable look. I would have thought she was giving me Trip to the Brain, but she wasn't performing. She was really struggling with what we were seeing.

"Sherry," I said again. "Snap out of it!" I snapped my fingers.

"Cecil!" she said. "What's up?"

"Do you have a safe house for us?"

"Yes," she said. "I'll activate it."

I looked at Mary. "I hope you can explain all of this, because this is unbelievable."

"I can," she said quietly. "I really can. We should go to my people, they'll protect us."

"The same way they protected you from getting tortured and raped? We're going to Sherry's safe house, then we're going to talk, then we may contact your people. Or we'll contact the police. My call, I'm in charge."

"Yes, sir," said Mary. Then she came over and put her arms around me and we cried together. I didn't even want to think about how close Larry and I had come to being in that slaughter.

After a few moments, Sherry came back.

"I called my boss, he's activating the safe house

and sending a car."

"Good, thank you," I said. "I doubt we'll be followed again, it looks like they got what they want."

"Not completely," Mary said. "There's a reason they didn't kill me."

"We'll have that talk when it's safe to do so," I said. Then I yelled, "When's that car supposed to get here?"

"Soon," said Sherry. "We'll meet it farther out."

"Well, we need to get out of here before the area is cordoned off," I said. "Larry!"

Larry stepped out at that moment with his backpack slung.

"Sorry it took so long, I had to grab a few other tidbits we might need. I take it we're not coming back here?"

"No sir," I said. I walked over to Vali. "You coming with us?"

"You really know what happened here?" he asked.

"Yes."

"Why couldn't you stop it?"

"We had no idea this was going to happen, no indications anybody even knew..."

He looked at me soberly.

"I trust you, Cecil. I always have," Vali said. "I'm ready whenever you are."

I took stock of my crew. I had the retired engineer that can do anything with a positronic system that can be done. I had the private investigator. I had the physics instructor who happened to have served in a special forces unit of some sort during one of the anti-communist revolutions. I had the secret agent that works for an organization that doesn't exist. And they were all following the fool.

"Ok, let's rock. Vali, take point. Sherry, you're with Mary, and Larry's on the rear."

About 10 minutes later, we were in the car, headed to safety.

"Ok Mary, spill it," I said.

"Ok. I'm sorry I didn't tell you any of this sooner, but, uh, you'll understand."

Chapter Seven

As you know, my father died 3 years ago. Legally, he had already been dead for 7 years, which I didn't know at the time of his real death. In the weeks after he died, I was contacted by one of his friends who explained about my father's previous legal death. He had apparently been living as a fugitive of sorts in our home, and over the years had been an active agent in a secret society.

The secret society really is a society, not really an organization. Membership generally goes parent to child, and outside recruiting isn't really done very often, except in exceptional circumstances or the situation where local chapters need to grow to be able to operate. Apparently my dad didn't want to pass the membership on, probably because my sister couldn't handle the job and because I had so many other things going on. Truthfully, he probably didn't think I could do the job anyway, and he was right, in a way. Anyway, the society contacted me because they needed a replacement for him, and he hadn't made appropriate arrangements, and so I've been involved with them for about 3 years now.

The data you found on the flasher drive is actually the founding report of the society. The CIA agents that wrote that report formed the society after being ordered to destroy the report. They kept it around, obviously, and formed a society. So, what's in the report?

Simple. The report details an interstellar civilization that existed thousands of years ago, traces of which were found on Mars in the early 21st century. Additional artifacts were found on Earth, Luna, and later in the asteroid belt. The information has been intentionally suppressed by governments that know about it for reasons of self defense. There still has not been a time in the history of mankind when government didn't depend on some sort of fear by the general public, and the knowledge that there may be interstellar civilizations would definitely destabilize general society. At least, that's what the governments would have you believe, and there are several that are aware of the information's existence, but not aware of additional research that has been done. We do a pretty good job of keeping tabs on all the science teams out there, but occasionally a report comes through.

As an example, there was a team of archaeologists recently that found evidence of life on Jupiter. Their report contained fairly detailed information about life-support pods found in Jupiter's atmosphere. They found our old civilization, the ancient one that had come through here previously, the one on which the society was founded in order to study outside the government's normal processes. We took steps to ensure that the research was thoroughly debunked and the scientists had their careers crushed, which is a sad event. The problem is, the team disappeared soon after that. There is a Family on Mars that, for some reason we can't figure out, believes the report. They sent their own agents up the tree and discovered our society's existence, and are now waging war to either expose us, destroy us, or get their own hands on the technology that has been uncovered.

About a week ago, two mobsters got their hands on proof positive of our existence. That flasher drive that you got. My partner managed to steal it back, and it was during that chase when he dumped it in your bag. You see, Cecil, he thought you would turn right around and show it to me and I could pass it up the line back to safety. Originally, my section leader had intended to contact you directly, but when he saw that you were forming your own research team, he decided to give you some room to operate. He's had at least one agent watching you at all times, but apparently you managed to slip them several times. You're good, Cecil, you should really consider joining the society. We will be attempting to recruit you.

In any case, the mob's agents somehow managed to track the device to you, and you can probably figure out the rest from there. What I know for certain right now is that the mob believes *you* are the agent, and *I* am the lover that knows nothing about any of this. And to be honest, the operation you guys ran to rescue me looked very professional. I take it this isn't your first rodeo?

They didn't kill me because they wanted to leave me as a warning to you. Something you've done has scared them, and these are people who don't scare easily. They were hoping you'd find me in the custody of those guys so they could take you into custody. Of course, now that I think about it, I think that was really just the B plan, since the A plan was obviously focused on the school.

So, going forward, we have to somehow stop the mob from getting anywhere with the information. There's no telling what damage they can do with it. While we have managed to leak a lot of new technology based on the Ancient Ones, there is still a lot that we can use but can't logically leak. If the mob gets their hands on some of that tech, they will be nigh invincible. At least, no government could stop them, and our society has been largely a research group, not an espionage group. This sort of underworld war between gangs isn't our thing, we just don't have the skills to deal with it.

Chapter Eight

It took a few moments for all of us to digest this information. Being scientifically minded, none of us could understand why there would be a secret society whose purpose is to suppress scientific research publicly while still pursuing it privately. It boggles the mind, really. Science is supposed to be transparent, not conducted in secret. Engineering, on the other hand, is usually conducted in secret for various reasons, but this is science! If there had been an interstellar civilization that came through our solar system, that's the sort of thing people should know, isn't it? Peer review processes become most important, then. Science does its best work out in plain view! And now here Mary's little group is, under siege by a powerful criminal organization who probably also wants to keep the information secret, losing agents, and now what? How are they going to deal with this?

"Mary," I said, "I think this is bigger than any of us. We have to enlist the government."

"We can't," said Mary. "It's a bit involved, but basically if we do that, we lose control of the tech, and it would more than likely lead to a big war. There's more research that we haven't talked about, there's a serious interstellar threat, and as long as we stay under the radar, our solar system won't be invaded."

"Whoah," said Larry. "You're saying these Ancient Ones are still around?"

"No," said Mary. "Their civilization collapsed, and near as we can tell, their homeworld no longer exists. But there are other civilizations nearby that have benefited from the tech left behind, and we're behind all of them in development. There is one about 20 light years away that has the capability to invade us and is probably even aware of us, but at this time doesn't see any reason to come this way. They're headed in a different direction, conquering everything that moves. If we suddenly show up with an interstellar capability, they will be here in force to take over."

"And governments can't be trusted to protect us?" Sherry asked.

"I don't really understand the specifics," said Mary. "I understand why the society was formed and what sort of obstacles they've faced over the last few hundred years, but I have to say, I've been questioning remaining a secret society myself. But I'm just a lowly agent, the command center is on Earth."

"Well, your society being secret just caused a massacre at a college on Europa," Larry pointed out.

"That wouldn't have happened if Cecil had just told me what was going on," Mary said. She looked at me. "I'm sorry babe, I'm not saying it was your fault, there were a few bad decisions made along the way, and truthfully you did a better job of protecting the drive than we did, or would have had we got it back, I'm sure. The society is weak because it's mostly scientists and engineers, not enough agents to protect it. We're feeling the weakness now."

"Does the drive contain any information that would directly lead the mob to new technology they don't currently possess?" I asked, trying to turn the conversation away from the massacre.

"No," said Mary. "It only contains the original report, and all of the artifacts included have already made it into existing tech, like the fusion drives you used to repair."

"So what does the mob need to turn it into something more useful?" I asked.

"Access to society records," said Mary. "Access to our agents. I know things they could use."

"But right now, they think you're the lover and I'm the agent," I said.

"Near as we can tell," said Mary.

"Has anybody else been exposed?"

"Not that's still alive," said Mary, with a tear forming in her eye. I put my arms around her and looked her in the eye.

"We'll get through this," I said. "And we'll get the bad guys, and do what's right, whatever that turns out to be."

"I hope you're not angry with me?"

"No, of course not," I said. "In a way, this has been kind of fun. In a lot of other ways, obviously it hasn't been fun. But we'll get through it."

"What about contact?" Vali said, catching everyone's attention.

"Contact?" Mary asked.

"Does this report contain any way for the mob to contact the alien civilization?"

"I suppose," Mary said. "I haven't really thought about it. Why?"

"That's what makes the most sense," said Vali. "The mob doesn't build anything, they buy and steal. They have no intention of discovering technology or running a scientific experiment. They intend to contact a nearby species and get new technology from them."

"Larry," I said.

"I'm on it," said Larry.

"Help him, Vali, this is your baby now," I said.

"Help him do what?"

"Read the report, answer your question. Mary, can you get in contact with your section leader without exposing the safe house?"

"Yes," she said. "That won't be a problem. I'm sure Sherry can get a message out for me, and properly encoded, well, you know. Why?"

"We don't need a mob that is beholden to alien civilizations. Vali's right, that not only makes the most sense, but also represents the biggest danger. We need to figure out how to stop that communication from taking place."

"That's a pretty big task," said Sherry. "Got any suggestions on how to prevent that?"

"Obviously we need to find out how the communication can happen, what technology is required, and take whatever steps we need to to prevent it," I said.

"It's still a pretty big task," said Sherry. "Really."

"Not that big," I said. "Maybe. I guess it depends on what it takes, and we won't know that until Larry and Vali finish reading the report. In the meantime, we have other problems to deal with."

"Oh yeah?" said Sherry. "Like what?"

"Well, we have to get into contact with Mary's secret society," I said.

"Why? They seem to be the ones who created this mess in the first place," said Sherry.

And she was right, according to my views of transparent science.

"Because," I said. "Because whatever mistakes they've made in the past, at this moment, we stand together. And that's more important than whatever silly mistakes they've made in the past."

"Ok," said Sherry. "I can't say I agree with that, or even understand it, but I guess you know what you're talking about."

"Secondly," I began again, "We need to figure out how the mob found out about this stuff in the first place."

"Explain," said Sherry and Mary at the same time. It was in stereo, it was so cool. Those two had always enjoyed each other's company, I wished they spent more time together, they'd make really good friends.

"The mob doesn't do anything even remotely to do with anything like this," I said. "Ergo, in order for them to find out, there almost has to have been a leak from the society."

Mary looked stunned. Sherry just chewed on it a bit.

"So you figure someone within Mary's secret society leaked the information, probably for money or power or something?" asked Sherry.

"Sure," I said. "Or they were getting back at their section leader, or something like that. Motive is irrelevant at this point, what matters is that the mob found out somehow, and the simplest solution that makes the most sense is that there was a leak from Mary's secret society."

"We had a betrayal?" asked Mary.

"Let's not forget some important data that Sherry turned up," I said. "The accident in which your father was declared dead included several other people. After that point, the mob has built up a list of victims that also didn't exist. For all intents and purposes, this 'war' that has been going on between the two underground organizations has been going on for 10 years."

"Well then, who was the leak?"

Sherry spoke up.

"Mary, dear," she said, "This will be hard to accept. Partly because we have no idea if it's even true, but partly because, well, the person involved is so close to you. In that accident on Mars, there was one survivor. The others definitely died in the accident or soon afterwardes, but one person survived who was declared dead. That was your father. This mob family we're dealing with is probably also from Mars. That's a hard coincidence to overlook."

"You think my dad sold out the organization to the mob?" Mary asked, incredulous.

"I don't think anything," said Sherry. "I'm just looking at the facts."

"No. No! No no no no," said Mary. "My dad would *never* sell out the organization to the mob."

"Not even to protect someone?"

"Like who?"

"Well, you, for example," said Sherry. "Your sister, your nieces..."

"How would that protect them?"

"The mob often works by threatening family members of their target," said Sherry. "You should know that. For all intents and purposes, what you went through the last day or so is exactly that, because they believe Cecil to be the target. If they were threatening your father's family members, well, I wouldn't judge how he decided to save them, just as I won't judge your own decisions to protect Cecil."

Mary was clearly taken aback.

"So you don't think it would have been bad for him to do that?" asked Mary.

"I didn't say that, I said I wouldn't judge him for it," said Sherry. "Also, he probably figured the organization could protect itself, and followed it up with sufficient warning so that it *could* protect itself."

"Then why enlist me? I have mob contacts," said Mary.

"Because your contacts are here on Europa," said Sherry. "And the society is dealing with Martian mobsters. You might be able to provide defenses through your contacts, a common ally. Enough to combat that threat your father may have invoked."

"Wait, stop," I said.

"That would imply the society recruited me to counter whatever damage my father did!"

"I'm not saying that--"

"STOP IT. BOTH OF YOU," I shouted.

Both girls looked at me.

"Look, we don't have enough to determine where and when the betrayal happened, and what you've got, Sherry, is indeed circumstantial. It's not to be ignored, but it's *also* not to be accepted," I said. "But what we have right now is an important point you just raised."

"What's that?" Sherry and Mary asked again in

- 169 -

rhyming unison.

"If the Martian mob is operating on Europa, than the Europan mob is going to want to put a stop to it, or collect a toll, or something," I said. "Mary, can you get in touch with anybody of significant rank in the Europan mob?"

"Yes," she said sheepishly. "I used to date...well, I don't want to talk about it."

"Fine," I said. "Send him a message that he needs to speak with me about a territorial violation. Keep it short and sweet, and fucking send it." I don't swear much, but that was definitely an occasion for swearing. "We need more guns on the scene, and the mob has plenty of those. And using the 'enemy of my enemy is my ally' doctrine, we should be able to enlist them without owing the mob any favors."

"I don't know if I'll be able to make that case," said Mary.

"You're not going to," I said. "I will."

"But--"

"Look, my only connections are low-life couriers. What you get in the street. You've got bigger connections. Use them."

"What if they want to, er, pimp me out?"

"Why would they want to do that at this point? We're not talking about business associates, we're talking about a mutual enemy that they need to know about."

"They don't work that way," said Mary.

"They're people," I said, "And I know people. Just get me the meeting, I'll take it from there."

"I don't know..."

"Trust me," I said. "I know what I'm doing."

"You've never dealt with organized crime before." It was an odd statement to hear.

"Yes, I have," I said. "Quit doubting and just fucking do it."

I love Mary, but sometimes it's a pain in the ass to get her to do what I need done.

"Ok," she said. "Right now?"

"Now's as good a time as any," I said.

So she picked up her pad and went through it. "I want you to hear the conversation," she said. So I sat where I could see and hear the pad, but wouldn't be picked up by its camera. I was more than a little shocked to see the Tortoise appear on the screen.

"Hey turtle boy," said Mary.

"Hi Mary," said the mobster. "What's going on?"

"You remember my boyfriend, the fool?"

"Yep," he said. "The, uh, *lady* with whom my boss would like to meet."

Mary and I were both stunned to hear that.

"Really?" asked Mary. "Why?"

"Apparently your, uh, *boy*friend has done some things that we are very interested in knowing about," said the Tortoise.

"Well, he's got a lot going on," said Mary dubiously. "I think we can arrange a meeting. When and where?"

"Tomorrow my boss is attending a party," said the Tortoise. "He's attending a party at which your boyfriend is supposed to be performing. That will be the best time to meet."

"Ok, we'll do that," said Mary. "Thanks."

"No problem," said the Tortoise. "We'll see you there."

Then Mary cut the connection and looked at me.

"Party?"

"I forgot to mention, I booked a gig for tomorrow," I said. "Well, you know, we broke up and all, so I didn't think you needed to know anymore."

"Cecil, oh d-d-d-ear!" Mary started crying again.

"I'm sorry," I said. "It really hurt, but I guess I shouldn't be trying to rub it in." I put my arm around her and squeezed her.

"It's ok," she said. "I probably deserve it, even though I was obviously trying to protect you."

"I take some blame for all of this," I said, "Since I was trying to protect you. If our communication had been more open when all of this started happening..."

"But it couldn't be, and you know it," she said. "I had to keep my membership a secret, and I couldn't involve you in something so obviously dangerous."

"On the other hand," I said, "Considering the series of special skills that I possess, I happen to be an excellent person to involve in something like this."

"It's not the skills," said Mary, "It's how I would feel if I lost you."

"And yet to protect me, you pushed me away."

"Doesn't make a lot of sense, does it?"

"Not really," I said. "But while we're confessing things, I have a question for you."

"Shoot."

"Who was the guy you were talking to at Homeboy's?"

"Which guy?"

"The one that offered to buy you a drink, and then you went off to a different table to talk."

She sighed.

"That looked really bad, didn't it?" she finally asked.

"Yep," I said. "It did."

"I saw you chatting up that one chick, made me pretty fucking jealous." She carefully enunciated the last three words of that.

"So, who was the guy?"

"That was my section leader," she said. "I gave him a hard time over how he approached me. He told me that if you weren't involved in the society, then as far as he was concerned, I was single. I was pretty pissed."

"So what were you talking about?"

"Society stuff," she said.

"Cut the crap, Mary," I said, getting quite annoyed. "I'm involved. The mob has tried to abduct me because *your* dead partner gave me something I was supposed to give to you. Oh no, he couldn't be bothered to use his last words to just fucking tell me I had to give you the drive. Instead he had to be all cagey about it. And you know me better than that, you know damned good and well that I would protect it and make sure it didn't fall into the wrong hands. But somehow your partner didn't know that, he just assumed I'd give it to you. And as a result of all the secrecy, dozens of innocents have been brutally murdered, and the people we were supposed to keep the information from in the first place have gotten their hands on it! You *must* divulge *everything*."

Mary looked at me with a hardness that was only marred by the tears streaming down her cheeks.

"Ok," she said. "I guess I deserved that. And you're right. You couldn't back out of this now even if you wanted to, and I'm sure you want to. Why would you want to be with someone like me? Don't answer, please. I don't think I could handle the answer."

She sighed and collected her thoughts before continuing.

"Simply put, the Tortoise was my assignment that night. We knew the mob had gotten to Pat, and I was supposed to arrange a meeting with Don Julian to find out what he knew about the Martian mob's operations here. That's why we were going to meet with him after we left Homeboy's."

"Did you still go on and have the meeting?"

"No," she said. "There was a sting operation in the neighborhood."

I chewed on that for a few moments, then had to ask the obvious question.

"So you used to date the Tortoise?"

"Yes," she said. "I did."

"Why didn't that one work out?"

"Well, because he was a mobster, duh," she answered.

"You knew he was a mobster when you were dating him?"

"Yes," she said. "That was part of the initial

attraction, but then he started telling me I should go the distance and become a hooker for the mob. He'd handle everything. It took me a little while to figure it out, but he had probably already made money on me having sex with one of his friends, so I dumped him."

"You were dating him and had sex with one of his friends?"

"He sorta pushed me into it," she answered. "It's kind of complicated."

"I see," I said. "You've had some strange relationships."

"Yes, I have," she said. "It was quite a bit later that it occurred to me he may have taken some money from his friend in exchange for the sex."

"I think you should let me be the secret agent now," I said.

She smiled at me. "Yes, you are much better at this sort of thing than I am. Why don't you let the society recruit you?"

"I'll take whatever temporary appointment they need to feel happy having me take over their field work, but I work for myself. Considering how they've handled you the last few days and the respect they've shown me after I stuck my neck out for them, I suspect they'd have problems letting me be a free agent."

"Yep," she said. "They will. They like to be in control. A secret society has a fair amount of paranoia built in, you know."

"I can imagine," I said.

Chapter Nine

I had just finished a long, hard day's work. I woke up at 8am, went straight to class, then to class again, then again. I came home and worked on homework for several hours. After finishing that, I cleaned the kitchen and cooked dinner. Then I put in another four hours or so worth of programming work. Then I took a shower and went to bed.

SHE came in from the bathroom wearing some silky pajamas.

"Hey sweetie," SHE said. "What's cooking?"

"Oh dear," I said. "I'm wiped out."

SHE smiled a bit. "That's ok, I can take care of myself."

Then SHE sidled up next to me. SHE put HER hand on my penis and started stroking.

"Uhhh, that's not taking care of yourself," I said.

"Just lie back and let me do the work," SHE answered.

"Sorry babe," I said. "I really just want to go to sleep."

"What? And miss this?" Then SHE took off HER pajama top and let HER F cups drop on my chest.

"Yeah, and miss that," I said. "I'm sorry, it's been a long day and I've got a long day tomorrow. I really don't want to be up late."

"Oh it won't take long," SHE said. "You never do..."

Then SHE dropped down and put HER lips on my penis and started to suck.

"No, please, don't," I said. "I really just want to go to sleep."

SHE pulled HER lips off of me with a popping sound.

"You say you want to go to sleep," SHE said, "But your dick says otherwise. Hmmmm, I'm going to have to study this some more."

Then SHE put HER lips back on it.

"No, my dick is just doing what it's supposed to do," I said. "I really want to go to sleep, please stop that."

SHE looked up at me, then pulled HER lips off of me. Then SHE climbed up on top of me and looked down at me.

"I want sex, and I have a right to it," SHE declared. "I'll have it, whether you want it or not."

Then SHE reached back and started guiding me into HER. I pulled it out. SHE guided it back in. I pulled it out. Then SHE put HER hands on my shoulders, pushing me down into the mattress, which had the effect of forcing my hips up, and SHE pushed herself down onto it. I felt HER warm juices surround me. I was disgusted.

"No," I said. "Do you really want to do this?"

"Oh yeah," SHE said. "And you do, too, even if you won't say so. You know you love me."

"It's not a question of love," I said. "I'm exhausted."

"Then you won't fight back," SHE said. "That's good enough."

"No, I will," I said. "Do you really want to do this?"

"Yes," SHE said. "You owe it to me."

Without another word, I reached behind HER neck and forced HER to post. SHE dropped forward, catching HERSELF on the bed with HER hands. I popped my hips out to the right and went to pull a knee up. My ankles were suddenly inexplicably shackled. I couldn't move them!

"Ha ha ha ha ha," SHE laughed at me. "You thought you'd be able to get away this time! You stupid son of a bitch! I want sex, and I want it NOW!"

SHE put HERSELF back on me and started moving HER ass up and down.

I put my hands on the right side of HER neck and swung my shoulders to the right. SHE rolled off me and off the bed, as expected. But when I went to free my ankles, my neck was suddenly shackled to the bed. SHE climbed back on the bed and crawled over to me.

"I see you've lost your woody," SHE said as SHE grabbed my right wrist and put it on HER tit. Then SHE moved it to the side and attached a wrist cuff. "We'll see what we can do about that after we deal with your pesky struggling." Then SHE grabbed my left wrist and started licking it. "I won't cuff this one, I think I'll like the way you struggle."

Then SHE was down again, sucking my dick.

"Please don't do this," I said. "I don't want this."

SHE said nothing. HER mouth was full.

"Please," I said. "Don't."

Satisfied with the erection SHE forced on me, SHE climbed back on top.

"I don't take 'no' for an answer," SHE said.

Then SHE started moving again. SHE moved, and moved, and shook back and forth. SHE moaned in my ears. When SHE put HER tit in my mouth, I bit it hard.

"Oh I love how you struggle," SHE said.

Then SHE slapped me in the face.

"Don't do it again," SHE warned. Then SHE moaned a bit louder. "Oh you're so sexy when you fight me."

"Please, stop," I said. "I don't want this."

"Will you shut the fuck up?" SHE yelled. "I want it, and that's all that matters. Why don't you get that?"

To drive HER point home, SHE started punching me. First with HER right, then with HER left, and going back and forth between the two. HER hip gyrations increased with every punch, HER pussy wetter with every thrust. SHE was really getting off on beating me!

Then the unexpected happened. I felt my own start to pump. I filled HER pussy up with ejaculate.

"Oh baby," SHE said. "I knew you wanted it. But I'm not done yet."

And SHE continued.

And I woke up screaming. Mary, cuddled up next to me, woken up as well.

"What's wrong, sweetie?" she asked.

"Bad dream," I said. "Go back to sleep."

"Oh dear," she said. Then she kissed me. "Are you ok?"

"I'm fine," I said. "Please, just go back to sleep."

"Well, if that's what you want," she said, "But I would rather know what's wrong."

I was quiet for a moment, then answered.

"It was a conglomeration of several episodes in my life thrown into a single rape scene," I said.

"Oh my," she said. "Was it triggered by, er, what happened earlier?"

"Probably," I said.

"Who raped you?"

"In my dream, or in real life?"

"Either. Both, I suppose."

"Nobody, in real life," I said. "In my dream, my ex-wife."

"Why her?"

"Because she tried to rape me in real life," I answered, "But I fought her off. It was dumb for her to try to rape somebody with a third degree black belt in Judo."

"Then what was in the dream?"

"Well, it contained every attempt to rape me that she, er, attempted, only with each counter that I made in real life, there was a dreamy counter that prevented me from escaping."

"So did the rape proceed all the way through?"

"Well, sorta. I came."

"While being raped?"

"It's a biological function," I said. "It's completely involuntary. So yeah, of course I came while being raped. A lot of women report having it happen too."

"So you don't think that having an orgasm automatically means it's not rape?"

"No, of course not," I said. "It's an involuntary system. Theoretically, any man can get any woman off, if he does it right. And in a rape situation, there's so much adrenalin flowing that the victim can have an orgasm. It's not common for women who are raped, but it does happen around a fourth of the time. Men, on the other hand, have orgasms much more often during rape. That makes sense since men generally have an easier time having orgasms than women. It's the way their bodies are set up."

"So if, hypothetically speaking, I had an orgasm when those assholes were raping me, you wouldn't hold it against me?"

I looked down into her eyes. This question clearly meant a lot to her.

"No, sweetie," I said. "Of course not, I would never hold it against you."

Then I kissed her.

After the kiss, I felt her shoulders shutter and the tears fall on my chest. I held her close to me while she cried herself out. It took awhile.

Finally, she was done crying, at least for the moment.

"Sweetie," I said. "It really hurts to think about how long the ordeal was for you that gave you an orgasm in that situation. I think I did the right thing when I killed those assholes."

"I think you did, too," she said. "I was surprised at how easy it was for you."

"I wasn't," I said. "Considering what they'd done to you, it was as easy as putting on a pair of shoes. It had to be done."

"We also couldn't escape without it, and they had the tactical advantage."

"True," I said, "But that's not why I killed them. Baby, my dream wasn't real, but it contained a lot of things that actually happened to me. And that's not all. There's a reason I don't work at the school anymore that involves a coworker trying to sleep with me. But I don't want to go into that. The point is, they needed killing, they didn't deserve to live. I can understand their desire to have sex with you, I have that desire hourly, but they went about it the wrong way and for the wrong reasons. They did it to traumatize you, make you ineffective as an agent, and to get at me and/or your secret society. We have to defeat that purpose, and we have to defeat it together. You're not alone here, you're never alone while you're with me. We're fighting this together, we're recovering together. It's almost like we were both raped. We're in this together, and we always will be."

"I love--" She couldn't finish. She broke out crying again and squeezed me to her.

We fell back asleep in that position, my chest wet from her tears, and from mine as well.

Chapter Ten

I woke up in the morning with Mary running around the room excitedly, dripping tears everywhere. She seemed to be getting dressed, but kept putting on a shirt, and then taking it off to put something else on. She likewise seemed to be arming herself, but kept putting the weapons down and putting different ones on, as though our small arsenal wasn't enough for her to feel safe. I climbed out of bed, grabbed her into my arms, and said "Stop." She stopped, looked at me quizzically, and broke down. I held her shaking body for a few minutes while she let it out. Finally, I asked her what was going on.

"My section leader has turned up dead," she said. "Last night, every single person on Europa involved with the society was murdered."

"Except you," I said.

"Yes, except me," she said. "They're probably coming after me next, and you too, since whoever did this thinks you're the agent and not me."

"But they won't get us," I said.

She looked up at me with hope in her eyes. But what she said denied all hope.

"Do you have any idea who you're dealing with?"

"Yes," I said. "I do. I grew up on Mars, remember?"

"Yes," she said, "I remember. There and the asteroid belt."

"I'm distantly related to some of these guys," I pointed out.

"Not enough to protect us," she pointed out right back at me.

"No," I said, "That wasn't the point."

"I know."

"How did you find out?"

"Sherry did," she said. "She called this morning, we're apparently moving to a new safe house. She thinks that will be safer."

"I think we're leaving the planet," I said, ignoring the fact that Europa was, technically speaking, a moon.

"Why's that?"

"Something in my dream," I said. "Hard to explain. Let's talk to Larry and find out what's in the report."

"Ok," she said.

"That will at least keep you from going off half-cocked and seeking vengeance or running blind."

She kissed me. "Have I mentioned that I love you, today?"

"Not yet," I said.

"I love you," and she kissed me again.

Then we went into the living room to get briefed by Larry. Larry had obviously been up all night.

"What's the skinny, Larry?" I asked.

"Interesting stuff," he said. "Apparently this secret society of Mary's is much older than previously thought. They have ties to freemasonry, and may well fit into the mold of the old Illuminati."

"That's a fun fact," I said, "But wasn't the existence of the Illuminati thoroughly disproved during the 20th century?"

"Yes, it was," said Larry, "But that doesn't mean the legend didn't have a factual basis. This society is very old."

"Ok, so what about the aliens?"

"According to this report, Mary's secret society's involvement with aliens and alien technology dates back at least to the 16th century. During the Inquisitions in the 16th and 17th centuries, the society had to reduce its numbers to protect the information and keep it out of government hands. The CIA report made in the 21st century was another situation where the society had to step in to suppress the information. Interesting stuff. I'm still trying to digest it, here."

"But I thought the society formed because of that report?" asked Mary.

"They formed because of the aliens," answered Larry, "At the time the alien technology was discovered, anybody connected to it would have been executed as witches, so the society had to be secret from the get-go. That report was merely the latest in a long line of contacts with the aliens. And sadly, it includes the information necessary to contact them at this time. That is probably the reason you're told the society formed because of the report. It has to protect its secrecy."

"So is all the stuff about the ancient civilization just made up to cover up the fact that the society is in contact with an existing species?"

"Nope," said Larry, "That stuff is all true. Apparently the evidence points to the ancient civilization sending out a small group of political refugees to a new place where nobody would ever find them. The map points to a particular location in Africa that could be their landing site. Within 100,000 years, they would have out-populated the natives and intermarried with them enough to look like natives themselves."

"So you're suggesting we're all descended from this civilization?"

"That's what it looks like," said Larry. "Which brings up interesting problems in our history."

"Such as?"

"Well, there has been a long standing argument over whether or not the Europeans that settled in America should have done so at the expense of the natives. But if that's how our species came to exist on Earth in the first place..."

"I see," I said. "Considering later occurrences in history, that might be information best kept suppressed."

"Not exactly," said Larry. "It happened so long ago, long before recorded history, and the natives that were destroyed no longer exist in any form. So the old arguments over reparations don't apply since there's nobody left to repay."

"Ok," I said, "This is interesting, but it still doesn't tell us what's going on now, and why the mob wants the report, and why they're killing off society members now that they have it."

"That one's a bit harder," said Larry, "But I will try to explain.

"Apparently the relationship goes back to the forming of the Italian crime families in the 19th century and has something to do with some of the initial mobsters being members of the society. Which sort of makes sense when you consider how the two are related in some fundamental sense. The two have not had much of a relationship due to a falling out in the mid-20th century, but there have been incidences where the mob's resources were used to protect the society, and the society's resources were used to liberate imprisoned mobsters. With both of them trying to avoid government attention, it seems there were times when they had to work together, another 'enemy of my enemy' situation.

"Vali?"

"It's my turn now?" Larry nodded at him. "Ok, so I called up one of my old friends who now works in intelligence. First, some background information.

"As you're aware, when mankind expanded into the other planets in the solar system, the various mob families came with us. They've never been considered a united organization by any stretch of the imagination, but the Italian families in particular gained a great deal in power simply by being the first in space. The Yakuza and the Russian families have all been struggling to gain a foothold in the outer planets.

"Anyway, about 12 years ago, a pirate ship owned by the Martian mob stumbled across some interesting technology while laying in wait out by Titan Station. As you know, most shipping traffic that comes through Europa heading farther into the outer planets passes by Titan Station, which makes that area of sky the most dangerous. But given the vastness of space, especially that part of the solar system, there are a lot of small objects nobody sees, until some ship or other happens to encounter one basically at random. Most pirates throw things away that they don't understand, but this particular ship happened to have a captain who was such a science buff, he had his own science officer. So they studied the device, determined it to be of alien origin, and proceeded to hand it back to their keepers on Mars. The Martians then took the device to the one group they knew would be able to identify it, and that group made the object disappear.

"So the pirate captain and his science officer got funding to pursue the society and get the object back, and also whatever information they can get. They apparently believe they can arm themselves with alien technology and make existing governments obsolete."

"How does your intelligence guy know all that?" Mary asked.

"He doesn't," answered Vali. "I filled in the blanks with information Larry had."

"I see," I said. Then, after a brief pause, "So this is a plot to rule the solar system?"

"Yep," said Larry, "By a single pirate captain and his science officer."

"Who's the pirate captain?"

"His name is Billy Studwell," said Larry. "He's not a terribly notorious pirate, and the mob was ready to dump him when he found this object."

"And he's managed to maintain his hold on this operation for 12 years?"

"The operation has waxed and waned, but he's been operating completely on his own for the last couple of years," said Larry. "That would explain the massacre, since that's really not the mob's style, but it is Studwell's style."

"But what about the two mobsters that didn't know how to fight in free fall?"

"It's more likely that you just took them by surprise and beat them with superior fighting abilities," said Larry.

"So they may have known how to fight, but because I took the initiative like I did...?"

"Yep," said Larry. "You were in more danger than you had any idea you were in, which seems to be a common occurrence for you."

"Not that common," I said. "But right now he's still in orbit, finishing his mission?"

"Yes," said Larry. "He needs to take out all agents of the society before moving on, because any remaining agents can get a message back to his Martian masters, and if they get wind of what he's been up to..."

"How is it that we're missing police involvement in all of this?"

"I don't know," said Larry, "Sherry might know better than we do."

"So hang on a minute," I asked. "If that report is just the CIA report, how do you know all this stuff about Studwell?"

Larry grinned fantastically at that point. "I identified the killers."

"Really?"

"Really."

"Ok, how did you do that?"

"Well, it was fairly simple," said Larry. "The bugged pads, you remember those?"

"Yes..."

"I kept listening, and they eventually mentioned something about the Big Boss, and I got to wondering. A few database queries later and I had it. The only person in the solar system who actually has an interest in this stuff and a history of these sorts of tactics is Billy Studwell."

"No other hits on your query?"

"There were," admitted Larry. "But none that matched up with what's happened. I'd bet my life on it, yours too, that this is Billy Studwell."

"You may very well be making that bet," I said. "Mary?"

Mary had been quiet up to that point, but when prompted, she had something to say.

"Larry's right," she answered. "We've been suspecting Studwell was after us, but we couldn't prove it, and you know how scientists demand proof."

"So, I guess it's settled," I said. "We're going off world. Where's Sherry?"

"Work," said Larry, "She talked to her boss about a new safe house, but is otherwise on a normal day."

"How are we supposed to contact her without exposing ourselves to Studwell?"

Larry handed me his pad. "Use this, I've secured it," said Larry.

I dialed up Sherry.

"What's up?" she asked.

"Where is the pirate ship *Sweet Dreams?*"

"Oddly enough, docked," said Sherry after a few minutes' worth of checking.

"Contact the captain, tell him Cecil needs him," I said.

"Old friend of yours?"

"We grew up together," I said. "He was the one who suggested I take up juggling."

"You *do* have an interesting collection of friends,"

Sherry said.

"Yep, I do. Let me know when you've contacted him."

"What's the plan?"

"We're leaving," I said. "On his ship."

"Should I tell him that?"

"No," I said. "Have him use a crew to kidnap us after the party tonight."

"That's a weird way to join a pirate crew," Sherry said.

"You join it the normal way, Mary and I will be kidnapped. Larry and Vali will go with you."

"So I'm quitting my job and leaving with you?"

"Pretty much, yes," I said. "The game is afoot." I smiled at her.

"Well, this is certainly much more interesting, anyway, and my boss is the biggest asshole in the world," smiled Sherry. "I'll make it happen."

"Roger that, and thanks a lot, Sherry," I said. "I really appreciate the way you've thrown yourself in and helped out."

"It's no problem," she said. "And if your pirate friend has a strong net hookup, I'll be able to continue accessing my PI databases."

"My pirate friend has one of the best netrunners around," I said, "Second, possibly, only to Larry. Larry's pretty damned good, too."

"Ok, let's get this show on the road," she said. "You can tell me what we're about when we're all safely on board and making tracks from this place."

"Roger that," I said as I cut the connection.

Larry had fallen asleep, so I didn't disturb him. I left him a note on his pad telling him what we were about to do. Then I went back in the bedroom to find Mary and get ready for the day.

"So, what's your plan?" she asked.

"Simple," I said. "I'm getting costumed, and you are, too. Then we're going out to perform, and we're ending at the party. After the party, pirates are going to abduct us--"

"NO!"

"Trust me, baby," I said. "They're friends of mine."

"You have pirate friends?" she asked incredulously.

"Yes," I said. "Good friends, too."

"How did that happen?"

"Long story," I said. "Asteroid friend, we used to overhaul derelicts together when we were teenagers. He's the one who got me into juggling during the divorce, in fact. He gave me my first lessons. Good guy, Captain Vallejo is. A real good guy."

"So why are we going to be kidnapped by pirates?"

"So that this Studwell character, who no doubt knows Captain Nick 'Naptime' Vallejo, at least by reputation, will have absolutely no idea that we'll be gunning for him."

"So we're going to hunt him down?"

"And kill him, yes," I said. "Once Nick hears about what's happened here, he'll do everything he can to get justice. And being on the side of the law that he's on, he won't be going to the police."

"Do you think he can take him?"

"Nick has the best crew in space, bar none," I said. "Studwell's as good as dead, at this point."

"I should have told you what was going on a long time ago," said Mary. "I love you, Cecil, more than I ever thought I could love someone." And she wrapped her loving arms around me and held me for quite some time.

When the embrace finally finished, we got to work. She didn't like dressing up as my assistant because I insisted she wear really skimpy clothes for her costume. Like most women who had a few extra kilograms, she felt quite self-conscious about her mass. I always enjoyed how she looked, and she'd wear anything for me in private, but out in public, she had difficulty with it. She felt that a sexy assistant should be a bit smaller than she was, but I felt that a sexy assistant for a jester only had to be sexy and that her mass was an asset for the job. We agreed to disagree, but in that particular instance, she did what I asked without question because she knew it was a life-or-death situation. Luckily, because of our private lives together, she had amassed a fairly extensive wardrobe of sexy clothes as well as the skills to show off her bigger middle-aged body. As a former stripper, she obviously knew how to show off a smaller body. The real problem was that the clothes were at home, the one place we couldn't go because of the crime scene we'd left behind and the fact that there were mobsters looking for us.

Now, you may argue that if there were mobsters looking for us, we shouldn't go out at all until we knew we were safely traveling to the party, where we'd be under guard of a well-funded local gang. And that would be a strong argument, really. But we had to do it.

For one thing, we had to warm up a bit and have our act together for the party. We were going together, and we had to *be* together for it. For another thing, we were safer out in public than in a private safe house, should it be compromised, and since Sherry was lining up a move to a second safe house, that meant she had reason to think this one would be compromised. Since I had arranged for us to be kidnapped after the party, we only had to be safe for this one single day. Larry could get lost and hook up with Sherry later and join us on the ship while Vali would be the kind of person to just go to the ship and ask to join, but Mary and I had to keep ourselves alive and free long enough to get to the party. But, you may ask, if the bad guys were willing to shoot up a school and take what they want, what would stop them from doing the same thing to get me and Mary? It's a good question, and it's one I didn't have an answer to. I had a feeling that wouldn't happen, though. We weren't as valuable as the information they were trying to get, which they already had in their possession, so they wouldn't go to those extreme measures to get us. So, when it came down to it, I felt safer going out with Mary in public, dressed in costume, and busking then I did staying in the safe house, and she trusted my judgment. Sometimes you just have to go with your gut feeling, and it took years as a fusion-drive mechanic for me to learn that lesson, but by this time it was a lesson well-learned.

The problem at that moment was that she didn't have any skimpy clothes. But I had a pocket full of money from having been working recently.

"Let's go buy some more," I said.

"Is that really safe?"

"Sure," I said. "I'll get dressed up and ready to go, and we'll hit up the clothing stores and get you dressed up in something new. We'll do your makeup after getting your outfit."

"Ok," she said. "I trust you." Then we went back into the bedroom to get ready.

So I did it. I always start with the makeup, because if I put the makeup on last, I always got it on my costume. If I put it on first, no problem. I put on the white base, which is actually women's makeup. The white base isn't a big seller for women because very few women have pasty white skin, but it can be found. So I stood there naked, powdering my neck, chest, and shoulders. This was required because the white blouse covered my shoulders and chest, and this particular covering gave me a blanket of white that extended from the blouse to the facepaint, and it didn't wear off easily, it required real makeup remover to get it off of my skin. Of course, while I was doing that, Mary had different ideas. She grabbed my butt and caressed my hips, pushing her belly into my back. Then she reached around and took my dick in her right hand. It responded as expected and became instantly hard. She's awesome, in part, because she can do that to me. I tried to focus on powdering my neck, which provided additional provocation for what she was doing with her hand. After I finished powdering my neck and breast forms and stuff, I moved on to the real work in putting on makeup.

Mary, of course, had different ideas. She brought her left hand up between my cheeks and started rubbing my anus. She had a way with that, it was amazing. I gasped as she rubbed, teasing my cheeks and the hole between them. She must have dropped down, because as I was applying the white part of my face she was breathing on the small of my back and licking the very top of my butt cleavage. I continued applying the white paint to my face, carefully drawing the swirly pattern I use on my face. She moved her left hand to cup my testicles and started massaging them while her right hand slid forward and back on my hard dick. I probably drew the swirl on my face incorrectly at that point as I could feel moisture on her right hand. I was starting to leak cum out of the tip, just a little. She rubbed it around, while her tongue worked its way down to the bottom of my butt. In an accommodating move, I spread my legs, and her tongue continued working between them.

So I did what any rational, reasonable man would have done. I put the makeup kit down and turned around. And she did exactly what she would have done and took me into her mouth. Fully. Completely. It was so hot. I gasped as she did it, feeling my knees go weak. She has that effect on me. That's just one of many reasons why I love her so. Then she did the unthinkable and stuck her tongue out to massage my balls while I was buried all the way in to her mouth. Amazing! That was definitely the first time she'd done *that* to me! I almost fell over, it was so awesome. Instead, she pulled back, all the way out, looked up at me and smiled.

"You're amazing," I told her.

She said nothing, put her hands on my hips, and started rocking her head back and forth on me. A combination of tongue, lips, and teeth brought me to the brink of ecstasy in nothing flat. I had to pull her head off of me. While I knew she loved for me to finish in her mouth, I really wanted something else. So I grabbed her hair and pulled her off of me, then guided her to the bed and laid her down. It's pretty cool what you can get someone to do simply by pulling their hair, and she loved every minute of it. So I laid her down and brought my tongue to bear, starting on her well-shaped breasts. She loves nipple play, but I felt like teasing around the base a bit, licking down her décolleté, and bringing my mouth to a tasteful suck on her right nipple. She gasped in response to it, and started a low moan. I moved up and gave her a kiss, then back down.

Normally, when I've got a full face of makeup, I don't do oral sex. It rubs off and gets into some odd places, and then I have to start over from scratch with the makeup. At that point, not only did I not care about the makeup, but I only had half a face done, and it wasn't really done. So I slipped my tongue down her belly, gave a small bite on her belly button, and move down into the nether regions. It didn't really fit my style to go straight for the clitoris, so I licked around the base of her right thigh, and then down the inside of the thigh. She gasped, somewhat predictably and quite satisfyingly, and put a hand on the back of my head. I thought at first she was going to guide my head, but continued what I was doing. I breathed a bit on her thigh, then moved straight to the other thigh and ran my lips up into her crotch. This, naturally, caused her to spread her legs wide. Seeing her obvious anticipation, and feeling the need to tease, I took in some recently shaved flesh into my mouth, feeling her clitoris pull tight against my chin. Then I rocked my chin back and forth against her clitoris and let the flesh out slowly. Then I looked up to her beautiful brown eyes tightly shut and her lips pulled into an expression of pleasure.

I love doing this to her. It drives her nuts.

So I dropped my tongue down between her labia and worked it back and forth, alternating between licking between and hitting her clitoris and pulling each labia in turn into my mouth. When I pulled them both into my mouth, she pushed her entire pelvic region up to meet my face and started fucking it. What else could I do? I took it like a man, and fucked her right back with my tongue and chin. She moaned an appropriate response. After a few moments of that, I brought my hand down from her hips and sank two fingers deep inside her. She recoiled, and then came right back with her own thrust. I could feel her juices starting to leak out of her at that point, and rotated my hand so I could rub her asshole with my thumb, using her juices as a lubricant. She pulled her thighs up beside my head and started squeezing, so I let her have it with my thumb, sinking it into her ass to the first knuckle. This had the desired effect of pushing her vulva tightly up against my mouth and cutting off my air supply, which I loved. I could feel my dick dripping its own fluids. She moaned louder and moved her hips faster, and it was all I could do to hang on while she fucked my face for all it was worth. It only took a few minutes before she fell back and I could feel her lips convulsing on my fingers, her juices squirting into the palm of my hand. I continued thrusting my fingers into her while she finished cumming all over my hand, then brought my face up to hers.

"How bad is my makeup?" I asked.

"Probably as bad as the makeup on my thighs," she answered.

I kissed her, and she responded with her tongue. There are kisses, and then there are kisses, and there are kisses like these that make me want to violently thrust my hips into something soft, warm, and moist. I always thought it was awesome that she could invoke that sort of reaction with just a kiss, and this time I managed to thrust into the bed. Oops. It didn't do any damage, and I quickly pulled off of it and brought my hips up to her belly.

"Oh yeah," she said, "You like fucking my belly."

"I'm in the mood to fuck something else," I answered. Then I lowered it down to her thighs, which at that time were pressed tightly together.

"No," she said, "That's not where I want it."

Then she grabbed my hips and pushed me off of her and climbed off the bed. She pulled my legs off the side of the bed and took me in her mouth again. I wasn't sure what to think, because she'd taken the thing I wanted away from me, but after a few minutes, I knew what she was up to. She'd covered me in a natural lubricant, then moved up and took me into her bosom. At that moment, I was faced with a flashback of the first time she'd used her breasts to bring me to an orgasm. It was a beautiful moment, a single gesture of love. So many times I had heard of that particular act as simply boob-fucking, and right then and there it was nothing but love. She was a wonderful woman, and she could do things to me that nobody else ever could, and she was doing it again, dammit. She grabbed her breasts each in a hand and squeezed them together, rocking her chest up and down on me, with her eyes locked firmly on mine. I was so turned on. Lubrication wasn't even an issue in this case, with her mouth having already provided plenty and my dick producing more every second. Every now and then, she'd stop and rub my dick against one or the other nipple, and push her breast hard onto me, then slip me right back in between and work it some more.

Now, there are times when a man celebrates his great stamina and endurance and his ability to please a woman for a long time, sometimes many hours. Then there are times when a man curses his lack of stamina and his displeased woman complains. This was neither of those times. I think she was down there for three minutes, tops, before I squirted her chin and neck. It was awesome, and I probably yelled out quite loudly. Ok, I know for a fact I yelled out quite loudly, because we heard Larry in the next room ask if we were ok. Mary answered him, but I have no idea what she said, and he left us alone. Then I watched her rub what I had deposited on her neck right into it, and then lick her fingers and palms.

But she wasn't finished, and apparently neither was I. The rest of this turns into a regular account of sex with a girlfriend, but I wanted to point out that at that moment there was nothing regular about it. There was a strong possibility this would be the last time we'd be able to do that together, because one or both of us might be dead in a few hours. On the other hand, if we survived, we'd have a chance to do it again in just a few hours. In any case, we spent the next hour fucking like it would be our last time. I think we managed to rewrite the kama sutra, and in the low gravity of Europa, there are a lot of possibilities you just don't get on a spaceship. As statistics go, I had a record-breaking three orgasms in an hour, which is a lot considering that like most men, I have a recharge time. She, on the other hand, lost track somewhere around six. Which, actually, isn't unusual for us even if it is somewhat uncommon.

When we were finished, I had to start the makeup from scratch.

Chapter Eleven

We set out that day ready to take on the world. We were both recently-sexed, energetic, and in love with each other, and nothing could faze us. We got the skirt at a stripper-clothes store. We got her a camisole and tight yoga pants at the local department store. She put her hair up and applied the costume makeup to finish the deed, and we hit up the shopping district. She was looking downright fuckable in her assistant's costume, so much so that I wished she'd dress like that more often. Thanksgiving was coming soon, so the shopping district was abuzz with shoppers. We took a pretty good take, keeping our eyes out for anything out of the ordinary. We also never left the public view.

That made using the restroom a bit tricky. You see, in all those spy novels in days gone by, nobody ever talks about when and how spies use the restroom. In fact, restroom scenes are usually oriented around the plot, where the villains and other contacts use the restrooms but the heroes never do. I guess that didn't make us heroes, because we had to use the restrooms together, and ensure there was always a fair crowd. Since I passed as a woman, we had no problems using the restroom together, but I still had to sit down on the toilet to pee. A person with a penis standing sounds like exactly that and is in danger of being outed, but a person with a penis sitting sounds like a person without a penis sitting, and is therefore safe.

As the day progressed into early evening, it was getting high time to get over to the party. So I pulled out my pad and dialed up Susan Hall, Event Coordinator extraordinaire. She answered readily.

"Hi Cecil," she said. "I see you're ready to perform tonight."

"Yes, I am," I said. "I wanted to confirm location and see if we could get a car sent."

"No problem," she said. "Just give me your location and I'll send one right over."

When I finished talking to her, I immediately dialed up Sherry to tell her where the party was located so she could send the pirates after us. She answered readily, and confirmed she was already with the pirates, as was Larry and Vali. The day was going swimmingly. All that was left was to attend the party and get abducted and the day would be a good day.

When the car arrived, I got the distinct impression that Susan Hall was going to a lot of effort to impress me and I couldn't imagine why. She'd sent a stretched limo, a rare and expensive piece of machinery for a place like Europa. Mary and I got in and seated, where we found the Tortoise holding beers for us.

"Welcome!" said the Tortoise. "Have a seat."

We took seats in the car.

"You are looking quite pretty today," he said to me.

"Thank you," I said, batting my eyelashes.

"You know, Mary," the Tortoise began. "I find it interesting that you're dating a crossdresser."

"Why's that?" she asked.

"That just doesn't seem to be your type."

Mary chuckled a bit. "Why not?"

"You're into real masculine types, are you not?"

"Trust me," she answered. "It takes a lot of balls for someone like Cecil to wear a dress."

The Tortoise whistled despairingly. "You got me

there."

"Besides," said Mary. "My girlfriend is *very* sexy."

"I can't argue with that, either," answered the Tortoise.

"So, why is Don Julian so interested in me?" I said, changing the subject to something I found less awkward.

"We've, uh, noticed that you've been doing a lot of running around," he answered.

"I'm a busker, I always do a lot of running around," I pointed out.

"No, not like this," he responded. "Look, I'm not authorized to discuss this with you except in the presence of Don Julian."

"That's too bad," said Mary. "All this secrecy is going to get someone hurt."

"Is that a threat?" amused the Tortoise.

"Of course not," said Mary.

At about that time, the car came to a stop.

"We're here," said the Tortoise.

"Already?" I asked. "That was quick."

"You did notice the car showed up quick, right?" asked the Tortoise. I blew him off and opened the door. He quickly jumped out to help us out, proving that the old sexist chivalric code wasn't dead yet. I let him help me out of the car because, while he may be sexist, it is always nice to be treated like a lady. I could see why so many women still want to be treated that way.

The party was being held in the type of clubhouse that required a password to get in, which the Tortoise supplied, vouching for the both of us. I briefly wondered how I would've gotten in if I hadn't called for a ride, but pushed it out of my mind. They'd probably have let me in thinking I was a hooker ordered by the boss. The party had already gotten started, so as soon as we walked in, we went to work.

Having discussed this earlier, we didn't hit the stage right away. Instead, we went table to table telling jokes and flirting with the seated party-goers. For the most part, our tableside show was oriented around cheap magic tricks and silly interactions with each other and the partiers. We made sure to hit every table, which took about an hour altogether, and didn't linger at any particular table. It was fun, and the liquor flowed pretty freely for us. Since I didn't want to get hammered, I tended to have the bartender water the drinks down a bit so that I could still drink socially without getting plastered.

I noticed that this was a high flying crowd. There were several politicians, as well as numerous prominent New Austin businesspeople throughout the crowd. The Julians were definitely holding a big party, and had I not been embroiled in the kill-the-bad-guy situation I was in, this would have been a great opportunity for me to expand my audience to some very powerful people. Judging by the number of ladies dropping me their contact information, I could also have expanded my sex life to the wives and a few husbands of some very powerful people. Glad I dodged that bullet, because there was no way that could end well.

After a few more tables' worth of tableside performance, Mary gestured to me that it was time to get stageside. So I took a moment to mentally prepare myself while she provided the playlist to the DJ. I retired to a somewhat private part of the room, closed my eyes, and breathed deeply for a few minutes. That moment of centering prepared me mentally for the rigors of performing on a stage, and in front of this crowd, I needed to be as prepared as I possibly could be. After I felt suitable prepared, it was time to get the show on the stage, to turn a phrase.

I glided through the crowd, grabbing a random drink from a server's tray, and moving onto the stage in the far corner from the door, I did a front roll, carrying the drink all the way through it without spilling and coming to a stand facing the crowd. Part way through my glide, the spotlight operator had spotted me and focused onto me, getting the crowd to focus on me. After standing from the roll, I took a bow, and walked over to the microphone, situated next to the stool that was still standard fare for this type of performance. I put my drink down and grabbed the mic. I switched it on and immediately started banging on it with my hand, yelling "Is this thing on?"

The crowd laughed about that, of course.

"So, I was out walking around the other day, and you know what I discovered? Apparently there's no atmosphere outside the domes. You shouldn't order a meal out there."

There were scattered chuckles over that one, and I figured I should have done the full set-up on that joke. Oh well.

"So, do you know who I am?"

The crowd didn't really respond to that, but I at least had all eyes on me.

"That's too bad. I was hoping you knew, because I don't."

Maybe the stress was getting to me, because I was

having a hard time even remembering my best hits.

"What? What was that?" I looked to Mary, who was yelling to me. "Oh, right, that's who I am. I remember now."

I squared my feet and faced the crowd directly.

"I am Cecil the Fool, and I am here to entertain you!"

At this point, the crowd gave me a nice and respectful round of applause. Since I was only there as a cover for a meeting with Don Julian, it didn't necessarily matter how good my performance was. However, given the events in the coming weeks, I was more than likely going to hang up my jester's hat for good, so I wanted to have the best final performance I could. Under the circumstances, I just didn't know if I had it in me at that time.

I decided to hide behind more athletic performance tricks that are generally considered even more impressive wearing the kind of heels I was wearing. I gestured to the Mary, who in turn gestured to the DJ to begin the song and I took up position in stage center. Mary would provide the props I was going to need for this interpretive dance. As the opening notes of the 1812 Overture began, I moved into a spiral, moving farther out from the center with each rotation, also rotating my body, going between arms crossed and arms extended, with periodic pirouettes tossed in for good measure.

This type of performance is more like figure skating, but without the ice. It had become popular a few decades after the first Lunar colony had formed, due to the low gravity making such a performance possible in the first place while also making the ice performance more difficult. Using various dance steps, I moved around the stage and performed stunts like flips, high jumps, high spinning jumps, and because of the basis of the music, mock punches, blocks, and rifle shots. As the first climax approached, I moved more vigorously, with more jumps timed to hit with cymbal crashes and such. As the music waned into the middle section, I worked down to the floor and performed more sensual moves, moves designed to bring about sexual arousal among the members of the audience but also miming movements of battlefield nurses and wounded soldiers. I never really knew for sure what Tchaikovsky was thinking for that middle section, but I always imagined it focusing on the part of the battle in Russia that highlighted all the dead and wounded soldiers and heroic efforts of the battlefield nurses to care for them the best they could.

As the final movement started picking up speed, I was up and marching like a soldier. Shooting and so forth. This is obviously the part that represents the rallying of the Russian armies and their allies and the ultimate defeat of Napolean in the field, leading to his subsequent trial and imprisonment. At the climax, with the cannon shots and everything, Mary tossed me my torches, unlit. I was feeling downright inspired, and when I fired up the torches, the audience let out a cheer. I obviously had them eating out of my hand at this point. I worked in numerous dance moves, at one point even throwing the torches way up into the air, and doing a side roll to get where they fell. I caught them and continued the act, of course. I worked in my light-up clubs as well, until I had six total objects flying around me in a whirlwind of fire, light, and movement. It was a fantastic orgy of light, as chaotic as it was mesmerizing. The waterfall pattern at the climactic ending gave me a perfect circle of alternating fire and light clubs, and as the last notes sounded, I tossed each successive club to Mary, who placed each in a different location near the front of the stage, until they were spread evenly across the front of the stage casting a vicious light in my direction.

Then I grabbed the mic and held it to my mouth.

"So, I farted not too long ago.

"I find it interesting that we live in a low gravity environment, and farting doesn't send us up to the ceiling. I mean, I've had some pretty explosive farts and all, and didn't get even a centimeter of lift. Why is that?

"I asked an engineer friend about this, and he told me, and I kid you not, he told me that the reason we don't shoot up to the ceiling when we fart is because our anuses are shaped wrong."

I let that set in for a moment.

"Your face is shaped wrong!

"Was my obvious response. Don't tell me my ass is wrong, you asshole. It's your ass that's wrong!

"But that's the thing, isn't it? Assholes? Think about it. What does your asshole do for you? Obviously it discharges shit you don't want or need. For some of you, it's a source of pleasure, in the right circumstance. For others, well, we'll leave that alone.

"But the question is 'what's an asshole good for?'

"And the obvious answer to that is cutting in line."

The crowd laughed it up a bit over this one.

"Now, I want to talk about some other things. You see, I'm a jester, and that means that part of my job is relating history to you. Also, part of my job is saying funny things. Putting those two things together doesn't always work out for me.

"So, there's an interesting pattern in human history where each century tries to outdo the previous century. Unfortunately, this usually involves a little bit of mass murder.

"Take, for example, the 19th century. Napolean conquered the world! Well, Europe, anyway. He mass-murdered his way across the continent, but managed not to kill a lot of people. Later in the century, there was the Boer wars and the Opium wars, and a few other wars, and a lot of people got killed.

"Then the 20th century said 'Oh, we can do better than that.'

"They started off the century by slaughtering people in Turkey nobody had ever heard of, and in the middle of the century, they killed like ten million people for no good reason, and ended the century with a last little bit of genocide in Europe. It's like they knew the century was turning over and they had to get in a little bit more killing.

"Weird people.

"Then the 21st century started off nicely, with a nuclear winter. It's like 21 said to 20: Hey, that's my girlfriend, go fuck someone else.

"Obviously there was some recovery from that, thanks to some people who thought that colonizing the solar system was a good idea. I wonder why they thought it was a good idea? I mean, do you really think that Mars is a place that is hospitable to live? There's no life on Mars, and there's a reason for that! Anyway...

"The 22nd century said 'fuck all that, we're too busy'. And that was a smart move. Unfortunately, the 23rd century didn't like that, and they were all 'orbital bombardment!' They were total dickheads. And you see that throughout human history, where the new century tries to one-up the previous century. It was nice when it was about technology, but it was also about war.

"So what's next? Here we are in the 24th century, and we've had no mass extinction event. What are we going to do?"

I let the silence speak for a moment or two.

"I think Ronald Spade has the answer to that one, honestly. He's already told all of us here that we're not welcome on Mars, and he's been moving ships into the asteroid belt at an alarming pace. I think he's worried that we all might suspect that he really does have a little dick.

"On the other hand: *aliens!*

"You've seen the movies, played the VR games, you know it's coming, right?"

I wasn't really feeling the comedy, so I decided to finish with a more physical show. Considering that that would probably be the last performance I would do for some time, I decided to end my act where I started it: juggling. Now, Mary can't juggle to save her life, but she can catch and throw, so I used her in her role as sexy assistant to keep a few balls in the air.

I moved the microphone and stand away from the performance area and threw a three sign to my fiance. She obediently took three fire balls from my bag, lit them, and tossed them to me one by one. I moved into a cascade as the music started, again, this time a newer pick, a 23rd century technical symphonic interpretation of the aforementioned orbital bombardment of Earth during the colonial uprisings that had happened a short time before the piece was composed. The piece had the same overall structure of the 1812 Overture I had already performed, with a light and quick beginning, a dramatic and tragic slow middle section representing the losses of the battle, and finishing with a dramatic and victorious sequence representing the bombardment itself, and ending when the colonies gained their independence. It was a terrible way to celebrate the deaths of billions of people, but it was an excellent piece for juggling.

As the light electric violins kicked in, I received all three lit fire balls from Mary and moved into a cascade, matching the tempo of the sequence. The balls moved through the air to match the soaring violin melody, while the catches and throws punctuated alongside the percussion section. It sometimes amazes me how beautiful a simple cascade can be made to appear, especially when your balls are on fire. I moved into the Mills' Mess as the electronic wind section played a counterpoint to the violins. The Mills' Mess is usually the first advanced three ball pattern that a juggler learns, and it is definitely an advanced pattern. Basically, the arms cross and recross a lot and there's a standard throw, an underarm throw, and a throw while the arms are crossed. The balls themselves move in a circular motion, alternating between clockwise and anticlockwise movement. It perfectly fit the section of the piece where the violins and electronic wind instruments are dueling. Then the electronic horns kicked in to dominate the remainder of the opening movement, and I shifted to columns, throwing in tempo to the horns with the balls themselves being simply tossed straight up, two on the outside of the pattern thrown together with the middle ball being thrown separate. As the horns continued to dominate the room, I shifted to Matt's Mess, where the middle ball in the column is moved to the outside and tossed into the middle. The outside balls continued where they were, of course. As the horns crescendoed, so, too, did my juggling. Throwing columns by grabbing the outside balls, crossing your arms, and then throwing them leads to a visual pattern where there's a horizontal line of fire at the bottom, and the bounding balls in the columns continue to make their movements plain for all to see. As the violins came in fast and loud, which they would ultimately climax to end the first movement, I switched to an alternating windmill. The alternating windmill is similar to the Mills' Mess in that I juggle a circular pattern clockwise, and then switch to the mirror image, but the alternating nature of the Mills' Mess is left out, meaning that I switched directions at will. As the climax approached, Mary tossed me the fourth ball and I worked it into the alternating windmill, climaxing by throwing all four balls high in the air with the last cymbal crash of the movement.

The next movement in the symphony was slower, of course, which doesn't lend itself well to a juggling routine, but I had been fooling around with contact juggling for some time and decided that it was time to put that on the stage. I let the fire balls drop, and due to their design they didn't bounce, and signaled to Mary to toss me two of my crystal clear light-up spheres. Matching the mourning tone and introverted nature of the middle movement, I basically rubbed the balls over my body. In contact juggling, which you may have seen in a certain popular movie from the 20th century, the idea is that the balls are in constant motion, but have to remain in contact with your body in some form. It's more than simply rubbing the balls around, however. The basic trick that kids learn in school is to roll the ball on the underarm, letting it pass over the forearm and onto the hand, and then whipping the hand up and turning it so that the ball rolls down the outside of the hand and forearm. Typically, with one ball, the juggler would then roll it off at the elbow onto their other hand and continue the motion. When done right, it's very graceful, almost like interpretive dance. I was using two balls, however, and that meant that I had to keep both in motion without them ever colliding, at least, not until the end.

I wondered how I appeared to the audience at that point. I was moving my arms in graceful sweeping circular movements, with glowing spheres rolling over my arms, chest, boobs, back, down to my legs, off my feet, and transferring back up to the shoulders to start the movement all over again. In front of me on the floor sat four evenly spaced balls of fire, and further in front of me sat the clubs, lighting up the stage with their alternating fire and light-up clubs. As the movement continued, I turned so that I was sideways to the audience and leaned back far enough to run a pattern of balls rolling over/between my breasts, down my belly, and then being transferred back to my shoulders by catching them off my hips and rolling them back up my arms.

As the second movement came to its inevitable end, I stood up straight again and faced the audience, with the balls rolling up and down my arms and ultimately colliding on the last whole note of the movement on my chest and dropping to the floor. Mary dutifully scooped them up when they reached her, turned them off, and put them away. During the very brief moment of silence that followed, I shifted the balls on the floor so that they served as the vertices of a large rectangle.

I wasn't doing this finale with balls.

Unlike the 1812 Overture, the third movement

started loud and brass, with the electronic horns coming in as a unit and marching with great dissonance. Beat by beat, Mary tossed me each club until I had all six in the air again, laid out in four columns with two clubs bouncing over the pattern like tennis balls in a tennis match. As the swirling strings came in to stand up to the bullying horn section, so, too, did my mix of clubs. Now, the six club Mills' Mess is impossible to do on Earth, and I'm still the only juggler I know of who has mastered it even in low gravity, but it is an impressive thing to see, and perfectly matched the warring movements of the obviously hostile symphonic sections. I imagined the violinists hitting the horn players with their elbows while the horns are stomping on the violinists' feet. In the final act of the movement, the horns took to a march while the strings and winds continued their dance of destruction, leading me to a column-based pattern with a cascade interweaving. It was a visual cacophony, a chaotic mess of light and fire. It was battle personified, visual warfare. As the percussion section set off the explosions of the orbital bombardment that ultimately secured victory and independence for the off-Earth colonies, I stamped my feet and separated the torches from the light-up clubs with the torches in my left hand knocking out the clubs in my right until all that was left in the air were the torches.

While finishing the routine with a simple three torch column pattern, the audience threw themselves to their feet with applause. The standing ovation I received as my performance came to an end told me that this was my final performance, and that it was over. I gave a bow, and exited the stage.

After I exited the stage, Mary and I were ushered into a private room where we found the Tortoise, a few miscellaneous wops, and a gentleman who I knew from jailhouse pictures.

"Don Julian, I presume," I stated.

"Indeed," he responded. "Have a seat at my table." Then, to his serving staff, "Get these people some drinks, they've been working hard all evening!"

"I'll have a ziegen," I said. Mary parroted me. The Tortoise was quiet.

Don Julian said nothing as we waited for our drinks, and we kept quiet too. I shot Well-prepared Defense at Julian, to which he responded with Nothin' Doin'. I always love it when I meet someone who knows how to properly express themselves with their face.

In due time, our drinks arrived, and I took a swig out of mine. Hey, I was thirsty!

"So," said Julian, breaking the silence, "I hear that you've been having problems with a rival of mine."

"Maybe," I said. "I have a lot of problems. You'll have to be specific."

"Studwell," said Julian. "The only asshole in the area who'd shoot up a school to steal a computer."

Since I wasn't surprised he knew about that, I had to say, "I'm not surprised you know about that."

"You shouldn't be," he answered. "We noticed them in orbit about a week ago and have been keeping tabs on them."

"Interesting," I said. "So, did you know they would attack the school?"

At that point, Julian had no choice but to shoot Empassioned Compassion.

"Cecil," he began quite seriously, "Had I any indication they were going to do that, I would have had an army there to defend your students. This moon and every single person on it is under my protection. My territory has been violated and I *will* seek revenge."

"I see," I said. "And you intend to help me in my quest to destroy this mo-fro?"

"I cannot promise anything," he said, "seeing as how you belong neither to me nor to the Illuminati."

I beamed What the Fuck at Mary, and she whimpered out "Well, we needed a name!"

To Julian, "What are your plans, then?"

"I believe that I will hire a fleet of privateers to pursue Studwell," he responded.

"I've got one that can take him, and he's ready to move pretty quickly, long before you can hire your little boaties."

Julian laughed uproariously. "Naptime Vallejo? You think he can take Studwell?" Then he laughed again. I have to admit, I was feeling a bit uncomfortable about how much Don Julian knew about me.

"Ok, spill it," I said.

"The man is out-manned, out-gunned, and outwitted," said Julian. "He's just not crazy enough to take down Studwell!"

"Really? You *do* know I've served with him before, right?"

"He was different then! Nowadays he just fires a warning shot and if his target fires back, he scuttles off behind an asteroid or some bullshit. He's not the captain you served with, he's not the man to take out Studwell."

"Well, he's going."

"Have you contacted him about this?"

"Well, no," I said. "Why?"

"Then you don't know," said Julian. "This is too much for him, he'll know it when he sees it."

I gave him Fierce Momma.

"Oh, don't get your panties in a wad," he responded. "Vallejo's still well-known to be the foremost tactical genius in the outer planets. With the right armaments, he might be able to take Studwell. He just won't step up and fight anymore, that's all."

I gave him Fiercer Momma.

"Fine, have it your way," said Julian. "I'll see if I can help, but I'm not promising anything."

"Fine."

"Good."

I chugged my remaining beer. "I seem to be out."

Julian waved a hand, making a beer magically materialize in front of me.

"Ok, Don Julian," I said, "You seem to know a lot about me."

"Yes, I do."

"Well, why?" I asked, tossing him a bit of Honest Pickings.

"I've been watching you for some time," he answered. "You see, I've known for some time that your girlfriend here is part of the Illuminati. We have usually had good relations with them, on the rare occasion we've had dealings, and I always found it interesting that she dated one of my underlings before she joined the organization."

He seemed to think that was a suitable explanation, so I shot him Unsuitable Explanation.

"I can see you're not satisfied with that explanation," he said, observing my change to Unsatisfied With Explanation. "I'll try harder.

"We tracked her joining the organization, and kept tabs on her afterwards. When you and she began dating, we first ignored you. But when you turned up as a, how do you say it?, a busker?, then we ran an extensive background check on you. I have spent the afternoon going over your dossier, in fact. You've had a very interesting life. I'm sorry your ex has kept your kids from you for so long that they probably hate you now." I inadvertently gave him Pissed Off Dad, but quickly replaced it with Who Are You Foolin'. He continued. "So, you served on a pirate crew, you've done some time rebuilding fusion drives, you've been a netrunner, I mean, come on man, you've done everything.

"That is, except for work for me. I had been preparing to offer you a job, because a man with your skills can go far in my organization. Hell, *you* could end up running the joint, making you the better boyfriend pick than Turtle Boy here--" he nudged the Tortoise with his elbow "--and, this most important of all, your loyalty to your friends is impeccable. That is exactly why I like you. And their loyalty to you is of likewise quality."

"What makes you think I'd side with organized crime?"

"Nothing at all," said Julian, again laughing uproariously. "Nothing at all."

"Then why this meeting?"

"Well, originally I had intended to find out what you knew about Studwell's operations here in the last few days," he answered. "Since we scheduled this meeting, many things have happened. The purpose of this meeting now is for me to tell you this:

"If there is any way I can help you, I will do it. I can't promise anything in particular, mind you, but if there is anything I can do, I will do it."

"Why are you doing this for me?"

"Loyalty."

With that said, he signaled for us to leave. Without another word spoken, we departed.

The party was still going on, but Mary and I had one more thing left to do, and that was leave the party. So we hurried out, stepped out into the corridor, and got ourselves shot with stunners.

Chapter Twelve

So we were on the pirate ship *Sweet Dreams,* and my old friend Nick was taking care of us. Because of how they chose to kidnap us, we slept for quite some time before waking for reveille. I swear that Nick had the only pirate ship in existence that used traditional military discipline to run the ship. We awoke and got dressed, without enough time to shower. I did my best with the sink to wash off the makeup, but I have to admit, there were traces. Oh well. I slipped on a pretty summer dress, took my girlfriend's hand in mine, and walked. We showed up to breakfast, which isn't a formal meal on this ship. Instead, you grab what you can, snarf it down, and then move on with your business. I had a note from Nick instructing us to meet in his conference room, so we took our breakfastses in there.

The command crew was already assembled, as were Larry and Sherry. We walked in and took the two available seats, which were obviously chairs cannibalized from some other room. This room didn't quite fit the group, but it had to, so we made due.

"Cecil, my old friend," said Nick. "You asshole. What kind of bullshit are you getting us into now?"

"I'm probably about to get you killed," I said.

"Oh good," said a quite attractive lady, "I always like to know when I'm about to be killed."

"Quiet, Shauna," said my old friend. "This is serious. Sherry has already briefed me on some of it, something about a massacre, and you're somehow involved, Cecil. So, spill it."

"Well, I don't really know where to start," I thought

out loud.

"Start at the beginning, then tell the middle, and finish with the end," my old friend said helpfully.

"Right, of course," I said. "That's good advice, where have I heard it before?"

"You were probably giving it to me," said Nick. "Now get going."

"Ok, we're hunting another pirate."

"I'm not a pirate!" said the lady, Shauna, who had spoken before.

"Me neither," said another.

"My lawyer fucked me," said a third.

"That's enough," said the captain, bringing his hand on the table to quiet everybody. "Cecil, who are we going to hunt and why?"

"We're hunting Billy Studwell."

The room was silent. Nobody spoke for several heartbreaking moments.

Finally, "Oh good," said Shauna. "At least we're not hunting anybody dangerous."

"Um, may I ask a favor?" asked Mary. All eyes were on her. "Who are you people? This is all new to me, I've never dealt with pirates before."

"Oh right, of course, forgive my manners," said Nick. "My friends are unfamiliar to you. I should introduce them. This chick who keeps dropping smart-ass comments is my Chief Engineer, Shauna Riley. My First Officer here is Martin Cruz. Tac and Helm, respectively are Jim Young and Darius with the unpronounceable last name--"

"It's Nikolakopoulos," said Darius, "And it's Greek, not Unpronounceable like these Spanish names you see buggering around."

"Right, whatever," said Nick, "He got his driver's license via email and the ship has the dents to prove it."

Darius nodded thoughtfully.

"My communications officer is Nika Veronin," continued the captain, "and my netrunner we just call Jared, because his last name is too boring to mention. And the wonderful chef is named Chino, and he happens to be the best aikidoka in the outer planets. He has belts in a few other arts, but I suspect he's probably not as well accomplished as your own loverboy there."

"Thank you," said Mary.

"You know Sherry and Larry already, of course," said the captain. "And I am Captain Nick Vallejo of the pirate ship *Sweet Dreams.* And you must be the sweet Mary that Cecil has told me so much about. I have to say, you are every bit as beautiful as he has said, and that's saying a lot considering what he thinks is beautiful. Welcome to my ship, dear lady."

"Thanks," she said. "I feel welcome already. This ship is a bit more well-equipped than I'd expect a pirate ship to be."

"We do alright," said Nick. "We haven't encountered any Spacers yet, but that's only a matter of time."

"Spacers?" asked Mary.

"Yeah, assholes," said Shauna.

"Murderers," added Darius.

Mary look askance at me.

"I don't know," I said. "Nick, who are the Spacers?"

"Vigilante force that's recently entered the solar system," said Nick. "They've been hunting down pirate crews for a few years and been remarkably successful at it. I believe I told you about them at our last meeting."

"You didn't mention 'spacers'," I responded.

"Oh," he said thoughtfully.

"Is there a chance we could enlist their help to get Studwell?"

"Nope," said Nick. "Nobody's been able to talk to them. Most pirates argue over whether or not they even exist, but we've seen them in action. We're one of the very few pirate crews to see them and live to tell about it. Probably helps that we look pretty legitimate from the outside."

"I thought you said you hadn't encountered them?" I asked.

"We haven't exactly encountered them," answered Nick. "It's a long story. I already told you most of it, and I'd rather we move on."

"Ok," I said. "Are they a threat to current operations?"

"Probably," said Nick. "But let's not worry about that. Why do we want Studwell?"

"Personal and religious reasons," I answered. "He ordered a massacre at the school, and has been hunting Mary's friends. In fact, Mary's the only one left of her group on Europa."

"She's not on Europa anymore," Jared pointed out helpfully. "So I guess her group has lost its Europan presence."

"Yes, it has," I said. "But not it's Europan frame of mind. Studwell stole some information in the course of the massacre that puts him in a position where he can acquire a great deal of power and possibly take over the whole solar system."

"So he's a nut-job that thinks he's going to rule the world?" asked Shauna.

"Yep," I said, "And he has the information to do it."

"Can he use it against us?"

"Not yet, but the window of opportunity is slim. Larry, how long before Studwell can get some advanced weapons, assuming he can make contact?"

"Hard to say," said Larry. "Could be as little as three months, as much as a year."

"That doesn't leave us a lot of time," I said.

"Contact with whom?" asked the communicator, Darius.

"We're not at liberty to discuss that," I answered. "I'm sorry, Nick, but while I can tell you what's at stake and who the bad guys are, I can't tell you why. When we meet them, they may have military grade weapons or worse. It won't be easy, and we may need help along the way."

"Cecil, we will discuss this later," said Nick. "In the meantime, we've been tracking Studwell's ship, the *Devil's Whore*, ever since Sherry told us to watch it. Tac, what's your analysis of the ship?"

"Well," started the tactical officer. "She's tough. She's got 12 bow torpedo bays and 4 aft, but apparently has some weak lasers. Our military grade lasers are certainly more powerful, and by the looks of things, she's got a number of blind spots her lasers don't reach. Her shields are pretty minimal, but that goes along with Studwell's reputation of blowing the bastards out of the sky and then collecting cargo from the remains. But he hasn't been doing a lot of attacking; it seems he has some other project going on. In fact, he hasn't even been seen engaging in any piracy for several years, so it's possible my information is out of date."

"So what are our chances in a fair fight?"

"Good, I'd say. At least half. But in an unfair fight, we could probably take him by surprise and take him down. It's the taking him by surprise that's the real problem," said Tac.

"Explain," said the captain.

"The man's got sensors that are well advanced of anything we've got. He's even rumored to be able to see cloaked vessels."

"Is the rumor substantiated?"

"He's taken down a few pirate ships that were undoubtedly cloaked when the fighting started," said Tac, "But other than that, no."

"So, basically, if we could sneak up on him, we could take him down, but since we can't sneak up on him, we're fucked. Is that what you're saying?" asked the first officer.

"Yep," said Tac. "That's exactly what I'm saying."

"Great," said the first officer. "At least we know we can win somehow."

"What kind of sensors does he have?" asked Larry.

"I don't know," said Tac. "The rumors don't include that. Why?"

"Well, some time ago, I did some contract work for the US Navy. They wanted to know if I could build a device that could hide from a particular sensor, but the contract was terminated before I could give them results. Apparently the project they were working on lost its funding. Anyway, the sensor was a Russian scientific sensor designed to look at pulsars that had apparently been adapted to see fusion-drive waste, which would theoretically allow tracking a cloaked ship. Naturally, the problem was..." Larry had the techies in the room interested, which included Nick, of course.

He finally finished. "So I had figured out how to conceal the exhaust stream, and also the initial infrared waves leaking from the exhaust manifold. It wasn't really that difficult, but involved being close enough to hack into the sensor net."

"That's brilliant," said the netrunner, Jared. "So you're suggesting we get close enough to hack into the sensor net, but still far enough that they can't see us yet, and then figure out how to hack in. How long did it take you to do that?"

"About four months," answered Larry proudly.

"Four months? We'll only have a few days at most!" declared Jared.

"Well, we could figure something out before we even get close if we can find out what kind of sensors they've got," said Larry somewhat haughtily.

"Are they still in orbit?" asked Shauna.

"Why does that matter?" asked Jared.

"Because you could hack in right now and find out what they've got," said Shauna.

"And if we're caught, they attack us right here and now," said Jared.

"I don't know about that," said Larry. "Getting caught, well, who's to say they'll catch us? And even if they do, we are just one ship in a sea of ships, how are they going to determine it's us?"

The captain interrupted. "I think right now is the best chance we'll get, but you're not doing it from the ship. Do you have a facility you can work from on Europa where you have everything you need?"

"Sure," said Larry, "The school. But it's a crime scene."

"If we can get you and Jared in there, can you do it from there?"

"If we can tap into the planetary sensors," answered Jared. "We can't use the ship's sensors to get to it."

"Oh that's not hard," said Larry, "I've done it before." Which, naturally, made me think that Larry had hacked into every system on Europa at one time or another, the old netrunner.

"Then do it," said the captain. "Find out what he's got, and don't get caught. We'll send a team to stand guard and get you out if the situation gets hot."

"Aye-aye!" Larry yelled, obviously enjoying becoming a pirate, even if only temporarily.

"Be nice to get that kind of attitude from my regular crew," said Nick. "Chino, set up a team and get it down there fast." Then he looked at me. "I know what you can do, and I'd rather you go on the team, but we need to have a little chit-chat before this gets too far along. What do you want to do?"

"I'm going with Larry," I said. "You know how it is, old friend."

Nick gave me a hug and whispered in my ear, "Take care of yourself, this is downright dangerous." Then he stepped back.

"This is not my first rodeo," I told Nick.

Chapter Thirteen

Chino looked over his team. He hand-picked everybody because that's how it works on a pirate ship. He was clearly satisfied with his choices.

"Cecil, I want you on point."

"Of course," I bowed my head at him.

"Vali, I want you to take up the rear."

"Of course," responded Vali, mirroring my bow.

"Larry and Jared, you're the package. I'll take up position right behind point, the two redshirts will take up left and right package escort." The two indicated redshirts grinned at each other for reasons I will never completely understand.

The shuttle approached the launch bay as we took up positions, preparing for anything.

"Cecil," asked Chino. "Are we likely to be attacked on landing?"

"No," I said. "They don't know anything, yet, hopefully."

"But after this operation?"

"They'll probably know we've found a, uh, um..."

"A ship?" asked Larry, helpfully.

"Yeah," I said. "A pirate ship, I mean."

The shuttle landed. I watched as the cargo bay door opened, slowly lowering itself to the ground. When it reached the ground, I rushed through, crouching near one of it's loading pillars. After surveying the bay, I signaled to advance.

I led the group down several corridors before we

stopped to take stock. We were still a few blocks away from the school, but we had made good time with no enemy contacts. It was a little disturbing.

"Chino," I said.

"I am here."

"We'll need to leave a rear guard."

"Where?"

"Near here, but not quite. We'll go another block, and there will be some gothic-esque buildings down there. That's where we should leave the guard."

"They'll have much cover."

"Indeed," I said. Then I signaled and we moved out.

As we passed the buildings I mentioned, Chino deployed the two redshirts to take up positions, instructed with watching everything and being ready to defend us should we come in hot. Another block later and we were in the school.

The school was covered up with security. I knew numerous approaches to the lab, so I chose the one least likely to be guarded. We approached the science building from the northeast, taking cover in the portable buildings that lined the northern end of a school that couldn't keep up with student body growth. Just south of that position, there was a door rarely used, and so unlikely to be heavily guarded. I moved forward and to my left, placing me across from that position. From there, I spotted the one guard, and he didn't show any signs that he had seen me. I signaled to Chino, and like a cat in the dead of night stalking a preying mantis, he moved in and took the guard down in one swift stroke.

I punched through the door, which was placed right next to the stairs. As I rounded the steps, I noted that the other door, the main traffic door, was heavily guarded, and that was just what I could see. Clearly they didn't consider this door a risk. I tried to avoid reminding myself how our police seemed to be more interested in beating people than in providing security, but in this case, it worked in my favor, so I moved to the stairs. Chino held the door and let the others in.

At the top of the stairs, there were two more guards on this side of the corridor. As I reached the middle landing, I spotted them and signaled everyone to a stop. I gestured for Larry to approach, since he had a gun that could stun.

"Can you get them both?" I asked in a whisper.

"Yes," he said, "But I can't guarantee any other guards in this hallway won't see it."

"I'll go up and signal you."

Without waiting for a reply, I fell to my hands and knees and crawled my way up the stairs. The guards were guarding the lab itself, which had three doors, two that led into the lab and one that led into the prep room. They were looking around the corridor expecting to see someone fully erect, so they didn't see my head sticking up over the top stair. I looked both ways down the hall and saw no other guards, so I signaled Larry to fire. The two guards fell one right after another, and I moved to the nearest door.

At that moment, another door opened just north of my position from a usually empty classroom. A cop stepped out, looking around.

"Who are you?" he asked.

I moved quickly and decisively, taking him down

before he even realized I was on the move. Then I knocked him out with a blood choke. As the others moved up, I signaled to Larry to stun the poor guy, which he was happy to oblige. Then I turned my attention to the lab. With my lockpicks I moved into it without even stopping.

Once in the lab, Larry went straight to his terminal and checked it.

"Apparently there's still power," he said. "That's good. I wouldn't expect them to depower a crime scene, but you know how it is."

Chino took the hall door and stood guard while I took the lab door.

Jared was clearly still shell-shocked by the evidence of the carnage that had happened here.

"These are the people we're going up against? The people that did *this*?" asked Jared.

"Yes," I said. "We will destroy them." I looked at Chino. "Even the aikidoka must respond to this injustice."

Chino nodded. "We must prevent these people from ever striking anybody again. However, I saw more than aikido in your fist, out there. I see you've branched out."

"Indeed," I answered. "You were my first and best *sensé*, but obviously not my only one." I honored him with a bow.

"You have learned to kill," said Chino. "And I suspect you have killed."

"Only that others may live," I answered.

Chino didn't answer, he only turned his head to watch the door. I wondered if I had let him down or if he felt I had done what had to be done. Aikido is a pacifist martial art, its purpose in combat is to subdue your opponent without harming either your opponent or yourself, and without receiving harm. As a result, it is very difficult to practice, and also difficult to use in actual combat. Where most other arts focus on power and strength and utilize a series of punches and kicks, or in the case of Judo, using the force of the ground on your opponent, Aikido specializes on circular movements designed to take your opponent down. As a result, there are very little punches or kicks, and the ones that are there exist solely to use as practice movements.

But as Chino taught me so many years before, the art is not in its use during combat. While an aikidoka must continue to be an artist during combat, the art of Aikido is in the heart and mind. Training and self-discipline are a common trait of all martial arts, but aikido stresses a respect and love of life. All life. The aikidoka would not swat a fly, nor smash a cockroach. And naturally, a person can't truly have a love for life unless they love their own life, so the aikidoka must live every day like it may be his last, miss no opportunities to laugh and love. The opponent who has nothing to lose can be quite dangerous, but nothing is more dangerous than the opponent who has everything to lose. The aikidoka goes into combat carrying his love, and the love of his family and friends, and the love he has for his family and friends. It is that love that makes him so powerful and so dangerous.

It is for that reason that whatever Chino may have thought about me having killed people, he still loved me, and I, him. It is also for that reason that Captain Nick 'Naptime' Vallejo came to his friend's aid, even knowing he and his crew may not survive. The pirate ship *Sweet Dreams* will enter into combat armed with its love of life, will know what is at stake, and will fight for all life in the solar system. After it is finished with that, it will continue to be a pirate ship.

I checked on Larry and Jared, who were both lost in their task. They had already cracked into the city's sensors and scanned the ship, but like most pirate ships, at least the ones that had any reasonably bright crews, some of their sensors were kept hidden. The reasons for that ranged from simply being stolen, so hidden from the police, all the way up to certain sensors being military grade, the possession of which would guarantee being boarded. When your cargo is all stolen goods, the last thing a pirate captain wants is to be boarded.

"You see," said Larry, "When you're a pirate ship and you're in orbit around some civilized place, you don't want the planetary defenses to know what sorts of gear you're packing. On the other hand, you need your sensor array to keep working as expected or else you're in orbit with potentially hundreds of ships and can't properly identify threats."

"That's right," said Jared. "You've served on a pirate ship before?"

"No," said Larry, "But I have helped law enforcement track a few down. No big deal, they weren't very good pirates. Anyway, what I found was that the first thing a ship does is figure out the sensor sweep interval, and then trigger their sensors to only work when the city's sensors aren't looking at the ship. The more active sensors that the city's passive detectors might pick up only get used when some other ship is using theirs, or when the sensor itself is pointed away from the city's detector."

"Right," said Jared, "So what's your plan to sense

these things?"

"We're going to break into Studwell's ship net and find the code that triggers the sensors to turn on, and then just follow the line to what's controlled. Simple enough."

Jared smiled. "Now you're talking," and got to work. "It's a fairly simple Barracuda class destroyer that he probably bought from a Russian arms dealer. Weak, out of date, nothing any respectable navy would use. The Russians do a pretty good job stripping the computer, but generally leave the armaments and sensors that have survived the salvage process. So Studwell has upgraded and stuff like anybody would, but is guaranteed to have an aftermarket computer of some sort, and not the Russian military-grade computer."

"You know about this ship?" asked Larry.

"Of course," said Jared. "I'm the one who's supposed to know all of this, aren't I?"

"I suppose," said Larry, "I never really thought about what it takes to run a good pirate crew."

"Well, Studwell's not someone's shitlist I'd want to be on, so I'd never attempt to crack into his computer," said Jared, "But I talked to a netrunner out in the Giovanni cluster a couple of years ago who told me a friend of his nearly got killed doing exactly that, and that Studwell has, get this, Studwell has a CRANE X-370! Can you believe it? That old piece of shit?"

"I cut my teeth on an X-330," said Larry. "Fine machines, good ship computers."

"Oh come on, man," said Jared. "That thing is so old, my grandma was using it as a doorstop."

Larry smiled. "I'm pretty old, too."

Jared stopped up short.

Larry went on, "If it is one of the old CRANEs, then we get in through the pulse field detector. Unless they've fixed it."

"Not likely," said Jared. "Studwell's reputation being what it is, he can't keep a good netrunner around. Let's get to it."

It always amazes me how dumb producers can be. Here, I was sort of watching Larry and Jared break into a pirate ship's computer, and they were both quiet, concentrating, and using their own pads. They moved things around on the touch screen, occasionally typing things with the keyboard, and otherwise looked like anybody else using their pads. But if you go to a show, and this is even worse if you watch any of the old "movies" made in the 21st century, this same scene would have Larry and Jared sharing a keyboard, typing excitedly, with a series of weird graphical things appearing on their screen showing what the intruder can see. But right there and then, Larry and Jared were working as a team, where Jared was watching for signs that anybody knew they were there and Larry was heading straight in to get the information he wanted.

All told, the operation took 20 minutes, give or take, and was both quiet and unexciting. Watching hackers is very boring unless you're a hacker. Larry announced his download complete, including sensor logs, and we prepared to remove ourselves from the school. We were going back out the same way we came in so we could pick up the two rear guards we'd dropped off.

Chino stepped into the lab, moved to the far door and held it. Then Larry and Jared caught up with him. I swung the prep room door shut and went through the near door. I gave the signal and we all stepped into the hallway together and hit the stairway. Chino and I leapfrogged our way down the stairs until I hit the landing and checked the hallway. With a gesture, the four of us made it to the door, where we were confronted with one of our guards standing handcuffed with two individuals standing on their sides, their guns pointing right into our faces.

The one on the left was the one who spoke.

"Well, Mr. Wendbury," he said, "Why does it surprise me to find you here?"

It was Detective Johns, which meant the other person was Detective Raymond.

"Detective Johns," I answered. "Seems that I forgot something in my locker and had to retrieve it."

"Using an insertion team, no less," said the detective. "Pirates, from the looks of them. I didn't realize you were in with pirates, this could make it go a lot harder for you in court."

"That reminds me," I said. "I never got a message telling me my court date. You wouldn't happen to have that information on you, by any chance, would you?"

"Cut the crap, fool," said the detective. "You're up to something, and you know something, and now you need to tell me what you know."

"Detective," I said, "We could go all night arguing ourselves in little circles. But you're right, we should cut to the chase. You let my man go and these gentlemen get away and we'll talk."

"Not going to happen," said the detective. "This man's our leverage."

"Hostage," I said.

"We're cops, we don't take hostages," said the

detective.

I looked at Raymonds. "What do you think of all this?"

"I seem to remember telling you to watch your back," said the man.

Johns spoke up again. "Look, Cecil," he said. "I know you didn't do any of this killing, except for the two mobsters in your compartment. And I'm pretty sure you'll get off with a justified killing exemption for those two guys. The only crime you have to answer to is the DWI. I've traced this massacre to a particular pirate, and now I see you with pirates, and that makes me wonder what your involvement in all of this is, exactly."

"Detective," I said, "My friends and I are going to hunt down the pirate captain that ordered this massacre and blast him out of the sky. You might be able to offer some assistance, but you are ethically and morally bound to let us go do our deed."

"But we are legally bound to arrest all of you," said the detective. "Why did the people who did this do this?"

"They were after particular information that we possessed."

"Did they get it?"

"Yes, they did," I grumbled. "And when they use that information, they will become extremely powerful, and you don't want *that* pirate crew to become so powerful. Quite the contrary, you want them gone as much as the rest of us."

"What is the information?"

"That is not something I can tell you," I said.

"We could take you downtown," he suggested.

"You could," I suppose. "Or you could let us go get the bad guys."

"It's my job to get the bad guys," he said.

"You're in over your head," I answered. "This whole struggle is about to go interplanetary, and that's beyond your jurisdiction. By the time you manage to get some space force to go after the pirates, he'll have gotten what he wants and then there aren't enough ships in the solar system to take him down. Had I thought the law could get Studwell, I would have gone straight to you. Instead..."

"Your pirate friends," he answered. "What makes you think your pirate friends can take Studwell down?"

"Simply put, they're the best crew in the solar system."

"Best *pirate* crew, you mean."

"Nope, best crew," I said.

"I can't let you go now that I have you," he said. "It would look bad."

"Just do one thing for me, you and your partner both," I said.

"What's that?"

"Don't shoot."

Then I signaled to Chino and he and I stepped up and did a wrist grab, threw the cops to the ground, and then tapped them into unconsciousness. In this series of movements, Chino performed the exact mirror image of what I did, and the two cops ended up on the ground with their heads near each other's and their feet spread apart. Chino quickly found the handcuff keys and freed our man, and we moved out. We picked up our last man and left campus in a diamond formation, with me leading. We made it to the tube station without difficulty, then into the capsule. Once in the capsule, we all heaved a sigh of relief.

All except Chino.

"What's up, Chino?" I asked.

"I think we'll be shooting our way out," he answered. "Get ready."

"Very well," I said. "Larry and Jared, stand back a bit. You two, to the front. Chino and I will take the sides. If there's any sign of firing near or at us, you two lay down a cover fire as soon as the door opens."

There was only a matter of seconds to get all this organized, but my team did quite well. And sure enough, as soon as the door opened, we heard the sounds of plasma cracking into concrete. From my perch, I could see a small group of people firing, but oddly enough, they weren't firing at us. I looked at Chino.

"Down," he said.

So I took the ground in a side roll out the door, and Chino did as well, making an X pattern in our movements, timing being the only thing that prevented a mid-X collision. I signaled and the two pirates stepped out and dropped to prone positions, ready to fire. Then Larry and Jared came out and dropped, one behind me and one behind Chino. I studied the scene for a few moments, determining the group on my left were police and the group on my right were mobsters. I watched them for a moment, then picked up my pad and dialed the Tortoise.

He answered, looking very much like he was in the same tube station we were in.

"Hi Cecil," he said. "How are you doing?"

"I'm doing fine," I said. "How's the gun fight going?"

"Decently," he said. "My boss said to watch and make sure you made it back to your shuttle. There's two other groups here, and the cops seem to think we're all their enemies. So they're firing on us all, and we're trying to keep the corridor clear."

"Roger that," I said, "And thanks for showing up. Got any plans after this?"

"Not really," he said. "Boss said to give you whatever support you need."

I gestured to Chino, then made a few hand gestures.

"I'm sending my best man to take down the cops, please direct your fire to Studwell's gang. I'm bringing the rest of my team to join you. We've got more guns to lend to this fight."

At that, I watched the mobsters turn as a unit and open fire on a third group that had been stationed there and watching the battle. Chino had already disappeared, so I took the front with the two pirate guards on my left flank and Jared and Larry on the right. We moved quickly, and as we moved, I heard the police fire die off, telling me Chino had done his job with his normal efficiency and love of life. No cops were killed in this fight. We joined the Tortoise under a rain of plasma blasts. His team was surprisingly small, consisting of only four people. But they were all armed, whereas only three of my team carried guns. We pulled them out and added them to the fire.

"Long time no see," I said to the Tortoise. "How goes it?"

"Pretty well," he said. "So, where are we going after this?"

"We have a shuttle in the shuttle bay, that's where we need to get," I answered.

"Figured," he said, "That's why we were waiting at this tube station. How did these guys get wind of your presence?"

"The cops were watching the school, that's probably how they figured out we were here. Their presence feels like we were allowed to do what we came to do just so they can watch and figure out what's up," I answered. "Studwell's men are here because they detected us cracking into their ship computers and are trying to capture us, is my guess."

"You've collected some interesting enemies," said the Tortoise. "How big is your shuttle?"

"Cargo shuttle," I said, "Used to unload the cargo bays of a bulk carrier."

"And your destination is that bulk carrier?"

"In a manner of speaking," I smiled.

"I have a gift from my boss in the cargo bays," he said. "We need to neutralize those assholes so that we'll have time to load the gift."

"What is it?"

"Let your ordnance officer tell you," he said, "I don't understand ship guns. Think of it as a little help to defeat a mutual enemy."

"That's quite generous," I said. "Please convey our gratitude to your boss."

"Of course," said the Tortoise. "Now, let's get down there. We'll lay a cover fire, you guys move over to the position."

"Sure, just don't hit Chino, alright? He's on his way

to take care of Studwell's crowd for us."

The Tortoise raised an eyebrow at me.

"Think of Chino as a ninja that tries not to kill anybody," I said. "One of the best, at that."

"Ah, I see," said the Tortoise. "Very well, let's get this show on the road." A signal from him and his men intensified their fire to a point where the pirates on the other side of the street had to take cover. At that, I took off and headed to the corner. When I got there, I hid behind a fake tree. Larry and Jared came up next and slipped around behind the building. When the remaining two pirates made it, I signaled for them to get to the cargo bay.

"If you find any more people firing guns, hit the deck and dig in, Chino and I will be along shortly."

"Roger," said Larry as the four of them took off down the street.

I turned my attention back to the firefight. Chino had slipped around behind the men, but didn't seem to be finishing them off. So I slipped across the street myself and came in from the other side, where I found Chino standing there, not moving. I leaned in close to his head.

"I am having a hard time doing this," he said. "I do not think I can kill these men."

I clapped him on the shoulder, then turned my gun and fired three shots, leaving three bodies.

"Even in cold blood," I said, "Some people must die."

"Understood," said Chino.

And we headed off to the cargo bay. The Tortoise and his men took a rear guard, which turned out to be absolutely needed because a much larger force of pirates appeared on the street. I couldn't tell who they were, but they were clearly not on our side, so Chino and I headed to the cargo bay. The Tortoise joined us personally.

"The crates are over there," he pointed. "There's a lift to move them, well, I'm sure your people know how to load cargo. I'm going to return to my men. It looks like Studwell's here in force. We don't have enough to defeat them, but we can at least hold them off long enough for you to break free."

"We'll keep a door open for you and your guys to join us," I said.

"No need," said the Tortoise, "And strategically dangerous. We'll make our stand here. Give Mary my love, and take care of her." And he turned back to fight. I choked back a tear, then turned to the cargo.

"Get those crates in the shuttle. Jared, you and Larry get in and fire up the engines. We're leaving."

"We won't be able to get clearance," said Jared.

"Fine," I said. "Nick said that shuttle had enough firepower to blast its way out the doors, get it ready and get moving! Chino, take the ramp." I moved to the shuttle as well to get the cargo doors open. It only took a few minutes to get all of the cargo loaded, since it was already palletized. It took slightly longer to get everybody into the shuttle and the shuttle doors dogged and ready to fly.

I got on the comm.

"This is cargo shuttle *Blake* requesting permission to depart."

"Shuttle *Blake*," responded the tower. "This is Detective Johns, permission granted. Please proceed, and good luck."

The last thing I saw when we got up off the ground was the Tortoise going down in a rain of plasma blasts, standing alone.

Chapter Fourteen

"We brought presents from the Julian family," I told Nick as he welcomed us back from the run.

"Really?" he asked. "What's all that for?"

"Apparently they wanted to give us some extra firepower," I answered.

"Great," he said. "I'll get Shauna and Tac to look it over. So, report."

"It went pretty well," I said. "All things considered. We had to blast our way out, but we had friends."

"Did you get what you went for?"

"Larry?"

Larry answered. "Yes, captain, we have a complete sensor dump, specs, you name it. As an added bonus, I got detailed information about armaments and defenses."

"You and Tac get on it and prepare a briefing. That's higher priority than inventorying our presents," said the captain. At that moment, the captain's communicator went off. He answered. "What's going on?"

Tac's voice came through. "Captain, Studwell's leaving orbit."

"Compute likely trajectories, then follow, but don't *look* like we're following," answered the captain. "We have quite a ways to go before we're ready to attack."

"Roger that," said Tac.

"They detected you," said the captain. It was not an accusation, just a statement of fact.

"Yes sir, they did," I said. "They met us at the gate with guns and shit."

"How did you get out?"

"Julian sent some operatives."

"Where are they now?"

"They didn't make it out," I said.

"With a gunfight behind you, how did you manage to get the doors open?"

"A certain detective showed up and opened the doors for us," I answered quietly.

"You have an odd collection of friends," said Nick. Then he gave me a hug. "Thank you for coming back alive, now let's get this show on the road."

"Yessir," I said. "I have to talk to Mary, then we can have our meeting."

"Fine," he said. "She was on the bridge."

"Can you signal for her to meet me in our quarters?"

"Sure," he said. "It's done, go talk to her."

A few minutes later, I found Mary already in our quarters. Obviously the bridge was closer to our quarters than the shuttle bay. She threw her arms around me as soon as I walked in the door and held me for awhile. Finally, I pulled out of her arms to talk.

"Your friend, the Tortoise," I started.

She sighed. "Yes? What about him?"

"I realize he was a mobster," I said, "But he was a good man."

"Where did that come from?"

"Mary, sit down," I said. She sat. "He showed up with a team and covered our rears while we made it off Europa. He, uh, well, you see, Studwell's men showed up in force. Under the circumstances, we couldn't leave a door open and still get out. He knew the score, your friend did. The last thing he told me, he said to give you his love."

It took her a moment to figure out what I was saying, and when it hit her, it hit like a tonne of bricks. She broke down crying, and I grabbed her in a tight hold.

"He gave his life so that we could get out of there," I told her, with tears streaming down my cheeks. "He did that so we could get the bad guys, and so that you could be happy, and with me."

We stood there in what felt like an eternal embrace. It took a few moments for her sobs to stop.

"How did it happen, in the end?" she asked.

"Do you really want to know?"

"Yes," she said. "I do."

"His team fought to a man, and the Tortoise was the last man standing," I said. "I watched the plasma blasts hit him, he must have taken like four or five at once. He was still firing when he went down."

"He fought to the last," she said. "I wouldn't have expected that from him."

"Apparently he did manage to reform his ways," I said. "He just couldn't leave his family, which is pretty reasonable when you think about it."

"Yes, it is," she said. "It's still very much unexpected. I'm glad he got the opportunity to show what he can do, I'm sorry it had to be the last thing he ever did."

"He still loved you," I said.

"Apparently," she said. "Apparently he also loved you."

"Possibly."

"Really."

"I love you," I said.

She smiled wanly and kissed me.

"There's something else," I started. "Something I've been wanting to give you, but haven't had a chance, and well, all things considered, I want you to have it now."

"What's that?"

"It's in my juggling bag, let me grab it." I reached into my juggling bag pulled out a present bag and handed it to her.

"A gift? What kind of gift is this? Should I wait for my birthday to open it?"

"No," I said. "You must open it now."

"Really? What kind of present is it?"

"It's a will-you-marry-me kind of present," I said simply.

She lost her breath, and almost lost her footing, but she opened the bag and took out the ring. Then she broke out in tears again, threw her arms around me, and said "Of course I will, sweetie."

Then we held each other again, eternally.

* * *

We walked into the galley together, hand in hand,

and found my old friend sitting at a table, drinking a beer. He gestured for us to sit and had Chino bring us some beers and also sit.

"So," said my old friend. "How the fuck did you get caught up in this?"

It took a couple of hours to relate the entire story, but I did it, and he listened patiently, taking notes and not interrupting. When I was finished, the questions started.

"Well, this is an interesting tale," said Nick. "Chino, what do you make of it?"

"Secret societies, aliens, it all has the making of a terrible science fiction novel."

"Don't forget the pirates," said Nick.

"Oh of course, the pirates," said Chino. "Cecil, only you would ever get caught up in something like this."

I chuckled. Mary smiled.

"Ok, so, Mary. How did you get involved with this society?"

Mary started. She was surprised to be asked that question.

"Well, I was recruited to take my father's place," she said. "Or so I thought."

"That's not really sitting well with me," said Nick. "You have no qualifications for the job, no skills, nothing. What was your job, exactly?"

"I was supposed to watch science reports and papers and look for signs of the society's exposure," she said. "I guess you can say I was in damage control."

"And your ability to do that job comes from ....?"

"Nowhere," she said. "I just read a lot."

"No science background at all?"

"None, other than a significant interest."

"No formal training, outside of regular public schools?"

"None."

"What did your dad do for the society?"

"He was a field agent," she answered with a sigh. "His job was to rescue members in trouble, move in with a society team to take over field research whenever new artifacts were uncovered, that sort of thing. He also had contacts in law enforcement that could issue ID's, edit public records, that sort of thing. Get our members out of jail."

"Then you couldn't take his place," he said, "Obviously."

"Obviously."

"Did you inherit his partner, or were you assigned a different partner?"

"I didn't have a partner."

"Then who was the guy that gave Cecil the flasher drive?"

"Oh, that partner," she said, flushing a little bit. "He was assigned to me a few days before he died. He was supposed to do the field work while I, well, I'm not really sure what I was supposed to do."

"And since you were recruited well before you and Cecil got together, the society obviously wasn't looking at him."

"Obviously," she said, "But it has been a wonderful

thing for Cecil to have gotten involved in this. I'd probably already be dead, and Studwell would be talking to the aliens already."

"The society got lucky," said Nick. "It's curious you were the only survivor on Europa from the purge that Studwell ran."

"It is? How?"

"Chino?"

Chino had been concentrating on her answers, but had obviously reached a particular conclusion.

"I think she was supposed to survive. At some point, whoever is running this thing figured that Cecil would come to us. They've all been tracking him, in spite of his numerous evasion skills. Face it, Cecil, you were the victim of a mass surveillance program by three different groups. Anyway, we are supposed to kill Studwell and prevent him from using the information he got, just as he was supposed to get it in the first place."

"But why?" asked Mary. "It makes no sense."

"Because the society was the target," said Chino. "Whoever is running this did it solely to get at the society and kill as many members as possible. This whole information leak was intended to also draw out all society members so they would be exposed, and thus easy to kill."

Mary was stunned. I had to admit, it sounded a bit out there, but it certainly made a lot more sense than a random notorious pirate deciding to go meet up with aliens and have a pow-wow. That made us the correction. So whoever was doing this clearly didn't want Studwell to get anywhere.

"So we still don't know who the bad guy is," I said. "I mean, we're supposed to end the operation by taking out Studwell, and we have to do that, the information he has is too valuable, makes him too dangerous."

"I think we're supposed to die in the attempt," said Nick. "That'll take Mary out, too."

"Then we drop her off, leave her someplace safe," I said.

"Where? She's safer right here than she'll ever be anywhere else," said Nick. "She stays. We fight. We win. We die. That's their plan."

"So who, exactly, are they?"

"Several suspects, obviously," said Nick. "As a mobster operation, this doesn't fit any profiles, but the families that have an interest in taking out Studwell are Giovanni, Julian, and the Martian conglomerate. The EIA would certainly have an interest in destroying the society, if they had their own alien research group. But there's too much left to chance. This doesn't have the feel of an EIA operation. The aliens themselves might be involved, assuming they even exist. If they were planning, say, an invasion of some sort, then destroying the society who exists to prepare mankind for invasion in the event of it happening would be an obvious first move."

"The operation went wrong somewhere," said Chino. "Probably when Cecil got involved. Whoever is running this, up to that point they were in control. Since then, they've had no control over the operation."

"That makes sense," said Nick. "That makes a lot of sense. Cecil has a way of disrupting the world. It's his special talent, and why he makes such a great fool."

"It sounds like the aliens are the ones who have the most to gain," said Mary. "Are they really preparing to invade?"

"If they exist?" asked Nick. "Sure, that makes the most sense. I'm suspending disbelief on that subject because we have to focus on taking down Studwell, but sure, if the aliens are real, they're preparing to invade. Chino?"

"Yep," he agreed. "I agree with that assessment."

"Further, I think you were recruited into the society for the purpose of ultimately running this operation," said Nick. "You are, um, cannon fodder."

"Then this operation has been in preparation for some time," said Chino.

"And your section leader, Mary, is now the prime suspect for the betrayal of the society."

"I don't believe it, I won't believe it," said Mary. "The betrayal had to be someone else."

"We'll leave that," I said. "It's not currently important."

"No, it's not," said Nick. "What's important right now is stopping Studwell."

"Wait," I said, "If it's the aliens running the operation, then why do we need to worry about Studwell? If we're set up to kill him anyway..."

"Because that wasn't part of the operation," answered Chino. "I think the aliens really intended to arm Studwell so he could loot and pillage and generally weaken the solar system. It's an age old strategy, actually. Before invading, a government would arm pirates and send them out to attack the target nation's shipping. What went wrong here is *you*, and the aliens are now wanting to take out you and Mary, and are willing to sacrifice Studwell to do it."

"What makes us so dangerous?" I asked.

"Me," said Vallejo, simply.

"You have an awfully high opinion of yourself," I pointed out.

"It's earned," my old friend gently reminded me. "If there's going to be an invasion, I'm the one in the outer planets to take out."

"But you're only one ship," I pointed out.

"That's only a minor inconvenience."

"Fine," I said, wondering exactly what he wanted to say but didn't say.

"So when we take out Studwell, we'll be making the aliens our enemy?" Mary asked.

"Yep," said Nick. "Absolutely. I always wanted an alien enemy."

"Then why not just contact Studwell on their own?"

"Because the society was watching for that sort of thing," said Mary. "So instead they had to infiltrate the society and destroy it, if possible, before they could contact Studwell. Otherwise, we'd have known and taken steps to prevent the contact."

"Right," said Nick. Then he sighed. "This is a real fine mess you've gotten me into, Cecil."

"When have I ever gotten you into anything clean?"

"Well, there was that one chick..."

"Never happened," I said. "Only clean chick I know is sitting with me."

"You're so cynical," said Nick. "Well, I guess it's time to find out what the Julians blessed us with that we can use to take out Studwell, and what information Larry and Jared managed to get that'll help."

* * *

The bridge crew assembled in the galley, and Chino prepared a giant steamed fish, pork lo mein, spring rolls, hot and sour soup, and rice. It was some of the best Chinese food I had ever eaten. I had known for years that Chino earned his nickname not because he was Chinese, because he wasn't, but because Chinese food is all he knew how to cook. That makes him something of an odd character since he's a master of a Japanese martial art, but at least he's a character. There was a good old bock to wash it all down, which was obviously Nick showing some hospitality to me and my friends.

"Alright, let's get down to business," said Nick. "Tac, report."

"Ok," said Tac. "Contrary to rumor, the *Devil's Whore* is armed with 10 torpedo bays, with 8 of them on the bow and 2 aft. There are 4 medium-powered lasers. Not quite as bad as mining lasers, but not quite the military grade stuff we carry. Simulations based on Larry's data suggest that she can't fire her lasers past the 50 degree mark, which isn't terribly impressive. Studwell obviously depends on his torpedoes, and he certainly carries enough. There are 120 torpedoes in stock right now. Do you want the warhead distribution?"

"Nah," said Nick. "You can give that to me later. What kind of sensors does she have?"

"Being a Russian ship, she happens to have that same array that Larry was talking about, only upgraded."

"So it can see us, even when cloaked?"

"Not exactly," said Tac. "The sensor logs for that array indicate that it gets readings slightly above background levels, which are difficult to distinguish. It would take a very complex algorithm to fish it out, and more computing power than we believe is onboard that ship."

"So how did they get their reputation for picking up cloaked ships?"

"Beats me," said Tac.

"They had their real computer powered down," said Chino. "That makes the most sense. They have the capability Larry described, but didn't need it while in port."

"That's certainly a possibility," said Tac. "In any case, Larry already knows how to fool this particular array, and he's already working on a solution."

"How far are you on that, Larry?"

"Not far, I really just did some preliminaries," he answered. "I should have it finished in a day or two, though. There's not much to it."

"What do simulations say about our chances against the *Devil's Whore*?" asked the captain.

"In 95% of runs, she destroys us with torpedoes," answered Tac.

"What about the other 5%?"

"Boarding parties," answered Tac.

"So we don't win in any of the simulations?"

"Nope," said Tac. "It's a suicide mission."

"Are there any where we manage to destroy them, too?"

"Nope," said Tac. "It's hopeless."

"No it's not," said the captain. "We can take them,

we just have to figure out how we're going to do it."

"We're attacking a destroyer," said Tac. "Granted, it's an older destroyer, one that no self-respecting first world military would use, but it's still a destroyer. That thing is armed to the teeth."

"Not anymore," said the captain. "They have to have cargo bays or else they'd make terrible pirates. And that means a loss of capability."

"Sure," said Tac. "So, what do we do?"

"We fight, and we win," said the captain. "First, the torpedoes. Why do we get destroyed by torpedoes?"

"Because our lasers can't reach around to hit everything," answered Tac. "So our active defenses are riddled with holes. Since the kind of ships we usually hit aren't well-armed, we do well against them, but send us barrage after barrage... In every simulation where we lose to torpedoes, he had to fire 50 to break through our defenses. Most ships, including us, don't even carry that many torps."

"So we need to upgrade our active defenses," said the captain. "Suggestions?"

Shauna spoke up first. "Extend the bend of our lasers."

"If we could do that, wouldn't we have done it already?" asked Darius.

"Sure," said Shauna. "Rather, we would have done it as soon as we could, and have not been able to do so until now. That package we got from the Julians happens to contain a rig that'll let us extend our laser coverage to a full 360 degrees."

"Really?" asked the captain. "That's awesome!"

"Might I suggest something?"

All eyes were on Larry.

"Sure," said the captain. "Whatcha got?"

"Well, first, how many torpedoes do we have?"

"20," answered Tac readily. "With 6 in the tubes."

"So, 26 total?"

"Yep."

"Are we fully stocked at the moment?"

"Overstocked, in fact," said Tac, "Because the Julians gave us 10 more torpedoes."

"The torpedoes carry their own dumb targeting systems, if I recall correctly," said Larry. "They're protected against EMPs, so firing nuclear warheads won't degrade their ability to hit the target, but the targeting systems themselves are pretty dumb. It wouldn't take much to fool the targeting systems into thinking the target is in a different place."

"What would it take?" asked the captain.

"Seems to me y'all should have a multi-phase generator somewhere around here," said Larry.

"We do," responded Shauna. "It's in the food banks, we use it to sterilize food and other things."

"It would be straightforward to configure it to generate a signal that matches our engine emissions, and then some simple positronics stuck into a torpedo warhead would let us fire torpedoes that look like us. It would probably even fool the other ship's sensors into thinking they were being attacked by a whole flotilla."

"That sounds interesting," said the captain. "Riley?"

Shauna answered. "It's theoretically possible, sure, and I've considered similar measures at some points.

But it's a complicated solution. It's also a one-off solution. To generate the fake engine signal would require us to burn out the multi-phase generator because it's just not built to generate those kinds of signals. We'd have at most 20 minutes of use. That's not tactically feasible most of the time."

"But if it would draw only 20% of their torpedoes, that would only leave 80 torps left for our defenses to fight off," pointed out Tac. "We can already expect to take out 50 of the torps with what we have."

"I like the idea," said the captain. "Do it. How soon can you have it ready to deploy?"

"About six hours," answered Shauna.

"Will you need Larry's assistance for it?"

"No, I can handle this," answered Shauna. "But I do want Larry to join the crew permanently."

"I can't do that," said Larry, "Sorry."

"What about speed? If push comes to shove, can we run away?" asked the captain.

"No," answered Tac. "We're just not fast enough. We can outmaneuver them in close quarters because of our comparative size, but we can't run in a straight run."

"Then they could get away from us without us even being able to attack," suggested the captain.

"Not quite," said Darius. "The problem for them is that their sprint range is fairly short. Ours is a bit longer, but their base cruising speed is lower than ours. For longer trips, they can't make it going any faster than that, and our base cruise is a bit better. So we can follow them forever, but we can't run away from the fight because they'd out-sprint us and destroy us before they needed to slow down."

"Or disable our engines enough that we'd lose our high base cruise," said the captain. "Ok, Tac, change your simulations to include these modifications and then let me know what you get."

"Of course," he answered.

"Next order of business," said the captain. "What exactly did we get from the Julians?"

"We got the 10 torpedoes and laser extenders previously mentioned," started Shauna. "We also got a higher-end targeting computer that I've already installed. There's a collection of hand weapons, mostly swords and knives, and some black powder weapons."

"That's sweet of them to give us the guns," said the captain. "Is there enough to issue one to every crewman?"

"Yes," answered Shauna. "But most don't know how to use those weapons."

"Still, it would give us an advantage if we have to board and they're expecting edged weapons."

"Why can't we use plasma blasters?" asked Mary.

Everyone suddenly stopped talking. Chino was the one who finally spoke.

"Well, you see, the plasma blasters are powered through the wireless power grid. Generally speaking, a ship doesn't generate enough power to be able to spare any to power plasma blasters because of how much power they need, and there isn't currently a battery capable of carrying enough to power a blaster for more than one or two shots. So, we don't carry them onto the enemy's ship. We can't even use them on our own ships because of that simple problem. Your registered guns use this fact to their advantage by not touching the power grid until they detect a plasma blast, which is also why you can't use them in self-defense against a sword. So in ship-to-ship combat, you generally have to go in with edged weapons. The old powder weapons are occasionally used, and are still issued to military personnel, but you have to accept the high probability that by the time you board, the enemy's artificial gravity system has probably been disabled. This generally makes powder weapons impossible to use, because every time you fire one, you get thrown backwards, and it's difficult to advance against an enemy when you get thrown back every time you fire. Zero gravity combat is very difficult. Since pirate crews are generally not very well-trained, they just carry swords and knives and clubs and stuff. It's cleaner, and simpler."

"Is it possible to extend the power grid to power plasma blasters?"

"If it were, I'd have already done it," said Shauna. "Also, if ours worked, so would theirs."

"But isn't there some sort of authentication in the power transmitter?"

"There is, but it doesn't work," said Shauna. "Even if it did, it would be dangerous to transmit power to a ship you're boarding that may very well have more plasma guns than you."

"What if our guys carried a portable transmitter?" asked Larry.

Shauna looked at him, dumbfounded.

"Because such a device doesn't exist?" she asked, sarcastically.

"It wouldn't take much to build one," said Larry. "A few batteries and a transmitter. I've built small ones for use in launching model rockets. For a big one, we'd just need an extra crew member to push it around."

"And if they hit it?"

"Cost of war," said Larry. "If it worked, it would be a small price to pay to have a massless gun in every person's hands."

"You'd think someone would have invented one by now if they were worth carrying," said Shauna.

"Necessity hasn't happened, really," answered Larry. "The only people who do armed boarding on a large scale are pirates, and the commercial market for pirate gear is pretty small."

"Good point," said Shauna. "The military does it, though."

"They have weapons designed for the job," said Larry. "Different situation, different resource level. I'd love to get my hands on some of that."

"Couldn't Larry and Jared hack into the ship's net and make their power generators generate overtime, and allow us to power our own guns?" Mary asked.

The room stood quiet. Some in the room thought she was talking out of her behind, while others thought she was just being given talk time to be polite. Larry didn't think either of these things, as he had an answer.

"Now that's totally doable," he said. "But it would take both power grids to be able to fire up the plasma blasters. Still, if the blasters themselves were tuned to an unknown frequency, the enemy wouldn't be able to figure it out, or would at least take some time to figure it out. We could take half the ship by then, or more, and then cut the power as soon as they've figured it out. It would give our boarders quite an edge."

"You're forgetting something," said Tac. "Boarding is a last resort. At least, armed boarding is. We don't do a lot of that."

"But you're forgetting something, Tac," said the captain. "Armed boarding may give us the best advantage. We have the best fighters in the solar system, and if we can give them a technological edge, that would make quite a difference. Larry, pursue this idea. I like what it represents. In the meantime, Chino, get the crew to brush up on their black powder skills. If Larry's idea pans out, we'll board with plasma blasters until the power gets cut, then use black powder to fight our way to the bridge. Our people know how to fight with black powder in free fall, theirs probably don't."

"Um, captain?" asked Shauna. "I just said our crew doesn't know how to use those weapons."

"That's why you're the Chief Engineer and Chino is responsible for combat. Chino?"

"In theory, we all know how to use black powder in free fall," said Chino. "In practice, well, how many rounds do we have? Oh nevermind, it doesn't matter. We can use cap guns for all it really matters. I'll start running drills in the morning."

"Morning?" Mary asked. "When will this combat take place?"

"Tac?" asked the captain.

"It will take us approximately two weeks to get into a fighting position," answered Tac. "We caught them getting out of orbit, but when you consider what it takes just to get out of orbit, they have about a week's head start. Then it can take anywhere from 3-12 days to get into fighting position, depending on where we're going. Add to it that we have to stay off their radar in the meantime, and it just takes some time."

"I see," said Mary, "I thought this was going to happen tomorrow. I don't really know much about space combat."

"Leave that to us," said the captain. "We are well-versed in space combat. We're pirates, after all."

Chapter Fifteen

Building up to a climax is always the hardest part, especially when there's a time delay between the events that trigger it and the climax itself. People who care notice this the most when having sex. You start with a little teasing, some foreplay, and try to build to an appropriate climax. It doesn't matter if you're male or female, the process is still essentially the same. Build stored energy so that when the climax happens, it can all be released at once. This is much harder to do when you have to expend a significant amount of energy to be ready for the climax, such as in the case we were faced with.

The next two weeks were some of the hardest weeks of my life. On the one hand, I had just started an engagement with Mary with the full understanding that one or both of us may not live to the wedding day. In fact, I may very well die on a ship full of my closest friends. Mary, on the other hand, is stuck on a ship full of strangers, where Sherry is the only person she really knows. Very different situations for us, each. Chino drilled at all hours of the day, and I took over when he wasn't there. So for 8 hours a day, I practiced with him as coach. Then I put in another 8 hours drilling the troops, knowing full well he was putting in an additional 8 hours without me. It was rough. Add to it the newly-engaged sex that Mary and I were involved with and I was lucky to get 4 hours of sleep a night. Some nights I didn't get any.

The bridge crew worked just as hard, if not harder. Tac ran simulations based on increasingly newer information, and at one point I heard we even had a thirty percent chance of surviving, while we were hitting an eighty percent chance of destroying the *Devil's*

Whore. That was the best news I'd heard all day. Nick, the captain, ran drills day and night. He'd set his alarm so he could wake up while everyone was asleep and run combat drills, and those of us who were training 16 hours a day had to answer the call along with everybody else.

We ran simulations for everything. What if the *Devil's Whore* noticed us following and suddenly turned back to hit us? What if they bumped up their cruise speed and we had to hit them before they got away? What if they had allies and we found ourselves being ambushed? What if we ran out of food? What if, what if, what if?

Tac estimated our combat readiness at 99.564%. I wondered where he got that number, because I was exhausted. I didn't think I could answer another drill, I was so wiped out. Mary had joined in the drills, even though she wasn't really considered a combat person. She had no training, which is even less than a regular pirate's training. Nick ran a tight ship, and the fact that he had our childhood aikido instructor in his crew meant that he was serious about training. His crew, for the most part, except for newbies, were aikido practitioners. Some of them achieved black belt status, but they had to be on the crew for quite some time to get there.

It says a lot about Captain Nick 'Naptime' Vallejo that his crew practiced a pacifist martial art. Pirates get such a bad reputation, but there he was making sure that his victims didn't get hurt. I wondered how Chino dealt with the situation where he was training people to use a pacifist martial art to steal cargo and then sell it. But the pirates we were going up against knew no such thing. They killed and asked questions later. They even had a reputation for raping the bodies before killing them, while killing them, and after they were done killing them. They didn't approach a bulk carrier and shoot a warning shot, they came in, disabled the engines and boarded immediately. They were skilled in fighting in a boarding party, and we seemed to think our best bet was to board them. That was due mostly to Chino's excellent combat instruction. Yet, he didn't want to kill anybody. Even when faced with a situation where he knew the people involved had to die, he couldn't kill them. How would our crew react to that? Could we even take him on a boarding party? I liked to think that after he saw the evidence of the carnage at the school that he'd be inclined to kill the perpetrators, but Chino can be quite pedantic. If he doesn't know who the specific people were that were pulling the trigger, he wouldn't kill. It was anathema to him to kill. I genuinely believed that if he ever killed somebody, he would drop dead himself. Luckily, he had no problems training others to kill. He made sure to teach the ethics involved, and to stress that we were able to kill the crew of the *Devil's Whore* only because of the atrocity they had inflicted, and the atrocities they would inflict if we were unsuccessful in our mission. He was on board with that. But as a person, would he do it, if he had to?

I brought these concerns to Mary one night, after spending the day training. She had a simple answer to it.

"If he doesn't, does it matter? He'll still disable his opponent and you still gain ground."

Mary is a smart girl. I have a love for her that's beyond any kind of love I've ever had for anybody. Now, you may ask, what about your kids? Go ahead, ask. Ok, if you won't, then I will. What about my kids? I love them in a particular way, the way a father loves his kids. I missed them, and I worried about them constantly. I wondered if they'd even know I was involved in saving the solar system, or if they wouldn't even get the memo. Their mom certainly wouldn't pass on that sort of information, not with her trying to play up her new boyfriend as the next greatest thing to their dad. Has he ever set foot on a pirate ship? Has he ever gone hand to hand to protect his lady's honor? She knew damn well I had done so, she was there! But would she let that affect anything? Obviously not, or else she'd still be with me. Wait, I left her, didn't I? I couldn't say if I loved Mary more or less than my kids because the relationship was completely different. I wanted to spend the rest of my life with her, but there was no guarantee that would happen. My kids would always be my kids, no matter what happened, I would always be their father, and they knew that. They loved me, and they knew that whatever I was doing, it was for a common good. My life had always been that way, and nothing that had happened over the last few weeks changed that. I was still fighting the good fight, living the good life, and always thinking about the ones I loved. Maybe that was why Chino didn't have a problem with me being a killer. He knew I went into combat armed with love, no matter what the result was. I never went into combat armed with hate. I had seen more than my fair share of combat.

The upcoming battle with the *Devil's Whore* wasn't any different. I didn't hate Studwell. I certainly didn't hate any of his crew. I didn't like them, that was for sure, but I didn't hate them. I had to do something, and I had to do it well. I was going to be a boarder, in part because I was the best fencer on the ship, and in part because I didn't know jack about flying a spaceship in ship-to-ship combat. I was going to lead my own boarding party, and we were going to go straight to the bridge. That was the plan, that was what I was preparing for. And Mary couldn't go with me. She was going to be stuck in an observer position, and it was clearly bothering her. She wanted to fight, but she didn't have any sort of fighting skills. She had never developed them, never been in so much as a street fight. Her skills lay elsewhere. She had mega-sex skills, of that I had plenty of personal experience. But she had no fighting skills, as much of a fighter as she was. She was going to be stationed on the bridge solely because it was the safest place to be in any ship-to-ship combat, even with boarding parties. I, too, would be on the bridge. Until it turned to boarding parties, in which case I would rush down several decks and get my team ready to penetrate.

After two weeks of training, Chino called a break. The crew spent a day sleeping. Mary and I had other plans.

* * *

"You want me to do what?" asked Nick.

"I want you to marry me," I said.

"Never knew you felt that way about me," said Nick.

"That's not what I mean, silly," I said. "All things considered, I don't want to die engaged to the hottest chick in the solar system."

"Then break off the engagement?" Nick suggested, helpfully.

"No," I said. "I want to die married to her."

"You're not going to die," said Nick.

"You don't know that," I said. "I *am* on the point team."

"You're not going to die, my dear friend," said Nick, "Because then you'd leave me to get Mary back to her people safely. She needs you to do that, because you're the only person that can."

I cried a little tear. No more words needed to be said.

An hour later, Mary and I entered the galley. Nick stood there in his finest dress skirt and blouse, his Aikido belt strapped to the skirt and his Captain's hat on his head. On his right stood Chino, and on his left stood Larry.

"What's going on?" Mary whispered to me. I answered by taking her hand and marching, slowly, to a point opposite the trio.

Nick looked around solemnly. The whole crew was there. In fact, everyone on the ship was there, minus a skeleton crew that kept us on target for the *Devil's Whore*. Even they, I learned later, had monitors to observe the ceremony.

And there, in a ceremony conducted by my oldest and best friend, I married the most beautiful, courageous, and sexy woman that ever walked any planetary body in the universe. Upon completion of the ceremony, a cold-blooded pirate crew broke out in spontaneous tears of joy.

* * *

I wish I could say what the wedding reception was like, but to be honest, I was so caught up in my wife that I didn't really see a lot. I recall a number of toasts to our success, fertility, and general sexual chemistry. I also recall being a little annoyed that nobody bothered to say anything about how we were wonderfully fit for each other besides noting sexuality, but I let that slide. In the vast training montage we were living at the time, the wedding provided a respite for everyone, and let me show my dear wife how much I wanted to be with her in spite of the fact that she'd dumped me just a few short hours before the wedding. Ok, that's hyperbole, but that's what weddings are all about.

People drank until they puked, danced until they fell down, and generally had a great time. We were showered with rice at one point, but the rice was fully cooked so it stuck to us. We were quite literally rubbing rice bits off when we consummated the marriage later that evening. That part was hilarious, but probably isn't something you care about. There was karaoke, during which I fingered my wife until she left a nice deposit on my fingers, sitting stageside, while talking to Tac who apparently had no idea there was sex happening right next to him. Poor guy.

Nick, my old friend, stepped up and gave a wonderful speech about loyalty under pressure, loyalty during the good times, and loyalty when someone wants to commit suicide. It was a beautiful speech, and I cried a bit during it, thinking about how all three points described not only my relationship with Nick, but also with my wife. It was quite moving.

Mary, for the most part, went with the flow. So she and I used any and every body that showed up to wish us well as an opportunity to flirt with each other. That, by itself, was nothing new, but on that night we were far more intensely flirting with each other than we ever had. We couldn't keep our hands off of each other, and we just kept kissing. I guess that's what I remember most of the evening, all the kissing. We'd kiss before eating, we'd kiss while eating, and we'd kiss while waiting for dessert. We just didn't really stop kissing.

I love Mary, don't ever question that. And I loved our first night of being married to each other.

* * *

Then I was asked to be on the bridge. The original plan was to spend four hours a day training and continue combat drills. We knew how to fire guns when the gravity was disabled, and we knew how to use plasma blasters when the power was on, and we knew when to switch to edged weapons. So I was on the bridge. Luckily for us, the training and drills were finally over.

"Well, Tac," said the captain. "It looks like this is it."

"It looks like it," said Tac.

"Can we get any closer?"

"No," said Tac, "I don't think so. Larry's done a great job hiding us, but it won't hold for much longer. We either need to attack, or back off."

"Then I guess it's time to attack. Lay out a spread and fire on my command. Target engineering, in particular the engines. Ready the laser defense system. We'll see if it's worth what we paid for it."

"Captain, it was free," pointed out Tac.

"Then we'll hope it's worth more than we paid. Got the targets set?"

"Just about," said Tac.

"I hope you respond faster in combat."

"Don't worry," said Tac, "I'm ready. Just give the order."

There were a few awkward moments of silence while the bridge crew exchanged glances. I wondered if Nick would take the opportunity to issue a brief, but very cliché pep talk, but I should have known better. He looked at me, looked around, checked his belt to be sure his pants wouldn't fall off, and gave the order.

"Ok, set course 331 Mark 27 and fire."

Chapter Sixteen

It was beautiful, if you like watching your first volley of torpedoes get shot right out of space. The *Devil's Whore*'s active defense systems took out the first six torpedoes fired.

"Apparently their defense can take out a wider angle than we originally believed," said Tac.

"That's fine," said the captain. "Poke some lasers amidships, let's see if we can set some fires."

And Tac fired some more. The thing about lasers is you can't see them fire on the view screen. They fire in such short bursts, and unless there's debris in the stream to inconsequentially defract the beam, you can't see the beam. All you can see is the effect, and in this case the effect was quite interesting. I watched as a long cut was carved into the side of the ship, opening cabins to the vacuum of space.

"Their shielding isn't very strong," commented Tac.

"The best defense is a good offense," said the captain. "Fire a volley of fakes, then a volley of nukes."

"Aye aye," said Tac. He worked his panel and made it happen.

You also can't see torpedoes on the view screen. They're too small, and anything you do to allow you to see them on the screen would allow your enemy to see them as well. As such, they were clearly visible on radar, so I watched the radar screen track them. A volley of 6 torpedoes left the *Devil's Whore*, and fully four of them turned off to chase the fakes. The remaining two were easily taken out by our own active defenses. Larry had been busy, obviously.

"Wow," said Tac. "Our active defenses are working better than usual. Did Larry mess with them?"

"Probably," I said. "He can't let a bad system go unrepaired, and he's had two weeks worth of thumb twiddling to deal with."

"Target those torpedo bays and fire," said the captain. "After you fire off the volley, throw some laser at it."

"Aye," said Tac. He dutifully fired.

I'd like to say I watched while he took out their torpedo bays, but I can't. What actually happened was a bit scarier. His laser shot reflected off the shielding around the torpedo bays, and it wasn't enough to distract the crew of the *Devil's Whore*. The torpedoes fired and flew directly to their targets. On the radar screen, one by one were taken out by laser fire until there was only one left, and it crashed into the target looking for all the world like it would destroy something. A satisfying nuclear explosion lit up the view screen, and for a moment I felt like we had struck a serious blow against our enemy.

"Glancing shot," said Tac. "We're lucky if we took out a shield generator."

"Fire another round," said the captain. "Set course 156 Mark minus 87, full speed."

"Yes sir," said Darius.

I watched on the view screen as the ship started to get bigger, and it appeared we were maneuvering towards the read.

"Target those aft torpedo bays and fire," said the captain.

As he said that, a volley of eight torpedoes left the

enemy and headed right towards us. I watched as the targeting computer picked them off one by one, first targeting the closest one, firing a short laser burst, and then moving on and hoping the torpedo it just fired at burned up. The thing about active defenses is that they don't try to destroy the torpedoes themselves because that would take too much power. Instead, they try to burn out the wimpy targeting systems on the torpedoes so they can't detonate. That way, even if they do hit the hull, they can't do any damage other than kinetic damage, and they never go fast enough to do serious kinetic damage. Torpedoes are fueled by old style solid rocket fuel simply because it's cheap, and since the torpedoes start at the velocity of the ships that fired them, they don't need a lot of delta-v to hit their targets. Of course, that simple property makes them vulnerable to active defenses, which is how active defenses came to be in the first place. Nevertheless, torpedoes remain the most effective way to cause serious damage to another ship in a combat situation. Lasers are too easy to redirect from vital areas, as we saw when Tac attempted to take out the torpedo bay with a laser shot, and ships just can't carry enough power to power ship-strength plasma blasters. So torpedoes remain the preferred weapon of spaceships, with lasers as the defense system. Many space combats simplify to who has the most torpedoes, and in this situation, we were definitely at a loss.

The targeting system cleanly disposed of all eight torpedoes, even as eight more appeared on the radar. It was going to be a busy night for the targeting system.

"Tac," said the captain. "Focus a laser beam on the source of the torpedoes, correcting with each torpedo. I realize we'll lose a laser from active defenses, but if Shauna made the adjustments she said she made, we should be fine. So see if you can get a laser right down the throat of that torpedo bay."

"Aye," said Tac, as he worked his control panel.

It wasn't long before a satisfying explosion showed on the view screen.

"I think I got a torpedo while it was launching," said Tac.

"Good," said the captain. "Turn about and stay to the rear. Find their fusion exhaust ports and target those. Let's see if we can overload the engines."

"Aye," said Darius and Tac in stereo.

The next series of movements were difficult to follow. You see, every ship is basically in orbit around something. At this point, we were both in orbit around the sun, having broken free of Jupiter's orbit. So you can't just turn around and face your opponent. Well, you can, but if you change your velocity, your orbit changes one way or the other. Increase your velocity and you start to drift into a higher orbit. Decrease your velocity and you drift into a lower orbit. If you turn around to face your opponent and then fire your engines, you will decrease your velocity and drop into a lower orbit. The advantage gained from having your bow tubes centered on your enemy is quickly lost when your enemy passes you by the simple virtue of being in a higher orbit than you. I didn't know for a fact, but I suspected the ship with the closest orbit had the advantage. But if you dropped your orbit too close to the body around which you were orbiting, then after the combat you still had accelerate back to a correction course, which could mean death for your ship if your new course was too much longer than your old course. It's all very complicated, and is the reason Nick was commanding his ship rather than me. Well, that and the fact that his pirates would do what he told them and didn't give a rat's ass what I said.

In any case, the enemy was clearly dropping their orbit, which gave us the advantage of several free broadsides, but the disadvantage of being exposed to several broadsides from them. The radar screen became a chaotic mess populated with torpedoes trying to find their way to a home where they could ejaculate their payload and cause as much damage as possible. Active defenses showed on the radar as a series of blip lines, appearing and disappearing, and then the torpedo hit would either continue on a straight course, or it would correct and continue aiming for the target.

I didn't see if our entire volley was destroyed, but I felt that the enemy's volley wasn't. A single torpedo hit somewhere over our heads.

"Damage report," said the captain.

"They hit C deck and took out the gym," said the first officer. "Looks like only two got through, and they hit the first target. They're still trying to find the engines."

"That's good news," said the captain. "How many of ours got through?"

"Just one," said the first officer. "We're detecting some air, but nothing significant. No way to tell what we hit."

"Fire again," said the captain. "And turn us in towards them, line us up for boarding."

"Aye," said Darius.

Just then, the ship rocked with another hit.

"Where did that hit?" asked the captain.

"Looks like we took a strong hit to one of our lasers," said the first officer. "Leaves us with one for active defense. No more offensive laser attacks."

"Fine," said that captain, "Then we'll do this the old-fashioned way. Cecil, go prepare your boarding party."

"Already?" I asked.

"Yes, already, we didn't expect to win this in ship-to-ship anyway. Get to it!"

"Yes sir!" I barked and headed below decks.

I moved as fast as I could down the ladder until I reached my deck. Gravity was still working, so I was able to run at a pretty good clip. I found my squad in their ready room, mostly hanging out and hardly in a position to start fighting.

"Get ready!" I said excitedly. "We're about to board."

They snapped to order fairly quickly, surprising me since they had never snapped to order that fast in practice. I guess the threat of real combat has a way of getting people ready for stuff they never expected to face. For my part, I had never expected to lead a boarding party expedition. Sure, Nick and I had served together previously as pirates, and we had boarded plenty of times, but we were different. He was usually in charge of the party I was in, and it was under a different captain. Here, I was alone with Nick as the ship's captain. This wasn't the same at all. I suppose life has a way of moving people forward and growing them right up.

But ready they were, and we all felt the acceleration as the ship approached boarding speed.

"Get suited up!" I shouted. There was chaos in the room as everyone tried to get ready to board.

Even amongst pirate ships, you generally board

using individual insertion devices. These are simply pods in which you surround yourself, much like a sarcophagus but more like a torpedo. In fact, the boarding party was launched in tubes similar to torpedo tubes, only slightly larger to accommodate the volume of a man. The tubes themselves would magnetically seal against the hull of the enemy ship, and then proceed to cut their way in. It could take several minutes, the entire time of which you feel exposed. In the meantime, the target ship's automated boarding defenses would seek out attached capsules and detach them. Under the best circumstances, you hope your ship will emerge victorious and retrieve you. Under the worst, you floated around in space, eventually dying from starvation. Usually, though, the victor picked you up and you either rejoined your crew or got summarily executed for piracy. Boarding parties are where you put your best man-to-man fighters into well-organized units, and the newbies and other worthless crewmembers you want to get rid of. You always hope that when the automated boarding defense system got somebody, it wasn't one of the good ones.

So we got into our tubes, one at a time, and were fired into oblivion. I was about fifth in the tube. The first four were to establish a beachhead, and then if all went well, I would enter and have at least two people holding a corridor. We wore vacuum suits, because we didn't expect to fight in an atmosphere. I had a plasma blaster ready to fire, if Larry's power grid magic worked, a black powder rifle if it didn't, a rapier for when the power was cut off, as well as two stilettos and a jo. In case you were wondering, a jo is a simple weapon. It measures 54 inches in length, usually with a 7/8 inch cross section. This particular jo was octagonal in cross section and made out of red oak. In aikido, it's used as a placeholder weapon for other things you may carry, such as a plasma rifle that can't fire due to lack of power, as well as a primary weapon. I carried it to be used as a primary weapon, but I expected my rapier would get more use. As much as it feels like an ancient weapon, in today's world of boarding parties, low gravity combat, and power grids, swords remain the most effective and reliable weapon to carry. As it was, I entered the tube ready to fire my plasma blaster, because if Larry did what he said he would do, I would be able to use it for quite some time before it stopped working. And when it did, I had a black powder gun to use after that. I felt a little insecure about the black powder weapon because while I had plenty of drilling with it, I didn't feel comfortable using it. I felt much more comfortable with the rapier. Black powder was just...dirty.

My tube launched, and I was either on my way to destruction or death, or more likely, both. I was leading the first boarding party, and statistics show that the first party doesn't usually survive for very long. I didn't worry about it, because I had survived quite a few initial boarding party raids.

This was no exception to that. I felt my capsule cling to the hull of the enemy ship. Then I watched as the capsule itself cut the hull. I waited the few tense minutes it took for the cut to complete, and then watched the entire sheet drop away. Then I dropped in, ready to fire.

The corridor was empty, except for my first four boarders. They had done their job securing the corridor. Even as I took stock, I could hear other sheets dropping as more of my crew came in. At the same time, the corridor was losing air, which I could also hear, from capsules ejected by the automated defense system. Pressure doors would be closing in front of us if we didn't close those holes quickly, and the first boarders that dropped out after me started welding them shut. Larry's portable power rig worked, and they simply used their plasma blasters. I cried a tear as I thought about all the times we couldn't weld fast enough and had to punch through pressure doors, realizing that at that moment ship to ship combat was forever changed.

I didn't sit around thinking about it, however, because we had to get to the bridge, and the pressure doors were closing fast in front of us. With a few gestures I set a point man and we started running down the corridor. The map I had been furnished of a standard Barracuda class destroyer told me which way to the bridge from here, provided Studwell hadn't done too much in the way of remodeling. Under normal, non-hostile circumstances it would take us about 5 minutes to get to the bridge. It was three decks up and about 400 meters from our current position. Under these circumstances, Studwell's crew would be fighting us every step of the way, with key guards placed at the lifts between decks. Military vessels are often equipped with hatches to allow easy traversal of decks in case artificial gravity gave out. I intended to use those as much as possible, because exiting a lift into an armed party is suicide. On most passenger vessels, that's your only choice, because the emergency portals are integrated into the lift system. Military vessels use them defensively against boarding parties, and each portal is self-powered and requires authentication to open. This way, boarders can't use them, but crew can. Unfortunately for Studwell and his men, Larry had extensive experience cracking such simple systems and had provided a device that should open any self-powered authenticated portal.

Now is as good as any for you to ask why we didn't

expect Studwell to defend the portals themselves. It's a fair question, so go ahead and ask it. Well, the answer has to do with two main factors. First, as a pirate crew running a military vessel, they had only one third of the crew complement required to operate a Barracude class space ship in combat operations. Second, as a cruel pirate captain, Studwell suffered turnover that rivals even the worst fast food employers. It's so bad, rumors say, that he doesn't monitor the desertion rate of his crew, he monitors the suicide rate. Other rumors indicate he doesn't even care about the suicide rate. In any case, the likelihood of his crew possessing anybody remotely versed in defensive boarding tactics, let alone how they apply to a military vessel, was very slim. I, on the other hand, had experience of my own which was further buttressed by Larry's briefing based on his time working as a civilian contractor for the US Navy.

Our strategy was therefore quite simple, and as elegant as a fencer could dream up. Our attack was the extension. A second party would be hitting two decks above the bridge, and quite a bit closer. The interval involved would force Studwell's defense commander to divide forces between the two groups, with most of his forces already en route to intercept us. In the time in which those fighters would be running around like chickens with their heads cut off, we planned to fleche. Simple, elegant, fast. The other party would then take up the rear and keep the bridge safe from intruders. We would set the self-destruct sequence and then retreat through the bridge's escape capsules. Larry's intelligence showed us the ship only had escape capsules in the bridge and in Studwell's quarters. Since Studwell's quarters had so many layers of security that only Studwell himself could enter, the crew was not going to survive.

We came to the first portal quite quickly. There was no resistance at this point because Studwell's crew hadn't had time to get to us yet. When they did, they'd find us one deck up from where they anticipated finding us. We went through the portal quite quickly, climbing the service ladder and using Larry's Lock Pick. The next portal required us to backtrack about 50 meters, but would put us on the same deck as the bridge.

As we moved down the hallways of the miserably colored Russian vessel, we could feel the shocks of additional torpedoes hitting the hull. Apparently Nick had managed to get through the *Devil's Whore's* active defenses. I decided it was time to signal Nick.

"Capo Ferro to the Sandman," I said into the comm.

"Sandman," responded Nick.

"What's going on? I thought we were far from getting through their active defenses?"

"Looks like your buddy Larry's quite the netrunner," Nick responded. "He's managed to confuse the main computer with a really complicated polynomial, so it's lost a fair amount of CPU time. We probably can't close in for the kill, but we can definitely do some damage."

As he said that, a small group of Studwell's crew came into view, running down the hall in our direction. We were near the next portal. My guys immediately opened fire, and they retreated.

"Looks like we've encountered a repair crew," I said. "If they're coming our way, you need to quit firing at us."

"Sorry," said Nick. "Apparently you're near a shield generator. That wouldn't happen if you would run instead of sashaying to the bridge."

"Capo Ferro out," I said.

Then we lost artificial gravity.

Having recently trained for this situation, we took our bodies that were now angling towards the ceiling because of our last run step, rotated slightly, and caught the ceiling on all fours, facing away from the portal. We should have bounced, but our suits were equipped with light magnets that would put a slight normal vector down, enough for our shoes to have some friction. We couldn't jump too high, or else the magnet would move us to the opposite causeway, but we could move a little bit. There were also lateral forces from the magnetic attraction to the walls, but they would only play in when it was time to hit the walls. Some of the best boarding crews actually sprint on the walls instead of the floor, and there's always a hot-dogger who falls into a side corridor by sprinting too long. In any case, we were now operating with the effective gravity of Europa, a gravity well I had lived in and juggled in for years.

We shimmied ourselves down the ceiling to the portal, cracked it open, and felt the burn of plasma fire.

"Sandman!" I called out. "Studwell's got plasma guns!"

"Roger," answered Nick. "Agrippa just reported the same thing."

"What the fuck?"

"Mary thinks they've already upgraded their power grid using information obtained from the aliens."

"Does this confirm the aliens' existence for you?" I asked.

"No," answered Nick. "But Larry's on the verge of shutting down their power grid. Whatever they've done, we can't hit the relevant reactor without destroying you. Which isn't a problem because we can't penetrate the shielding anyway."

"Roger," I said. Then I poked my head up, pointed my own plasma cannon in the direction of fire and opened up. In the brief period of stun that our opponents suffered when answered with plasma, I threw myself against the wall and another of my own party managed to get on the other wall. Coverage was bad because the walls were relatively smooth, but from prone positions, we continued firing. Having gained some ground, we could also see that our opponents were at the lift and had no cover of their own. It didn't even look like they were equipped with body armor. I had to wonder where the body armor was, since Studwell had a boarding reputation. He had to have crew equipped with body armor. I didn't have time right then to consider the possibilities, however, because I was too busy rolling and firing again.

Rolling in low gravity is difficult. The initial push to a side roll that comes naturally usually pushes you off the floor. In this situation, it would push me not only to the middle of the corridor, but also on a long line to the ceiling that went across the middle of the corridor, i.e. the place most target practice targets. Luckily, I had been doing acrobatics on Europa for quite some time, so the roll came naturally to me. For my companion on the other side who wasn't used to using this kind of penetrative tactic, it was a fatal error. He drifted to the middle of the corridor and suffered the kind of plasma burns that would have required extensive facial reconstruction surgery if his brain hadn't been burned out by the blast.

I didn't stop to think about that, either, as I was shimmying towards the nominal cover of a doorway, firing as I went. Two more of my crew had successfully entered the corridor and were fighting, this time from the floor. Yet another behind them went speeding up to the ceiling and executed an excellent low gravity front roll, coming out firing. Now we outnumbered and out-gunned our immediate competition.

I made the doorway just in time to watch plasma tear up the wall in front of me. At least they were still fighting back. A quick glance told me they had moved to protective doorways of their own. We exchanged several more volleys of fire.

During pistol recharge periods, I looked at the door that I was laying on. It had the look of a residential door, and indeed the map I had memorized indicated this was supposed to be a residential area. I considered for a moment the fact that these compartments were all inter-connected. I wondered if the enemy even knew that. These quarters would be used by low-ranking crew in a military vessel. As a converted pirate ship that could only put up a third of the crew, it was more likely these rooms were used as storage facilities. I took out Larry's Lock Pick and put it on the door lock. The door slid open and I drifted inside and around the jamb. I signaled to my boarders to keep fighting while I regained my footing on the floor.

Surveying the room, I decided it was definitely a storage facility. Gear was scattered and drifting everywhere, so badly in fact that I took a quick glance around, found the interconnecting doorway, threw myself at it, and shut off my suit's magnet. When I reached the doorway, I grabbed the handle on the side, applied Larry's Lock Pick, and floated through. I proceeded this way until I reached a room that should open behind our opponents. Turning my suit magnet back on, I opened the door to the hall and, though surprised to find him, shot the pirate that was hiding in the doorway. Then I grabbed the pirate I had just killed, turned him towards the pirate across the hall, and moved his hand to fire his own weapon at him.

Two down, two to go. If my calculations were correct, I was now behind them. I glanced into the hall and confirmed it to be the case, firing at the one on the other side of the hall from me. By the time they had oriented themselves on the fact that they had been outflanked, only one was left standing, and my other three guys took him down by brute force.

Then the power cut out. All of it.

"Sandman, report!" I barked into the comm.

"Well, we have good news and bad news," answered Nick.

"Spill it," I said.

"The good news is that Larry managed to cut main power to the *Devil's Whore.*"

"Ok," I said, "What's the bad news?"

"He managed to do it just in time, in fact," answered Nick.

"Just in time for what?" I said.

"Just in time for our own main power to get cut," answered Nick. "Apparently we're being boarded. Gotta run. Ciao!"

So that's where the body armor had gone. No use worrying about it now, I had to get to the bridge. With Studwell taken out, it was unlikely his crew would continue to do his bidding. I looked at the lift and considered options. On the one hand, that lift let out 30 meters from the bridge opening. That would get us there fast, at least. On the other hand, I had originally intended to forego lifts, even when unpowered, because they're the traditional defense points for pirate crews. One look around the damage here convinced me otherwise, however. Studwell had no doubt redeployed his crew to take the portals, and it was time for us to use the lift and get into the bridge.

Larry's Lock Pick not only opened the lift for us, it also provided enough power for it to move itself up a level, saving us a bit of shimmying. When the door opened, all hell broke loose.

Studwell's crew had moved to the portal, expecting us to come up through it. The lift dumped us out between the portal and the defenders. But there were only 8 defenders total, and two were guarding the lift. I grabbed one and pulled him into the lift while another guy shot the other with his black powder pistol. He had miscalculated several things, however. First, he hadn't braced himself. Newton's Third Law threw the poor sot banging into the wall behind him. Second, having not braced himself, his shot went wild. His wild shot had the unfortunate effect of hitting *me* in the back, and bullet wounds are notoriously difficult to survive when you're in the field having not accomplished your objective. Third, his arm grazed his backup man, causing him to fumble his sword.

With power lost and my back bleeding just above the left kidney, I drew my rapier and made a break for the bridge, signaling for the others to take a rear guard. I made it to the bridge and Larry's Lock Pick opened it just as the two groups collided behind me.

Moving into the bridge was difficult, but not impossible. Between my sword training and my aikido, I could take the five people that were there, with one small exception: Studwell. He was a notoriously good swordsman, rumored to have assumed a secret identity to compete at the Olympics. I took out the navigator, communicator, and helm all with the first three thrusts, moving quickly across the floor, and all before the crew noticed they were being attacked. Thinking quickly, Studwell brought his hand down on a switch that closed and locked the bridge door, cutting me off from reinforcements. He drew his sword and went to en guarde.

"We finally meet," he said to me. He gestured to the tactical officer to stand back. "We've got time before our boarders take out Naptime Nick, and I'd like to know who's the best swordsman here."

"Egotistical villains always lose to a sucker punch," I informed him. "Why do you want to fight me, anyway?"

"Come now, Cecil, your reputation precedes you! Eight time winner of the Europan Private Swords Competition? You've gone against Julian's best and stand undefeated. I've always wondered where you learned to fight. Now I know. You've served with Sleepy Ass Prick Vallejo."

"Nick and I go way back," I said. "I taught him everything he taught me."

"That doesn't make sense," answered Studwell.

"Neither does your hair cut," I said, stepping towards him.

He didn't waste any time, leading with a lunge in four. I parried easily and leaned back. His renewal in six was too predictable. I grabbed his blade and shoved it off to the side while I lunged. He barely managed to dodge, but did learn a valuable lesson at that moment: I have studied Capoferro. I snapped my blade to the right on my way out and nicked his rib cage.

"First blood," I said. "Now surrender your ship."

"This is to the death," responded my opponent.

I didn't have time for this shit. A prolonged duel at the last minute? No way!

"You're stalling for something," I said. "It won't work. I am the greatest swordsman in all the land."

"No, I am."

"No, I am."

"I AM!" And he lunged again. I took a step back and with my left hand I grabbed my stiletto. Why didn't I grab my jo? Because my attack would require two weapons, that's why. I kept the grab out of view, disguising it as a simple retreat, and managed to get it in hand all while he redoubled. I never did understand the point of a redouble. For me, when I lunge and someone backsteps, I find it better to recover and fleche, but I can do that because I'm scary fast. As usual when someone redoubles, I smacked his blade to the side and riposted, with a disengage. He managed to bring his blade back in line and parry me, if you consider taking a grazing shot to the shoulder a successful parry.

"Now I've blooded you twice," I said. "Surrender your ship."

"No," he answered. "I will destroy you."

It was time to make a move. I extended, just to see what he'd do. He went for the parry, so I disengaged to six and waited for his parry to come back into six. Then I began a circular movement that included smacking his blade so far he was in six-squared. As my left hand came around, I extended the stiletto and jabbed it into his neck. With his last remaining moment of consciousness, I said this:

"The good guys always win with a sucker punch."

And then he died.

At the precise moment, a circular section of steel plating flew straight down, bounced off my right shoulder, and hit the remaining bridge officer in the face, knocking him out cold. Surprised, I looked up to see Vali's vampiric face looking down at me.

"A little late to the party, eh?" I mentioned.

"Much like your last final," he said. "Did I miss any of the action?"

"You missed the climactic duel, Vali," I said. Then I activated the comm. "Capoferro to Sandman, what's your status?"

No answer.

"Vali, have you heard from Nick?"

"No," he said. "Communication dropped a few minutes ago, why?"

"This isn't good," I said. "*Sweet Dreams* was boarded."

I walked over to the navigation station and activated the sensor net. What I saw made my stomach clench. *Sweet Dreams* was a dog covered in ticks. I couldn't even imagine the horde they were fighting on that ship, with my sweet Mary stuck in the middle of it. I ran a sweep to see how many of the capsules were still occupied and my heart sank. Vali had made it to the comm by then and pinged all active comm gear.

"It looks like there's 28 hostiles on board the *Sweet Dreams*, and only 5 left here," he said.

"How many of our guys are here?"

Vali called for roll.

"Looks like we have 7 still. They've finished capturing the remaining crew. This vessel is now under our control."

"How many bridge-certified guys do we still have?"

"All of them, apparently," answered Vali, "But it doesn't matter. It'll take them too long to get in the bridge. That door is welded shut, and the passage I took was pure luck. They'll never find it."

"So it's just us, is it?"

"Yes," he answered. "Do you know how to drive this thing?"

"Does a carpenter ant know how to build a catapult? Are there any boarding capsules left on this ship?"

"No," answered Vali. "It looks like they launched all of them, probably to confuse our boarding defense systems."

"Smart," I said. "I wouldn't have expected it."

"Why didn't we do that?"

"We don't have enough," I answered. "We can't waste any on decoys. Not unless we're willing to go in understrength."

"So what do you want to do now?"

I took another look at the sensors. Shit! *Sweet Dreams* was bleeding air and launching escape pods, and on the edge of the screen was another ship! It was coming right at us!

"Hail the approaching ship," I said.

Vali did so. "No answer."

"Hail Nick!"

"HAIL NICK!" Vali called out even while he was doing it. "We got him!"

"Nick, we have control of the ship now," I said.

"Great," he said. "We've got problems, Cecil. Apparently they launched an all-out boarding attack. Everyone is fighting in the corridors. All that's left on the bridge is me and Tac, and I'm about to go out and lend my blade to the fighting."

"I'm surprised you're not already there."

"Heh, I was on my way out until Mary pushed me back and told me to stay here and wait for your signal. So, without further ado, I take my leave of you."

"Nick!" I shouted. "You have to stay on the bridge!"

"Why should I stay on the bridge while my crew is getting themselves killed protecting the ship?"

"Because we have incoming, and they're not answering hails," I answered matter-of-factly.

"Shit," he said. "Studwell has reinforcements?"

"Check your sensors," I said. "I don't recognize this ship."

There was a brief silence, then:

"It looks like a spacer," said Nick. "We're fucked."

"What the hell is a spacer?"

"Vigilante force hunting down pirates. We've talked about them before."

"And we're two notorious pirate ships, crippled from fighting each other, ripe for the taking."

"That ship could probably take us both even at full strength," answered Nick. "I've got Tac and me, so we can fight. How much of your ship is left that can fire back?"

"Looks like we have 16 torpedoes left, all of them fore, lasers, and some sort of weapon that I can't identify," answered Vali.

"In addition," I started, "We have maneuvering thrusters and orbital keeping. Main engines are down right now."

"You're in better fighting shape than we are," said Nick. "We've only got lasers. Our maneuvering situation is similar to yours, but our main engines are still powered up. We can probably manage twenty percent, tops. As long as the boarders stay out of the engine compartment, at least."

"You're the tactical master," I said. "What do we do?"

"First thing we do, we get free from each other. Make it two distinct targets instead of one ambiguous target."

"Are you sure being distinct is such a good idea?"

"I try to fight with distinction," he answered.

"Cecil," said Vali.

"What's up?"

"Those escape pods, they're all empty," he said.

"How can you tell?"

"I've checked the internal readings on each one. None are reading any sort of life form."

"That's interesting," I said. "Nick?"

"That's a standard Studwellian ploy. Jettison the escape pods to make the crew surrender."

"I think you should tell the rest of the crew to surrender. Those that can't barricade themselves, that is."

"Not to Studwell, not ever," answered Nick.

"Studwell's dead," I said.

"His men don't know that," he pointed out. "They'll continue operating under his orders until they can confirm his death."

"We can put his body on a boarding capsule and send it over," I said. "Once we can get out of the bridge, anyway."

"Use a bridge escape capsule. Set it to home on us. I'll have our automated retrieval system nab it. In the meantime, no surrender."

"Gotcha. Vali, give me a hand," I said.

In zero gee, moving the corpse wasn't really all that difficult, at least not in terms of weight, of course. What made it hard was the old coffee table problem. A coffee table is usually light enough for one person to carry, but too bulky for one person to get it in the air. This isn't true on Europa, of course, but Studwell was hardly a coffee table. It was but the work of a minute, tops, to get Studwell loaded, set the escape pod's course, and jettison it. It would take about three minutes to cross over to the *Sweet Dreams*, so we could expect hostilities to end relatively soon. That is, as long as Studwell's remaining crew didn't decide that they wanted to own *Sweet Dreams.*

"Done," I informed Nick. "So, what's your plan?"

"Kill the bad guys, win the sweet lady, and spend the evening attempting to make as many babies as possible," he answered easily.

"Mary's mine," I reminded him.

"That's fine," he answered. "It's the thought that counts right now. Hmmm..."

I went ahead and started moving away from the *Sweet Dreams*.

"How many boarding capsules do you have?" asked Nick.

I checked the ship's inventory.

"Looks like we have twelve, all on the starboard side. You know, the side that stayed away from us the entire fight. What do you have in mind?"

"Those plasma cannons," mused Nick, "They need the wireless grid to be able to power a shot. How did Larry's portable power supply work out?"

"It burned up," I said.

"It still has some significant power cells in it, though," mused Nick. "Can you get your crew to rig up the power cells to detonate?"

I looked at Vali who nodded back at me.

"Yes," I said. "No problem."

"Fill up as many of the boarding capsules as you can with those power cells, and any other power cells you're not currently using. You have five minutes."

I went on the intercom and gave the order.

"This is Captain Cecil Wendbury of the interplanetary vessel *Smeghead*. All hands! Get the power cells out of Larry's power supply as well as any other cells we don't need and fill as many of the remaining boarding capsules on the starboard side as possible. Then rig the cells to explode on signal. Commander Vali will provide support from TacOps. You have five minutes to complete this task."

"Nice job!" admired Nick. "I knew you had a good Captain's Voice."

"Thanks," I answered.

"Technically, though," interjected Vali, "I'm a Colonel, Retired."

"Sorry Vali, I'll correct that next time."

"You'd better, you might regain a whole letter grade," the ever-instructing physics teacher responded.

"So, what's your plan?" I asked Nick.

"I think we're going to do the old Jack Sparrow/Will Turner Maneuver. We'll go down each side and blast them!"

"But we don't have any cannons!" I answered sarcastically.

"That won't be a problem," answered Nick. "Use your remaining torpedoes to draw their active defenses. We've got a few torp shells laying around that we can send out to look busy. Fire your lasers down their bow and we'll see if we can't blind them. Then, when we pull alongsides, we'll blast the shit out of them."

"Brilliant," I said. "We're going to get killed making the worst naval attack in film history."

"It's better than being taken by the spacers," answered Nick. "And we've taken out Studwell."

"Roger," I said. "My crew is reporting back, hang on."

"They've completed the task," said Vali. "They will continue working on the task as we advance, but as it stands right now, we have 5 loaded capsules. We should have 5 more by the time we engage."

"Good," I said. "So now all we do is drive. As soon as we're in laser range, start firing. Ready torpedoes. Nick?"

"Already moving. Let's do this."

I pushed our station-keeping thrusters for all they were worth. They'd be empty by the time we reached the ship, but they should keep pace with *Sweet Dreams*. We were going to get ripped to shreds, I could just tell.

The next four minutes were extremely tense. As we entered laser range, Vali opened fire with an aggressive and futile attack on the enemy's bow. He wasn't having any trouble hitting them, but the hits weren't doing any damage. It was like the whole ship was made out of a reflective material. Now, you'd think that building a ship that's intended to be fired at by lasers would be built out of reflective material in the first place, but the truth is that any optics get torn up by all the space dust you have to take the ship through. So optical defenses are reserved for vital areas and usually themselves shielded. That's why you can count the number of torpedo launchers with your bare eye: they all have reflective outer coatings to deflect laser attacks on the launchers. Nick could usually find a way into the launchers with a laser, but he's different, he's trained his crew for that move. It's one of his signature moves, in fact. Other captains just take the time to cut behind the reflectors and allowing the two or three extra salvos that get fired in the meantime.

In this case, it was like the whole ship was made out of polished obsidian or muscovite. Nevertheless, Vali kept plugging away at it, managing to score a few hits on the way in. Unfortunately, it wasn't as much as expected. The enemy ship fired off a salvo of ultra-fast torpedoes, and our active defenses went to work on them. Even so, the ship was rocked by torpedo blasts. Normally, damage reports would start flooding in. On this ship, the only crew not in the bridge was occupied improvising explosives. On my partner ship, the crew was fighting hand-to-hand for possession of the ship.

It was hopeless. I may as well have written my last will and testament during those four minutes. Exactly how the two ships stayed together during that barrage, I'll never know. Maybe these 'spacers' just weren't expecting a full frontal attack from two crippled ships.

Another thing that probably saved my ship, at least, was the fact that the enemy stayed on target for *Sweet Dreams*, firing fully twice as many torpedoes at my wife. Obviously they had run a sensor scan and figured we'd be the easier ship to pick off second.

During the last of those four minutes, I dreamily remembered what was about to be my shortest marriage. My first marriage had lasted 12 years. This one hadn't even made it 12 hours. At least it would be death that finally parted us. I always said my second marriage would last to the end of my life, I had just expected my life to last longer after the wedding than this. How was it going to feel? Would I miss Mary? Would she miss me? It was times like these that I wished I believed in an afterlife. The thought that I'd see her soon would be quite comforting. Instead, all I had was the empty satisfaction of killing both the men that raped her and the man that ordered it. That wasn't the feeling I wanted to take to the grave, so I tried to focus on our last sexual encounter together. It had been nice. Newlywed sex. We hadn't done anything kinky at all, which was unusual for us. Just plain vanilla stuff. Yet it was the most stimulating it had ever been and the most satisfying. It was the first time I'd ever been intimate with someone that I wanted to spend my life with. My eyes teared up at the thought that I wouldn't be able to hold her while we died.

The last minute was terrifying. The boarding capsules fired and made it smoothly under their active defenses and penetrated their shields just fine. We passed so close they couldn't risk radiation burns from hitting us with lasers or torpedoes, so there was quiet. We were now past the point where I had already expected to be destroyed, and continuing to breathe. The ship was long, but we were finally passing its stern.

"Vali, do we have any aft torpedoes?"

"Two," he answered.

"Fire them."

"Already did," he said. "Now we have none."

Vali dutifully continued firing aft lasers back at the ship as we coasted off. Meanwhile, I looked in the aft view screen and watched the explosions.

It's a common misconception that because there is no oxygen in space, you can't see an explosion. Now, it's true that you can't hear it because human ears can't detect the sonic frequency that can pass through space. But seeing it is no problem at all. First, any release of energy will emit EM radiation, some of it usually in the visible spectrum. Secondly, a chemical explosive has its own oxidizer packaged inside it, so it doesn't need an atmosphere to explode. The result is that there is still a brief flash of fire. Finally, the argument continues that there's no smoke because an atmosphere is required for smoke. That one also falls down when you remember that smoke is just particulate product from the explosion, and that will happen regardless of the presence of an atmosphere. The end result? I had no trouble at all watching the series of explosions that rocked the spacer ship, and it was quite the site to see. Each capsule fired at once, tearing a hole in the side of the ship that was a hundred meters in diameter if it was a centimeter. The concussion waves rippled across the hull and the sensors registered power fluctuations throughout the ship. Finally, Vali's last two torpedoes had no trouble piercing the active defenses and made it right up the engine's exhaust ports, creating an explosion so powerful it rained debris all over our stern section.

I checked the sensors for *Sweet Dreams,* and to my relief she was right next to us, moving easily.

"Nick," I spoke into the comm. "Come in, Nick."

"Nick here," he answered. "That was fun! Let's do it again!"

"No more ships on the sensors," I answered. "Looks like we got 'im."

"Luckily," answered Nick. "Studwell also arrived, and random parts of his crew started surrendering. During that pass we were able to subdue the rest, and they're all on their way to the brig."

"I'm surprised anything could happen on board your ship under that bombardment."

"It was rough," he admitted. "I didn't expect to make it out the other side, that's for sure."

"Now let's rendezvous and start repairs."

At that moment, the spacer ship seemed to come alive again. It turned on it's side and opened fire once more at *Sweet Dreams.*

"Those fuckers are persistent," commented Nick. "Got anything left?"

"Nope, you?"

"Nope."

"Well then."

"Well."

"Give Mary my love, and take good care of her, Nick."

"What?"

"I heard me," I responded. Then I cut the comm.

I didn't want to, but I had to meet Vali's eyes before I killed him. He nodded quickly.

"There's just one thing I'd like to know," he said.

"What's that?"

"This button here," he pointed, "It's some sort of weapon, but it doesn't say what it is and doesn't apparently have any targeting system."

"Maybe it's tied to the regular targeting system."

"Maybe," he said. "Or it's not finished."

"Push it," I said. "It can't fire yet, it has to have something else there."

"What makes you say that?"

"As a software designer, I know that you never create an unmarked button that doesn't at least trigger a confirmation dialog," I said.

"Good enough, I trust your expert opinion."

With that, he pushed it. As soon as he pushed it, the panel it was on swung down, revealing another panel.

"Signal strength, mass reduction, what's all this?" I asked.

Vali was quiet for a moment. He had time, it was

taking me time to turn the ship around.

"I'm thinking this is some sort of battering ram," he said.

"Convenient," I said. "What does that mean for us?"

"It means we may survive, yet," he answered. "If I'm reading this right, we can't activate it until we're within one hundred meters of our target."

"What good can it be? We're going too slow to do much damage."

"Then what were you hoping to accomplish?"

"Embedding ourselves in what's left of their stern and engaging the self-destruct."

"Might I make a suggestion?"

"Certainly, O Physicist," I answered.

"Overload the main engines. That should give us enough velocity for this ram to do it's thing."

"We still die."

"Maybe not," he answered. "Trust me, as I have trusted you."

We locked eyes again.

"Is anybody in the engine compartment?" I asked the comm.

"Yessir," answered somebody.

"Do you know how to overload the main engines?"

"Yessir," the unnamed individual answered.

"Do it, on my mark."

"Yessir."

It took another 32.4 seconds for the ship to be oriented for the ram.

"Vali, arm the ram."

"Done."

"Overload the engines: mark!"

"Mark!"

"Now we wait."

It didn't take long. The crash was incredible. This I could hear throughout the ship. Bulkheads buckled, atmosphere leaked, power couplings blew up.

Now, our ship was quite a bit smaller than the spacers'. The ram apparently added what amounts to a force field in the front shaped like a cone that expanded as we went through the ship. The result would have closely resembled a banana peeling from the inside. The spacer ship was instantly destroyed and all hands lost. I found it quite fitting to destroy the enemy with a lunge at close quarters rather than with dirty distance weapons. We survived. Barely, bleeding atmosphere, and with only another hour left in our personal tanks, but we survived.

Chapter Seventeen

"Nick, we're dead in space," I said.

"That sucks," he answered. "We currently have no way to retrieve you."

"Tricky," I said. "How soon before you can get a shuttle out?"

"Two hours."

"That's about an hour too long," I said.

"That's the best I've got," he answered. "Any escape pods left?"

"No," I said. "We used the only bridge pod to send a dead guy to you. It'll take days to break the security to get into Studwell's quarters, so we've got nothing."

"Well, then, it looks like that fancy weapon bought you an hour of life."

"We'll see what we can do," I said. "Has Mary been located yet?"

"No," he said. "She's not among the dead, at least, but her beautiful living flesh hasn't been found."

"Keep at it, will you?"

"Of course," he answered. "We won't give up until we know what happened to her."

I cut the comm. Talking about what was happening was starting to bring me down.

"Vali, do we have any boarding capsules left?"

"No," he said. "But they should have this door open soon."

"After they open it, is there any chance we can all

bunker down in here and conserve oxygen?"

"No," he said. "The oxygen generators are all offline. It would take more than an hour to bring just one online, assuming we could find one that actually functioned."

"So we're dead? I can't—I won't accept that. There's gotta be a way out of this!"

"Could we propel ourselves across space to your friend's ship?"

"Nah, these are environmental suits, not pressure suits," I answered. "Assuming we can find a suitable vessel, got any suggestions for how to propel ourselves?"

"Newton's Third Law," Vali answered sagely.

"Hmmm," I said. "We just need a mass to throw behind ourselves."

"Baseballs?"

"You're thinking like a physics teacher," I said. "Think like a rocket scientist. We need--"

"BLACK POWDER RIFLES!" we both shouted at once.

"Yes!" I said. "We can even aim ourselves with them!"

"We'll tie everybody together tight and put someone behind us to fire the rifles, directing us towards *Sweet Dreams*."

"We just need enough pressure suits. Lemme see what I can do with what's left of maneuvering thrusters."

I hit the board again. It looked like I had one single thruster left with about a quarter tank of gas. Working a few controls, I got the one single thruster to burn itself out reorienting ourselves towards *Sweet Dreams* with a small push. The change in orbit would last forever, of course, but it probably only made for an orbital distance of a few meters. Sometimes you do the best you can, even when it accomplishes nothing.

"Ship's inventory says there are 20 pressure suits aboard," said Vali. "I've ordered everyone to grab the nearest suit. Shouldn't there be oxygen tanks attached to the suits?"

"There should," I said, "But typically those tanks are filled before use using the ship's artificial atmosphere."

"That's dumb," said Vali. "That renders them useless in case of emergency."

"This isn't a professional crew," I said, "They don't think about emergencies until they happen. We'll have to use our own oxygen tanks on their suits. There should be some on the bridge."

A few minutes later, we had our pressure suits collected and ready to wear. A few more minutes and we'd forced open the door for one of the bridge escape pods. It wasn't missing so much as it wasn't fueled. We expected that. Vali found the factory sticker that gave the mass specifications and spent some time figuring out how our makeshift pulse rocket would perform with the escape pod as an airframe with eight pirates in it.

"It looks like we're going to come up short a bit," said Vali. "We need another four kilograms of bullets to get to the right orbit, to say nothing of fine adjustments."

"Right, we don't want to end up in the right orbit but a kilometer back. Would the tanks from an oxy-acetylene rig help?"

"They would be more than enough to make up the

difference," answered Vali. "Of course, we'll still need the rifles to get us to the ship."

I hit the comm and got an automatic relay to Nick.

"Nick," I said, "Do you have the capability to retrieve an escape pod that comes to the ship?"

"Yes," he answered. "You have to come within a hundred meters, but we can grab you. I thought you couldn't get to one?"

"We can use the bridge pod, but it's unfueled. It probably doesn't even have an engine."

"So how are you going to move it?"

"Rifles," I said. "You know, these things we can't fire in freefall because it pushes us away?"

"Nice," he said. "I'll have Larry keep an eye out for you. He's the only one on the bridge right now."

"Ok," I said. "Capoferro out." Then, to Vali, "Let's get rocking on that door."

I gave the order to retrieve the torch that all spaceships carry from the engine compartment and then help us get the door open without using the torch. Within 20 minutes we had the bridge door open and all eight people suited up and ready to go.

"This is going to be tight," I said, "But it's our only way out of here. If this doesn't work, we're probably going to suffocate. If we don't try it, we will suffocate. I can't order any of you to do this, so now is your chance to back out."

Nobody backed out. We all got in the escape pod. I hit the magnetic repeller and we were off. I left the hatch open so we could actually fire our weapons behind us, and the battery in the escape pod powered the instruments, so we could actually aim ourselves.

Vali and I had rigged a frame that would show us the axis of the center of mass so we could shoot straight out with anything we needed. He started by emptying a clip from one of the rifles straight back. Then he used another clip to angle us into the direction of our current orbit. Finally, he put the torch tanks in place and opened the valves through the simple expediency of knocking them off with a hammer. After a brief period of adjusting the tanks, all we had to do was wait.

It took about five minutes for both tanks to empty themselves, after which time we were on bullet power only. We discarded the tanks and spent some time launching various gear out of the pod. Every throw gave us a small change in velocity and reduced the total mass that had to be moved by the bullets.

I looked at the view screen and checked the computer's calculations.

"Vali," I said, "This is actually working." He just smiled. "We're now in a higher orbit than *Sweet Dreams*. We should overtake in about ten minutes. It's going to be close."

"Yep, it is," he responded. Then he leaned out and fired a couple of rounds from his rifle. When we could see *Sweet Dreams* through the portal, he fired again in the opposite direction to stop the rotation. We all watched as the ship got bigger and bigger over the next few minutes. Then Vali started firing again, now pushing us into a tighter orbit and bringing us in fast to the ship. It was still a race to get to the ship before our tanks ran out of oxygen, but it looked like we had a chance, at least.

Unfortunately, my calculations were off a tad, as we started passing out from oxygen starvation a few minutes later. My last thought was something along the lines of horseshoes and hand grenades.

* * *

I came to in a corridor that was obviously lit by emergency lighting. I had a terrible headache and could feel burns on my chest and see a very pretty lady lying on top of me. Sadly, she wasn't Mary, just one of Nick's medical staff. She had obviously just saved my life, too.

"That was close," she said. "It looks like everybody made it. Nice work!"

I stripped off the pressure suit immediately and stood. The gravity plating was working already, so the repairs were obviously going swimmingly.

"What's the situation?"

"We still have four people lost. Five dead, everybody else is injured in some way. The captain would like to see you."

"Ok, where is he?"

"He's back on the bridge," she answered.

I didn't need another prompt.

* * *

"Nick!" I nearly shouted when I walked onto the bridge.

"Cecil!" He did shout. He grabbed me in a big bear hug. "My old friend, we seem to have survived yet again."

"Indeed," I said. "So, where's Mary?"

"The nurse told you there were four still unaccounted for?"

"Yes," I answered.

"She's one of them."

I sat down feeling heavier than I had in weeks, even though the gravity plating was only at a fraction of its maximum.

"Ok, so where did the four go?" I asked.

"Several places," answered Nick. "Mary just grabbed a gun and moved out into the corridor. Initially, she did very well, shooting attackers and keeping them away from the bridge. She saved us with that move."

Nick looked at me pointedly.

"I guess you're happy with my choice of girlfriends?"

"Not completely," he said. "She acquitted herself nicely in battle, but still got us into this mess."

"Ok," I said, "But where is she now?"

"She moved down the corridor and fought, and then the section she was in was depressurized. I assumed she was lost, but we have recovered the bodies that were in that section."

"She wasn't one of them."

"Nope," he said. "There was an escape capsule nearby, and it's not there anymore..."

"You think she got out on it?"

"Yeah," said Nick. "At least, I'm thinking it's a possibility."

"Where would she have gone?"

"That's the thing," said Nick. "I've been going over the sensor logs, and they don't track the capsule. However, there's a large gap, right around when we were battling the spacer."

"Meaning?"

"Meaning she could have gone anywhere and we wouldn't have seen, and by the time we could have seen, she'd have been off our scanners."

"So she ran away?"

"I don't know," said Nick. "The capsule itself was damaged, according to the computer. There's no way she could have gotten anywhere that our sensors can't see."

"How damaged are the sensors?"

"Not so much, now," said Nick. "We've got most of them online. We never lost passive sensors, and the active sensors, including the life form scanner, are online right now."

"So where do you think she went?"

"There's only one place she could have gone."

I sighed.

"She went to the spacer?"

"Yep," said Nick. "I know you don't want to hear that, all things considered."

"I don't think she did," I said. "Unless she thought the spacer would survive and she could use her special secret agent skills to convince them to keep her alive."

"You don't think she went over there expecting good treatment?"

"Like she knew them? Or had diplomatic relations with them?"

"Right," said Nick.

"No," I said. "She didn't. We know this for a fact.

This was almost certainly the ship that Studwell intended to meet. She found us defeating Studwell and came in to finish us all off. That was how they intended to ensure there'd be no trace."

"So they're aliens?"

"I don't know that," I said. "They're spacers, and they could be anything. Humans allied with aliens?"

"Like who?"

"Well, there's ISIS," I said.

"Why would they be interested in *her*?"

"Well, they are the Islamic State of Iranus and Saturn," I said. "That little militant group has an interest in this sort of thing."

"I don't buy it," said my old friend. "But we'll search the remains."

"If she didn't go to the ship, where else could she go?"

"We'll look," said Nick. "I promise."

"I know," I said. "I just, I, uh, I don't know what to do."

"Leave it in my capable hands," said Nick. "If she's out there, we'll find her."

"Yes sir," I told my captain. "What can I do?"

"You can go and rest," he answered. "You've been through a lot and you need to rest."

So that's what I did. I went and rested. Nick came and delivered me hourly reports for the next couple of days, but the hourly reports were always the same. They searched something, they found nothing. They tore through the spacer ship, and not only did they not find Mary, but they also didn't find any other bodies. I found that weird, considering that the ship had to have a crew, and yet there were no remains to be found. The technology found on the ship was quite different than anything previously known to be made, but it still had the interface that you'd expect 10 digited humanoids to operate, so we determined it was a human ship. Ruling out aliens was a positive step, and was confirmed when it was determined they used the Latin alphabet. I was still a bit skeptical, but what do I know? I'm just a fool, after all.

We searched nearby bodies as well. There was a comet passing us that we could reach by shuttle, and a nearby asteroid that was big enough to have an atmosphere. Besides the crazy odds that we'd be this close to both bodies, we still didn't find Mary among them. There just weren't that many places to look. We picked over the *Devil's Whore* ten times over and didn't find anybody left on the ship. Hell, it had all started venting atmosphere after the Big Fight, so there wasn't any place to find anybody.

In the end, we were forced to abandon the search for Mary. We had to repair our own ship, and we had nothing indicating she was even alive. We didn't have a body, which would make for an interesting reappearance should someone make a sequel of this story, so we went with that. Nick even spelled it out for me.

"Look, Cecil," he said. "We haven't found evidence she's alive, but we also haven't found evidence she's dead. Maybe she'll be in the sequel?"

I just nodded and cried. My baby, taken from me.

A week after the battle, we were hailed.

"This is the USN *Ulysses* signaling. Please identify

yourself."

"We're a private yacht," answered Nick. "We've run into a spot of trouble."

"Yes," responded the voice of the *Ulysses*. "We can see that. We were sent by Detective Johns of Europa. He said there might be a fight out here."

Nick looked askance at me, I grabbed the con.

"Thank you, *Ulysses*, for answering to Johns," I said. "We are in need of repair, and possibly towing. We also have missing crew that we need to find."

"We are prepared to offer any assistance we can," answered the voice of the *Ulysses.*

"Thank you," said Nick, recovering himself. "We need repairs and a search and rescue."

"Who are we rescuing?"

"A valiant member of my crew," answered Nick.

"Our scans show that your sensors are fully active."

"They are," said Nick, "But we can't give up. We don't leave our people behind."

"Understood," said the voice. "We're coming into towing range now."

The USN *Ulysses* moved into towing range and hooked onto us.

Over the next three days, they assisted us dramatically in repairing our ship. They had numerous spare parts which, while not completely compatible with our ship, were able to be installed with some modifications. Shauna showed herself to be a fantastic engineer, which wasn't unusual for her. It was more like this was a situation that really showed her skills as well as her command over her engineering crew.

The search and rescue turned up nothing. They launched every shuttle, but came up with nothing. In the end, there was only one conclusion.

"Cecil," said Nick. "I'm afraid we have to give up this pursuit."

"Why?"

"Because we've searched every place a person can survive and we've found nothing."

"We haven't found her body."

"True, but we've only found two of the four missing bodies, and they were both dead," said Nick. "The likelihood is that Mary is dead."

"I don't believe that to be the case."

"Yet the fact is that it probably is the case," said Nick.

"I suppose," I said.

"Look," said Nick. "I don't want to give up the search if you believe there's a chance she's still alive, but we have to. We have to get to port. We've finished repairs that enable us to get to port, and then when we're there, we can get further repairs. We have to do it."

"I understand," I said.

"But you don't want us to abandon the search," said Nick.

"No," I said. "But there are other lives at stake, and you have to make decisions based on that. Let's get back to port."

"And if she's alive and we abandoned her?"

"If she's alive," I said, "Then we're not abandoning

her. She's found a way out of this. If she were here and needed us to rescue her, she'd have found a way to signal us."

"What if her escape capsule was damaged and she couldn't even put together a transceiver?"

"Irrelevant," I said. "We've searched everywhere. Let's go."

"Ok," said Nick, "We'll go."

So we departed, heading to Titan Station, that being the closest shipyard capable of repairing the ship. Thanks to the fact that we had fought off a gangster, the USN was more than willing to repair the ship.

So that's what we did. We flew into port and got ship repairs, and we didn't think about the lives lost. That would have killed us.

Chapter Eighteen

"What are you thinking?" Sherry asked me. We were in port, back on Europa.

"I miss Mary."

"Do you think she's out there, still?"

"No," I said. "I have to practice radical acceptance. There's no way she survived that fight."

"Does that mean you're giving up on her?"

"No," I said. "It means I'm accepting what happened."

"What if you're wrong?"

"How could I be wrong about this?"

"Well, consider this," said Sherry. "When you look back at how she behaved, she never told you anything. Ever. Even after we rescued her from the rapists, she still only told you what you needed to know. She didn't say anything else, and sort of revealed additional details only when we figured something else out, or it was of strategic significance."

"What are you saying?"

"I'm saying that she had her own thing going on," said Sherry. "Maybe she managed to get rescued. Maybe she's not dead."

"If she's not dead, and she used the combat as cover to get away from us, what does that say about our relationship?"

"I can't comment on that," said Sherry. "I know this is hard for you."

I looked out the window, looked at Jupiter rising. It

was a beautiful site, but also one that I'd seen numerous times. I watched the Red Spot show up, and I thought about the hurricane that was happening there. It had been going on for centuries, possibly longer. I thought about the hurricane in my heart and wondered briefly if Jupiter had lost a great love, and if that was the source of the hurricane of the Red Spot. In that moment, I felt a deep and personal connection to the gas giant. We had both loved and lost, and as the great poet says, it's better to have loved and lost. Yet, I felt like the poet hadn't experienced that, because the feeling of lost love is so deep and painful, it permeates your entire existence. Every atom in your body feels the loss and expresses it in some way. I would have preferred to not have loved that deeply, so I could avoid feeling the loss.

"Are you ok?" asked Sherry.

"I'm fine," I said, with a sigh.

"We'll find her," she responded.

"We're not looking for her," I replied.

"She's not lost."

"Yes, she is," I said.

"Are you giving up?"

"Think about it," I said. "If she's not lost to us, she would have somehow come back to the ship, assuming she survived. If she survived and didn't come back to the ship, then she's lost to us. She's doing something else."

"Do you think she's still out there?"

"You think so, apparently," I said, somewhat cynically.

"I'm trying to comfort a friend in pain."

"She's dead," I said. "And in the extremely improbable event that she turns up alive, she's dead to me."

Sherry put her arm around me and held me, but said nothing. We watched the planetrise together.

"Cecil!"

I turned to look at my new accoster. It was Nick.

"Yeah, what up?" I answered.

"Tac and I have been going over the sensor readings, and we've found some interesting anomalies," he said.

"Anomalies?"

"Basically, we think there was a fourth vessel present during the fight."

I was taken aback, and I could feel Sherry pulling her arm tight in response.

"Fourth vessel?"

"It was cloaked," said Nick. "We wouldn't have detected it normally. The only reason we were able to see it was because of the sensors on the *Devil's Whore*. Larry cracked it and prevented it from seeing us, but that didn't prevent them from seeing other ships."

"What does that mean?"

"I don't know for sure," said Nick. "It probably indicates there was more firepower available that didn't join the combat."

"They didn't help us."

"They also didn't hurt us."

"Did you get an energy signature?" Sherry asked.

"We did," answered Nick.

"Can we track where they went?"

"We have some probable orbits they could have taken."

"I say we investigate," said Sherry. She looked askance at me.

"I suppose that's the likeliest place Mary would have gone if she survived," I said. "Let's track her down."

"I can't help you," said Nick. "I'm sorry, but we've been contacted about a special cargo, and the pay is really good. We might be going legit, but we have to pay back our expenses for this mission."

"I understand," I told him. "You do what you need to do."

"As will you," said Nick. "Take care of yourself."

"And you," I said. "Take care."

Author's Note

Hello, dear reader. You've made it all the way through this book, and I congratulate you for that. And now you're here, and you are reading this. What is this about? I don't see author's notes very often. Why is this here?

I want to talk about the history of this book, so that, for those of you interested, you can understand more about this book. As a reader, I generally appreciate the author taking some time to tell me more about the book.

Like all other authors in the world, I base my characters on real people. At least, in part. Cecil, Larry, Sherry, and Mary are all based on real people that I have known in my life. I've distanced the characters from their inspirations, so that I can explore their personalities in ways that the real people involved would never do. The pirate crew of Captain Vallejo, however, are very different. Each member of the crew represents a different part of my own personality, but enhanced to levels that my own personality cannot support. There's an interesting bit here.

Some background. This book that you are reading was my winning entry into the 2011 National Novel Writer's Month, which is a competition each November where you're expected to write a 50,000 word novel in 30 days. This was a winning entry. I didn't get accolades or anything, and I had to buy the trophy T-shirt. That's how the competition works. In any case, when I started working on this novel, I had no clear idea of a story, I just had a few characters that I threw together and made stuff happen.

I chose to tell the first two acts simultaneously

because it sounded like a neat idea at the time. As the revisions have happened, I considered rearranging the story so that everything was in sequential order. I actually printed it up and arranged the chapters in sequential order, and I found the story to be a lot less interesting when laid out like that. Now, I hate flashback sequences, so I wasn't going to use those. But I wanted to tell the story out of order, in part because I didn't know what story I was telling. I found myself in the middle of November several thousand words ahead of my word count goal, and having to stop and make a story outline. I found that after my story outline was finished, I had no endgame. I had no idea where the story would end.

But I knew one thing I absolutely wanted, if I could manage it: pirates! In 2009, I started a story for Nano about pirates in an interplanetary civilization. Here I had a story about an interplanetary civilization. In 2009, I made it something like 600 words and then quit the competition, but in those 600 words I had some clearly defined characters. That is where Captain Nick "Naptime" Vallejo originated. In this book, I needed a climax, and I wanted a space battle. So I tapped that story for characters, and the third act finally came together. It took some revisions to include Vallejo in earlier parts of the story.

So that's how the story came together.

Now, my prereaders had some problems with the story with which I disagreed.

One problem they had was that the fact that Cecil was a crossdresser, other than the plot device where he used that to hide from the police during the second act, offered nothing to the story. I disagree with that. The fact the Cecil is transgender is an important part of the story. The Star Trek franchise has been criticized for being unable to show gay couples in the background on Ten Forward, even though that should be commonplace. Not looking for a story, just looking to see these people. If these sorts of relationships are acceptable in the Federation, then we should occasionally see people in these relationships in the background of social situations. That meaning isn't lost on me. I found it reasonable that the lead character in a story could be a crossdresser, which is generally a transgender identity, and have it not be a big part of the story. It's in passing. It's as much a part of him as his blue eyes. It also has very little, if any, impact on the story. But it's in his character, which is why he wore a pretty sundress to a briefing about how to kill a maniacal bad guy.

Another criticism I got, which I partially addressed, was the expectation of more physical descriptions of the characters. There are two sides of this argument. The side I got from prereaders was that they'd like to know what the characters look like. My response was that I was intentionally not describing them because I wanted the reader to be able to relate with them. Maybe you are a Mexican-American reader, and you'd like to relate to the main characters. If they're all white, you can enjoy the story because that's what you experience in America. But if I left it ambiguous, you can fill in the blanks with what you know, and you could easily wind up identifying with the characters because I emphasized personality traits, thoughts, and so forth, and not physical traits. I want everybody who reads this book to be able to identify with the characters, to the extent that they are able. I want you to like the story, and I don't want ethnicity to be a problem. So I only described a few characters. I made a round of edits to describe characters, and I honestly got bored after I got to Larry. I had given a detailed description for

Cecil, and another one for Vallejo, and then I got to Larry. I knew there was a description of Mary in the narrative, and I got bored. I'd rather you read the story and identify with the characters, and I grew up on Heinlein, and he doesn't describe his characters either.

So that's what I did.

As far as physics goes, I had a post-graduate physicist read it, and he mostly approved of my use of physics. I didn't use Hollywood physics, I used real physics. The only real criticism he had was on the ships' cruising speeds, and it was a solid criticism that I couldn't answer. I made that choice on the ships' cruising speeds to serve the narrative, and we had no physical basis to support that. So, in at least that area, I know the physics are wrong. But everything else is close, and mostly spot-on, conceptually. He said it was a nice break from all the Hollywood physics that's put everywhere else, particularly in other novels. He appreciated that I actually cared about orbital dynamics, even when it wasn't exactly right, but that it was Right Enough. We had some detailed conversations about it, and the result was worked into the narrative. I want the physics to be right.

So then there's the question of Mary. As you can guess from the end of the book, she's not dead. But I can't promise that. I may have killed her. Let's look into that a bit.

When I finally made a story outline, it included all the stuff she was doing. But since the story is first-person, I couldn't tell you what she was doing. So in the narrative, she comes off as being a bit of an airhead. I added an entire chapter just to discuss her, as a character, and what she was doing. That chapter is easy to interpret as she survived this book, but I'll be honest, I don't know if she survived. She's a character inspired by my current wife, and I have my own emotional needs for not including her in future writings in this story. So, I don't know if she survived. But that's irrelevant. I considered her a failed character based on her presentation here, and was willing to determine she died in the combat. I spoke to my physicist friend, and I told him my concerns. I also told him that she was doing things that we can't see in the narrative, and he said that he figured she was and that I shouldn't write her off. So she's ambiguously dead, but she's also unambiguously not dead, based on the chapter I added after that conversation.

I guess we'll see what happens. I still haven't made up my mind.

One final note. This book has two copyright licenses available to you. The first is the standard All Rights Reserved that everybody uses. That's the default given by US copyright law. There is a second license, the text of which is found on the website www.creativecommons.org. It is a Creative Commons license, and it gives you additional rights. One right, in particular, that it gives you is the right to share this book with your friends and anybody else who might be interested in this book. So long as you don't try to make money from my work, and you don't try to pass it off as your own (or somebody else's), you can and should share this book with anybody who might want to read it. Please do so, and don't be shy about it. You can also make derivative works based on this one, provided you don't benefit financially by doing so. So, if you want to make a musical stage play out of this story, feel free to do so, at your expense. If you want to profit from it, however, I am going to want a piece of the action.

In the end, I believe that everybody who reads this

book should visit my web comic, located at www.davefancella.com. You will also learn about new books I may have written, and get to read my blog. It's a stick figure comic, so don't expect great artistry from me or anything, but do enjoy yourself while you're there.

About the Author

Dave Fancella is a juggler, musician, and ace fry cook. He has experience in automotive repair, website development, and education. He currently resides in Austin, TX with his wife and family.

Made in the USA
Middletown, DE
13 October 2022